★

"Congressman Hamilton?" I asked in a hushed voice. If he was asleep, I didn't want to wake him.

It was then I was struck by how quiet it was, what could only be described as a chilling silence. I rubbed my arms as if to ward off the cold.

Shaking off my unease, I stepped farther into the room. The congressman lay in the bed, his face turned away from me. I raised myself on tiptoes to see. It seemed the congressman's eyes were open.

"Congressman?" I said in a conversational volume.

When he did not respond, I moved closer until I rounded the foot of the bed. A prickly feeling crawled up my spine as I leaned forward. Even in the dim light, I could see a glassiness in his eyes, and I realized he wasn't breathing.

★

Masquerade

LIZ OSBORNE

WORLDWIDE®

TORONTO • NEW YORK • LONDON
AMSTERDAM • PARIS • SYDNEY • HAMBURG
STOCKHOLM • ATHENS • TOKYO • MILAN
MADRID • WARSAW • BUDAPEST • AUCKLAND

To my grandchildren, Jake Hulett, Trevor Hulett, Jeneveve Osborne, and Keegan Mallon, for the joy and fun you've brought into my life, I love you all.

Recycling programs
for this product may
not exist in your area.

MASQUERADE

A Worldwide Mystery/December 2008

First published by Five Star.

ISBN-13: 978-0-373-26657-9
ISBN-10:   0-373-26657-X

Printed in U.S.A.

Acknowledgments

I'd like to thank the members of my two critique groups, Megan Chance, Elizabeth DeMatteo, Linda Lee, Jena MacPherson, Melinda McRae, Karen Muir, Joanne Otness, and Sharon Thomas for their suggestions, advice, support, patience, and friendship. Thanks to those who worked with me at Group Health Cooperative, the physicians and staff, especially Kristine Leander, Sandra Matisse, Beryl Schulman, Glenda Anderson, Harry Shriver, M.D., Jim deMaine, M.D., Hal Leland, M.D., and James Van Ostrand, M.D., all of who made a challenging job manageable, and even fun at times. Thanks to Cyndi Osborne for sharing her police expertise. Thanks also to members of the Society for Healthcare Consumer Advocacy, especially Donna Davison-Smith, Ellen Martin, and Lolma Olson. Any mistakes in medical or police procedures are all mine.

ONE

YOU KNOW IT'S GOING to be a bad day when...

I knew it was going to be a bad day when the hospital alarm bells went off at six a.m., pealing so loudly that only the profoundly deaf could have ignored them.

My name is Robyn Kelly and I manage the Patient Relations department for Madrona Bay Hospital and Medical Center in a small suburb east of Seattle's Lake Washington. Last weekend, I turned forty. I am not thrilled with the prospect of searching my black hair more frequently for silver, but at least I don't need glasses to do it. Yet.

I had come in early that Monday to avoid the usual rush-hour gridlock, planning to finish some paperwork before the phones started ringing. But as I sipped my Starbucks latté in the outer office with my assistant, Connie, who had also come in unexpectedly early, the alarm bells startled us.

"What the heck is that?" Connie asked. She had graduated from college earlier in the year, and working here was her first job. She was usually full of youthful confidence, but, right now, her brown eyes were wide with concern.

"The alarm," I said, trying to remain calm for her sake. Unannounced drills did not occur at six a.m.

Connie rolled her eyes. "I know it's the alarm. Why is it going off?"

"I don't know why. You're the one who claims to be psychic," I quipped.

"I'm working on it. You're the one who's fey."

"Not me, my grandmother. And, she wasn't fey; she had dreams about family members."

She scowled. "It's just that—"

I waved my hand to stop her. A muffled voice was coming over the PA in the hall. Our office was not wired for the PA system, so we opened the hallway door to hear the announcement.

"This is a Code Yellow. I repeat, this is a Code Yellow. This is not a drill."

My heart pounded as I tried to remember the different kinds of codes. Code Yellow. It wasn't a fire; that was Code Red.

"What should we do now, boss?"

"Lock up your purse and bring your keys." To mask my own growing nervousness, I hustled into my office and grabbed the red "Disaster Manual" off the shelf. The hospital had disaster drills twice a year, and even though we took them seriously, there was always an element of play-acting. This was the real thing. "It doesn't matter what the color code is. We go to A103. Ready?"

I pulled my cell phone from my purse and propelled Connie through the door, locking it behind us. I wished I knew what we were getting into. At this time of day, there were not many staff in the building to handle it. Whatever "it" was.

We strode down the hall toward the closest elevators. As we walked, Connie undid her long blond hair, then twisted it into a coil and reclipped it in the back. I recognized it as her version of a nervous twitch.

The four-story hospital-clinic complex was shaped like a rectangular box with three wings sticking out, to the south, west, and north, each with a stairwell and a pair of passenger elevators.

Connie and I rounded the corner to the west wing. The lighted numbers above the doors indicated both elevators were stopped on the floor below us and heading down.

"Let's take the stairs. It'll be faster." I was grateful that this forced exercise was down, not up. I glanced at Connie. With the naiveté of youth, she now appeared more excited than anxious about whatever it was we faced.

When we reached the basement, we joined the smattering of people trickling into the large meeting room. I didn't know most of them since they usually left before I arrived in the morning.

Charley Anderson stood at the far end of the room, urging everyone to take a seat. Charley is about my age, and a registered nurse who rose up through the ranks to be the ER manager. Tall and lanky with a dry sense of humor, he's also a great person in a crisis, having worked in war zones prior to coming to Madrona Bay. I was relieved to see him in charge.

"Come on, people," Charley called out. "No time for chit-chat."

The urgency in his voice rippled through the group, and we quickly gave him our full attention.

"The State Patrol has notified us that there's been a multi-vehicle pile-up on Snoqualmie Pass—"

My stomach roiled. *Oh God, anything but that.* I swallowed hard, forcing myself to stay seated, concentrating on the present, not the past.

"—It sounds like black ice turned I-90 into a skating rink. We don't know the total number of casualties, but it's high. The worst will be airlifted to Harborview, the next worst will go to Overlake, then what's left will be sent to us. The best guess is we could get thirty to fifty victims in the next hour."

We listened in stunned silence. Thirty to fifty victims?

In an hour? We were a two-hundred-bed community hospital. Our ER would have injured people stacked in the halls, and ancillary services such as Radiology and the lab would be inundated.

"We can do this," Charley said, his voice calm, his determined gaze scanning the room. Then, he smiled. "O.R., your docs are already en route for this morning's surgeries. Cancel your schedules, but tell the urgents to wait. Maybe we can fit them in later in the day. Who's here from Two-West and Three-West?"

Several nurses raised their hands.

"Good. I need a free-bed count in the next ten minutes. Housekeeping? We need a full-moon-Saturday-night's worth of supplies in the ER in the next fifteen minutes."

That broke the tension and everyone chuckled, knowing how busy Saturday nights are anyway, even without the lunacy factor.

"Any questions?" Charley looked expectantly at the group, then clapped his hands. "Okay, let's do it. Rob? You come with me."

I nodded, then shoved the disaster manual at Connie. "Take this to the main lobby," I said hurriedly. "Everything you need is in here. Find a phone to call Social Services. They'll help with victims' families. Then, call Human Resources for backup. Then snag some volunteers in case we need runners for something."

Connie nodded, her eyes wide with tension.

"It will be fine. Just like Charley said." I patted her shoulder. "Everything you need is in the manual. Okay?"

She nodded again.

"I'm going to the ER. Call me if you need anything." I watched her blend into the crowd moving quickly out the door.

One floor up, I caught Charley as he strode down the

long hallway toward the reception desk and ambulance entrance. Double-timing it, I followed him past supply, special treatment, and staff rooms on one side, and exam rooms on the other. We dodged people rushing with supplies, calling and shouting to each other as they raced to prepare for the worst.

"This is a nice way to start the week," I quipped.

Charley snorted. "Yeah, right."

"How can I help?"

"Call the family practice docs from the clinic. And the P.A.'s. I'm hoping most of the victims sent here will be T-and-R's," he said, referring to treating and releasing rather than admitting patients to the hospital.

We reached the front desk. Charley opened a cupboard and pulled out his disaster manual. Actually, his was divided into two very thick volumes because the ER had a lot of responsibility.

"Here's the list," he said, releasing the page and handing it to me.

Before I could comment, a nurse rushed over and dragged Charley away. I took the list into a small physician-dictation room and shut the door. If any of the docs questioned the urgency of the situation, I figured I would just open the door and let them hear for themselves.

I was surprised how quickly I lined up half a dozen docs and a couple of P.A.'s, or physician assistants. It was probably more than we needed, but they would have to be here for rounds in another hour or so anyway. None of them wasted time asking me for details and they all sounded energized about being part of the action.

I stepped from the dictation room into an empty hall, then found everyone gathered quietly around the front desk, watching the ambulance entrance. It reminded me of a scene from the television show, *ER:* that moment of total silence before all hell broke loose. But this was not fiction.

Then, from a distance, we heard it. A siren. Then another. The ebbing and soaring wails grew louder as they approached.

I swallowed hard, suddenly nervous. This was my first real disaster. Could simulation drills possibly prepare me for the real thing?

The first docs I had called arrived in a rush of controlled intensity. They quickly traded raincoats for white coats, pinned on their name tags, and shoved stethoscopes into pockets. Charley teamed each of them with an ER nurse as the ambulances began pulling in front.

He signaled for me to follow. Filled with trepidation, I caught the pair of latex gloves Charley tossed me and pulled them on as I followed him and an ER nurse, Jamie Rice, out the door. The first of the victims were being pulled from the ambulances—

The squeal of tires. The sickening crunch of metal against metal. Shattered glass. Blood everywhere. David. Oh, God. No—

"Rob!" Charley's sharp call pulled me back to the present. Taking a deep breath, I donned the emotional armor worn by those who deal with people's fears and anxieties on a daily basis, the only thing that keeps us sane, and hurried to his side. I blocked out the groans and whimpers, the metallic smell of blood. The memories.

The rain had stopped, so at least the victims lining up in the circular driveway did not have that added misery. I could only hope we had everyone moved inside before the next downpour.

Charley did the initial triage of each new victim, an as-sessment of how serious the injuries were, then Jamie or I tagged the patient with a colored card that identified for the docs which patients to treat first. If Charley suspected something critical, we looped a red tag around the victim's arm and waved for an orderly to take him straight to an exam room. Broken bones got a yellow tag, while cuts and bruises earned a green tag and an interminable wait inside.

At one point, I looked up. The scene unfolded, wild and chaotic at first glance, but amazingly efficient. Not quite *Gone With The Wind* when Scarlett walks through the hundreds of injured soldiers, but as close as I wanted to get.

"Yellow tag," Charley called out, then moved on to the next victim with Jamie close behind.

I moved to the yellow-tag victim. He looked vaguely familiar, a handsome man I guessed to be in his mid-thirties, with dark wavy hair and those long, thick eyelashes that are wasted on a man. He grabbed my arm and jerked me toward him.

"Where's the doctor? I hurt."

I wrapped the yellow tag around his arm. He needed help, but not until after the red-tagged victims. "What do you need?"

He squeezed my arm hard enough to bruise and I flinched. "Get the doctor," he snarled. "I want something for the pain."

I extricated my arm and glanced around. All the docs had gone inside with the red-tag patients. "They will be with you as soon as they can. They're all with other patients right now."

"I don't care." The man struggled to sit up. "I want something for the pain and I want it now."

I tried to ease him back down, surprised at his strength despite his injuries. "I know this is hard for you. I'm sorry. But we can't give you pain medication until the doctor has thoroughly examined you. He could miss a serious injury if you can't feel—"

"Come on, nurse." His voice took on a whiny, cajoling tone that gave me the creeps. "Just a little shot."

"I'm sorry, sir," I said again. "I'm not a nurse. I can't give you anything, but I will check to see how much longer it'll be until a doctor can see you."

"You're not a nurse?"

"No, I'm a patient representative."

The man looked at me, an oddly speculative expression crossing his face. "What's your name?"

"My name's Robyn. A doctor will see you soon."

"But, I want—"

"Rob! Red!" Charley hollered. He was getting ahead of me. I didn't have time to linger. I moved to the "red" patient and waved for someone to take her inside immediately.

Within a relatively short time, Charley, Jamie, and I had finished, leaving yellow-tagged victims lining the halls on gurneys, while green-tagged people overflowed the waiting room, many grumbling into cell phones. During a lull in new arrivals, I slalomed around the line of gurneys, taking names and numbers of relatives to call. I tried to give each victim a kind word and a reassuring pat on the shoulder. Not being a doctor or nurse, there wasn't much more I could do for them, but it seemed to calm several people down. Most responded with a hesitant smile, but I saw the fear ease from their eyes. I took a deep breath and had a good feeling that, for some people, I had made a difference today.

Finally, all I wanted to do was take a break, even if only for a few minutes. I found an empty spot outside some exam rooms and leaned against the wall. My eyes closed, I breathed deeply and felt the tension start to seep away.

I heard something. A moaned scream. A giant pit formed in my stomach. Then I heard the rattle of curtain hooks pulled across a metal rod. A woman dressed in green scrubs stepped into the hall.

Darlene Skaggs, one of our midwives, cast me a sardonic look. "I suppose you're the best I'm going to get under the circumstances. Get over here, Rob." She disappeared into the exam room and I heard the curtain whipped closed.

How could I refuse such a gracious request for help? I rounded the curtain and saw a laboring mom in the throes of a contraction. I moved to the other side of the bed and waited until the exhausted woman sank against the pillows as her contraction ended.

Darlene smiled gently at the patient. "This is Linda. She lives in Ellensburg. She was on her way to Sea-Tac to pick up her mother when they were in the accident. She's a bit early, but this baby decided he wants to pick up Grandma too."

"Who's on upstairs?" I asked, since there was always an obstetrician in our hospital.

"Dr. Kyler. He's doing an emergency C-section not related to the accident. We'll take care of Linda here, then move her upstairs." Darlene turned to the patient. "This is Robyn. I know you wanted your mother to be your coach, but it looks like Rob will have to stand in for her. Okay?"

Linda nodded and smiled weakly. Then she groaned, signaling another contraction. I took her hand, and she squeezed so hard I lost my breath. I tried to mimic the Lamaze breathing technique. If it helped with labor pain, it should help my hand. As the contraction subsided, Darlene excused herself and left the room.

I wiped the woman's forehead with the corner of the sheet. "How are you doing?"

"Okay." Her chin quivered. "I really wanted my mom to be here." Her ash-blond hair was damp, lying limp around her face.

"I know," I said, patting her hand. "At least she'll be here to help you with the baby."

Darlene returned, and Linda looked at her anxiously. "Have they found my husband?" Her fear was palpable, or was it my own memories causing my heart to pound, my knees to weaken?

"Not yet," Darlene said. "We'll call the other hospitals. Don't worry about him right now. You have your hands full delivering this baby."

"What's your husband's name?" I asked, the calmness in my voice belying my inner turmoil.

"Ben. Ben Tucker," Linda said. "We were in a white Toyota."

"Can you describe Ben to me?"

"He's my age. Twenty-eight. And he's real good looking."

I smiled. "I'm sure he is. What color is his hair, and how tall is he?"

After Linda gave me more details, I took a minute between contractions to call Connie at the information desk, and asked her to have Social Services locate Linda's husband.

"Sure, Rob," Connie said. "I called the Human Resources people too, and they're on their way. But it's pouring rain outside and rush-hour traffic is awful."

"Are you doing okay?" I asked.

"So far. I've been listening to the radio, and it sounds like all the reporters went to Harborview with the most serious cases."

"It's probably too much to hope the reporters will stay there."

I hung up as Linda started another contraction, and I focused on this young woman and her breathing. In between contractions, Linda told me her story. This was her first baby after three miscarriages. She'd spent the last four months in bed. It sounded like a high-risk pregnancy to me. Alarmed, I glanced at Darlene.

As if reading my mind, Darlene said, "I called her OB in Ellensburg. Keeping her pregnant through the second trimester was the hard part. She's been doing fine since her contractions started."

Darlene checked Linda, who was amazingly calm. I figured she was now so totally focused on delivering her baby that nothing could distract her.

"Okay," Darlene said. "I see the head. Next contraction, I want you to bear down and push."

Linda nodded, her mouth set in a straight line of determination, and I squeezed her hand in support. The contraction came and we pushed, Darlene calling out instructions, and me offering encouragement.

"Okay, here he comes…here he…oh, he's a beautiful baby boy, Linda." Darlene quickly cleaned the infant, swabbed out his mouth and made sure he was breathing before she wrapped him in a blanket and handed him to his mother. Then she massaged Linda's stomach to finish the birth process. I looked over Linda's shoulder, a lump forming in my throat as she checked the baby's fingers and toes and cooed with maternal pride and delight.

Reminded of my own son's birth, I swiped at the tears blurring my vision. That was the happiest day of my life, rivaled only by the day I married David. Josh had been a joy to me, but now, in his late teens, there was an underlying friction between us and I struggled to understand it.

"Well, how are things in here?"

I turned to see the obstetrician. "Hi, Stan."

"This is Linda Tucker, Dr. Kyler," Darlene said. She proceeded to give him a technical status report.

There was nothing more for me to do here, so I washed

my hands and waved to Linda, who smiled back, then I slipped from the room. In the hall, I hesitated a moment.

Wow.

That was all I could think. Wow.

I had just helped bring a new life into the world. Me. I smiled broadly, feeling quite pleased with myself.

The self-administered pat on the back lasted only a moment before I remembered what I was doing before I heard Linda's groan. Oh, yes. I had been taking a break. The hallway was now empty of gurneys, so I hurried down the hall to the reception desk.

"Hi, Patti," I said to the receptionist as I leaned on the high counter. "How are things?"

"All the reds and yellows have been seen. Some are in the O.R., and the rest were admitted. All that's left are the greens."

"Do you need me?"

"Not unless you want to take temps and prep rooms."

I laughed. "I'll pass."

Patti grinned back. "I thought so. Now leave. Having you here makes me nervous."

"I don't know why. You're the one who got six compliments from happy patients last month." One of these days, I planned to observe her in action, maybe even video her with patients, to use as examples in customer-service training for other receptionists.

"Seven compliments. But, who's counting?"

I waved good-bye. The adrenaline rush had worn off. I wanted a shower, and I wanted either a nap or a caffeine IV. I was accustomed to mentally strenuous days, but this morning I'd run the gamut of emotions. And, it was barely 9:00 a.m., a long way from going-home time at 5:00.

When no one rushed forward to offer me the rest of the day off, I started down the hall toward the front entrance.

We needed to prepare for the reporters who would show up eventually and for the accident victims' families.

I pushed through the double doors to the main lobby and was immediately caught up in the crush of day-surgery patients. I had forgotten all about what the disaster response had done to them. It was worse than the airport with last-minute flight cancellations. The situation was ugly, and looked about to get worse.

From behind the registration desk, the beleaguered lone receptionist was dealing with patients one at a time. In her early thirties, Nicole was soft-spoken, and probably weighed one hundred pounds dripping wet. She said something quietly to the man in front of her. He was in his late fifties and overweight, with a baseball cap pulled low over his unshaven face.

The man scowled and boomed, "What'd you mean, my surgery's been cancelled? I missed breakfast and drove all the way from Kent in this storm, and I'm not going home until my hernia's repaired."

I sighed. Handling this agitated crowd wasn't a receptionist's job, but the supervisor wasn't in yet. I pushed my way through the throng, vaguely aware of the sour looks as I passed by, as if I was cutting in line ahead of them. I ducked behind the counter and put my hand on Nicole's shoulder. She looked at me, relief shining in her eyes.

"Mind if I say something?" I asked her.

"Please do." Nicole couldn't scoot her chair away fast enough.

"Folks, could I have your attention?" I called out. "Quiet down, please?"

It took a moment before the cluster of people stopped talking and milling and I could continue in a more normal voice. "My name is Robyn Kelly, and I'm the manager of Patient Relations."

"Well, you better start relating, lady, 'cause—"

"Sir, if you would give me a moment, please." I gave the man my "icicle manager" stare, then returned my attention to the whole crowd.

"I'm really sorry about this delay. I'm sure you're all aware that we've had an unexpected event," I said. "There was a serious multi-vehicle accident on Snoqualmie Pass this morning."

"So why's that my problem?" It was the same man. Were some people just born obnoxious?

"We are one of the hospitals responding to the accident," I said calmly. "We had a number of victims brought here who needed emergency surgery, so we had to cancel elective or non-urgent surgeries. I don't know about you, but I'd be willing to accept some inconvenience if it meant saving someone's life."

Many of them nodded in agreement. Most people were reasonable if you were up front and treated them with respect. The others were sent to departments like mine.

"I'm really sorry this has happened," I said. "If you'll give Nicole some information, we'll call you to reschedule your surgeries. Thank you for being so understanding."

I wanted to make a blanket offer to write-off their insurance co-pays as a good-faith gesture, but Will Slater, the administrator, would have a fit if I didn't run it by him first. As my Irish grandmother used to say, he'd skin a flea for a ha'penny and sell the hide.

Stepping out of Nicole's way, I watched the people talk quietly among themselves, with only a minimum of grumbling.

When it looked like Nicole had matters under control, I ducked into the restroom to salvage what I could of my appearance. The mirror view was worse than I had imagined. The best I could do was run wet fingers through my hair and dab around my face and neck to rearrange the remnants of my make-up. At least the waterproof mascara had lived up to its advertised claims.

My new blue silk blouse, however, was a total loss. It had been my birthday present to myself, along with dinner at the Metropolitan Grill and tickets to the Seattle Symphony with my friend, Andrea Van Dree. The blouse had been a real splurge. What had possessed me to wear it today? Now it was covered with a variety of "mystery spots." Even Nordstrom would balk at accepting it as a return.

My shoes were wet too, and I didn't look forward to a day of cold, clammy feet. Thank heaven for the cell phone. I called home to ask Josh to bring a change of clothes before he left for the university. He had heard about the accident on the news and wanted all the gory details. It took some fast talking to deflect his quizzing. I was left wondering if the only reason he agreed so readily to bring the clothes was to get a closer look at the action.

I couldn't hide in the bathroom until I was presentable, so I headed across the lobby where Connie had stationed herself. One reporter was already on the scene with a cameraman in tow.

"Hi, I'm Robyn Kelly. Can I help you?" I extended my hand to the reporter.

"Melanie Cole, Channel Eight. We tried to interview someone in the ER, but they told us to leave." She gave me what was supposed to be a disarming smile. "Can you give us some information?"

I had never been "the spokesperson" before, but a quick look around the lobby offered no other volunteers. "I don't know how many accident victims we received, but it went as smoothly as could be expected. We canceled our scheduled surgeries for the emergencies, but it's going okay. Only a few people with minor injuries were left untreated as of a few minutes ago."

"Anything newsworthy?"

I thought for a moment, then smiled. "Well, we did deliver a baby." Before I said another word, the reporter and cameraman bolted down the hall. "Wonder where they think they're going? Call Social Services, Connie, and see if they've located Linda Tucker's husband yet."

"That's just the kind of human-interest story reporters eat up," Connie said as she punched in the extension.

While Connie was on the phone, I saw Irene Hamstead, a nurse manager, rushing by with a clipboard in one hand and a portable radio in the other, her long black braid swinging in rhythm with her steps. At night, when all the administrators were gone, a nurse manager was in charge of the hospital.

"Irene, are you 'it'?"

She changed direction and headed for me. "I'm 'it.' Wouldn't you know, today's the big executive retreat at Port Ludlow. No one's scheduled to be here at all today." She sighed, then looked at me with an impish grin. "Although, that may not be all bad. Thank goodness Charley came in early. And you, I understand you've been a busy girl this morning."

"I came in early to avoid the traffic and try to catch up on paperwork. At least I avoided the traffic."

She gave a short laugh. "An empty in-box is an urban myth. If we caught up, we wouldn't know what to do with ourselves."

I nodded in agreement. "By the way, the first reporter's already arrived. There will probably be more soon. I'm media relations until PR shows up."

"Lucky you."

Ignoring her quip, I asked, "Any info on the victims that I can share without violating privacy laws?"

"Charley's supposed to call any minute with the numbers." At that moment, her radio beeped. She pushed the speaker button. "This is Irene."

"Where are you?" Charley's voice.

"The main lobby with Rob."

"What's the extension there?"

Connie glanced at the phone in front of her. "Five three two four."

"Five three two four," Irene repeated into the radio, then turned it off. "Whatever it is, he doesn't want to say it over open radio waves."

That didn't sound good at all. What could he say that he didn't want heard by the other two departments listening to the radio, Security and Engineering? Curiosity building, we stared silently at the phone. When it rang, Connie picked up the receiver and handed it across the counter to Irene.

"Charley? What've you got?" Irene crooked the receiver between her ear and shoulder and started scribbling on her notepad.

"Uh-huh…uh-huh…okay…Great. Thanks. What?" She looked at me and frowned.

"What? You've got to be kidding?" Irene sighed heavily. "Yeah, Charley, I've got it. I'll take care of it. Thanks."

"Well? What is it?" I asked as Irene handed the receiver back to Connie.

"Charley gave me the numbers you can share with the press. They saw forty-three people. Sixteen are either in surgery or waiting to get in. Another seven were admitted for observation. The rest were treated and released."

I frowned. "That isn't privileged. He could have said that over the radio."

"I know," Irene said with a pained expression. She squeezed the bridge of her nose and sighed again. "One of the patients filed a complaint against you."

Her answer stunned me. That was the last thing I expected her to say. "A patient complained—oh, I know who it was. That man who demanded pain meds." I shook my head. "I told him a doctor would be with him as soon as the more serious injuries were treated."

"Well, that's not why he's complaining."

"It's not?"

"No. He wants to file a formal complaint that you were rude, unprofessional…and that you deliberately downgraded his color code when he asked for help."

"I what? I'd never do that. Charley triaged him as yellow, and that's what I put on his arm."

"There's more, Rob. The man who filed the complaint is Jake Hamilton."

"Jake Hamilton?" I repeated. "That name sounds familiar."

Irene nodded. "It should. He's Congressman Jake Hamilton."

TWO

"A…A…A CONGRESSMAN?" I sputtered. "Filed a complaint? That I deliberately…you must be joking."

I could tell from Irene's grimace that she wished she were. Indignation—no, fury welled up inside me. Ten years and a wealth of compliments, and now someone had filed a totally false complaint against me. And not just any someone, a congressman, a well-known congressman. I'd thought he looked familiar, but under the circumstances, I probably wouldn't have recognized Brad Pitt in that crush of bandaged and moaning people.

I shook my head in dismay. This was the kind of thing that destroyed careers. "Where is he?"

She flipped her long braid over her shoulder. "He was admitted, but I don't know where."

"Hmmm." A vindictive congressman. Just what I needed.

In a hospital, we dealt with unhappy people every day. Let's face it, patients seldom wanted to be here. Even happy occasions are fraught with anxiety, like Linda having her long-awaited baby, but not knowing where her husband was, or if he was even alive.

A story like Linda's might make today's news, but this was different. This could stay in the news for weeks. Jake Hamilton was not only a political figure, he was a prominent person. Every word he spoke would be parroted by the press and scrutinized by the public. And, his complaint was a serious one—that I had deliberately tried to harm him.

But, why? Then I remembered that odd look that had crossed his face when I said I was a patient rep. Good heavens, did this have something to do with the patient-rights legislation we were trying to push through Congress?

I groaned. "PR's going to kill me. If Will doesn't do it first." I glanced at Irene. "I don't suppose we can forget to call them?"

Irene shook her head. "Wish we could. But you can't talk to the press if this complaint gets out. Call PR. I'll page Will and another administrator. They get paid the big bucks to protect the hospital's reputation, right?"

Her implication that I had jeopardized our reputation made me wince. "Right. But we're here and they're not. In fact, if they are already at Port Ludlow, it'll take hours for any of them to return." I thought for a moment. "I wonder how long we can keep this quiet? I don't suppose we can keep Hamilton sedated until the press finds a serial murderer to focus on?"

Irene shook her head again, but smiled sadly. "No, Rob, we can't sedate him unless it's medically indicated."

Another reporter and cameraman came through the front entrance, Channel Three this time. "This is going to be a very long day. I want my Excedrin," I said with a heavy sigh.

"I'm out of here." Irene eased away from the reception counter.

"Coward," I muttered after her.

She squeezed my hand and said, "Hang in there. I'll be back when I have something to report. We'll keep the complaint quiet for a while."

I turned to Connie. "Ready?"

She nodded, her mouth may have been in a serious straight line, but her eyes sparkled with anticipation.

She wasn't disappointed. For the next hour, we were swamped. Security helped us convince the local press that if they stayed in one area, we would give them regular updates. With promises of coffee, donuts, multiple phone lines, a fax machine, and all the victim information we could legally provide under HIPAA regulations, they were happy. At least for the time being.

Until they learned one of the victims was a congressman.

A congressman who had filed a serious complaint about me.

Despite all the chaos, I had borrowed a clean white jacket and slipped it on to cover my bedraggled blouse. It made me look more official, but caused minor confusion whenever someone assumed I was a doctor or a nurse. I wished Josh would hurry up with my change of clothes.

Connie contacted Dietary to place the food order and argued about whose budget to bill it to, while I sent another E-mail to all departments that combined all their latest status reports. The worst of the crisis may have been over for the ER, but the effects were rolling through the building like a storm surge.

At the opposite end of the building, the clinic was open for regular appointments, but the surgeons were behind schedule from the emergency consults and surgeries. I hoped the clinic patients were as reasonable as most of the cancelled day-surgery patients.

At one point, Tom Geralding, the security manager, strode by. A barrel-chested, retired marine, he had a way of drawing himself up that made him seem taller than he really was. That, and his booming voice, made Tom someone I wanted on my side if things got ugly. He slapped the counter and stopped in front of us. "You two doing okay? Can I get you anything?"

"Thanks, Tom, but we're fine. And you?" I asked, partly for our next update and partly because everyone expected me to know what's going on.

"I've got our guys stationed at the main entrance. They'll let in staff, patients and their families, and, unfortunately, reporters," he grumbled. "Everyone else is turned away. And, I got rent-a-guards at the other doors. Only people with hospital photo ID get past them."

I glanced at Connie and saw that she was adding it to the next all-department E-mail. I told Tom, "We caught some reporters sneaking down the back hall. One was in a wheelchair and the other was wearing a white lab coat and pushing him."

"Hmm. That was smart," Tom said. "I'll add masquerading as staff and the need to control access to lab coats and wheelchairs to my final report when we wrap this up. How'd you recognize them?"

"The local TV reporters are easy to identify. We shooed them back to the clinic waiting area."

"The guy behind them lugging camera equipment was a dead giveaway," Connie piped in. "It's the radio and newspaper people we don't recognize."

"The last thing we need is reporters running amuck. Slater will have my head if we lose control of the building." Tom scowled and shook his head. "He'll have my head anyway when he sees what this extra security is costing us, but there's no getting around it."

I nodded in sympathy and tried to reassure Tom. "It's not like he can blame you for something like this."

"Don't be too sure. You should've seen him when we called in snowplows to clear the parking lot two years ago. We do that, what, every four or five years? It's not something we budget for. And, we sure as hell didn't budget for this."

Tom leaned over the counter and lowered his voice. "It's bad enough we got police all over the place investigating the accident. Not to mention the families running around, not knowing which hospital they should be at. But with a congressman involved, the press is gonna go nutso." He looked around to be sure no one was standing too close. "That's when the you-know-what hits the fan."

"I guess we just wait and hope it doesn't happen until after we've gone home," I said.

Tom must not have recognized my attempted humor, because he nodded sagely and pushed himself away from the counter. He slapped the laminated surface again. "I better call for more security guards to watch the stairwell entrances. That's the only way we'll keep reporters out of the rest of the building."

"I'd just block the doors or lock them," Connie said as she picked up the ringing phone.

"Too easy," Tom replied. "Fire codes say no can do. You ladies stay out of trouble, you hear?"

That was easier said than done, I thought with a sigh. The whole thing with the congressman had given me a headache. Or maybe it was all the noise and confusion.

Connie hung up the phone and laughed. "Do you want to hear the latest one?"

"Sure." Rumors and stories were running rampant.

"A trucker going to a rendering plant skidded on the ice and dumped a load of beef carcasses all over I-90. The State Patrol's closed it again to all westbound traffic. An environmental group is holding a press conference," Connie said in a clandestine whisper. "They're citing this as an example of why we should pay more attention to the hazardous waste hauled by trucks every day."

I shook my head as I sorted through the most recent internal E-mail updates. "What a mess. Ice and grease."

"Where is he?"

I looked up to see a young woman in her early twenties. Her shoulder-length brown hair was tousled and her silk blouse collar lay half-in and half-out of her tailored suit jacket. Her distraught gaze jumped from me to Connie and back again.

"I'm sorry, where is who?" I asked.

"Jake. Jake Hamilton." She had a soft, girlish voice that clashed with her professional clothing.

"Are you a relative, Miss…?"

"I'm Jake's—Congressman Hamilton's aide, Cynthia Martin."

"I'm sorry, Ms. Martin, but he's not—"

"You don't understand. I have to see him. I have to know he's all right." From the way she clawed at the attaché case she clutched to her chest, hysteria was not far away.

"I'm sure he's going to be fine, but I don't know if he's been assigned a bed yet. If you'd like to wait over—" The woman started down the hallway. I hurried around the reception counter and caught up with her. "Wait, Ms. Martin? Cynthia, where are you going?"

"To Administration."

"But I can—"

"My mother's Brenda Martin," she said, lifting her chin. "She'll help me see him."

It clicked then. Cynthia was a willowy version of her mother, our Director of Nursing Services. I touched her arm to comfort her. "I'm sure she would, Cynthia, if she was here, but she's not."

"What do you mean?" Cynthia wailed as she spun away from my hand. "Of course she's here."

"There's a management retreat at Port Ludlow today."

Cynthia sagged against me, and for a moment I was afraid she'd fainted. I felt her shudder and then, her body shook as she began to sob. Over her shoulder, I gave Connie a raised eyebrow look. This was one very loyal congressional aide. Given this reaction, if it turned out her feelings were more than strictly professional, I wouldn't be surprised. Congressman Hamilton had a reputation for eliciting the total devotion of any female who came in contact with him, regardless of her age. Not that I could understand it, based on my own encounter with him. I must be the glaring exception to that phenomenon.

I led Cynthia to the empty waiting area and settled her into one of the overstuffed chairs.

She fumbled for a linen handkerchief and glanced around to see if anyone was watching. "I'm glad Ja—Congressman Hamilton didn't see me fall apart." She blew her nose. "He says emotional displays are a sign of weakness."

"I see," I said finally. I could understand why he needed to be careful about his own behavior, but why his young aide? "How did you know to come here, Cynthia?"

She blew her nose again. "I flew in last week from D.C. We're hosting hearings around the region on salmon runs. I was leaving for the Renton hearings when I heard about the accident on the news. I just knew he was involved."

Connie would have appreciated Cynthia's psychic abilities. Over the young woman's shoulder, I saw the Channel Three reporter and cameraman coming down the hall and silently groaned. I didn't need to be clairvoyant to know I had to get Cynthia out of the public area.

"Do you usually live in D.C.?"

She nodded. Good; chances were the local media wouldn't recognize her, but I didn't want to risk it, especially with her as fragile as she seemed to be.

"You know, Cynthia, we don't have any information on Congressman Hamilton. We could use his address and phone number, and the name of his regular physician," I said in a calm, soothing voice. Keeping myself between Cynthia and the reporter, I eased her from the chair and guided her into the confines of the Business Office.

The Business Office staff was amazing when it came to ferreting out information, but it was the quickest way to get Cynthia out of public view. "Maybe you could help us with that, and I'll let you know when you can see him. How would that be?"

Cynthia nodded meekly. Relieved that she had acquiesced so easily, I turned her over to an admitting clerk.

I had barely returned to the reception counter when the phone rang again and Connie answered it. "Uh-huh. Uh-huh." She glanced at me, and I didn't like the way her expression went from animated to bland. "Uh-huh. Okay. Thanks for the warning." She hung up the phone and scowled at it. "Thanks for nothing."

"Are you going to keep me in suspense?" I asked.

"Oh, you're going to love this one. That was Daniel in PR. Essentially, he said, they'll be here when they can, but it'll be a while. The bridges and interstates are still a mess because of the storm."

"When they can?" I looked at her in disbelief. "You're kidding. Someone must live on the Eastside. And what about beepers and cell phones?"

"I don't know," Connie said, shaking her head. "Maybe you can get a better response from him."

"Does he know about Congressman Hamilton?"

"No. He didn't give me a chance to say anything."

"Hmm. That might not be all bad. If he doesn't know a congressman is here, he doesn't know about the complaint."

"Good thought, boss. Oh, and Social Services found Ben Tucker. He was taken to Overlake and he's doing fine, but he'll be there for a day or two. Social Services called the airlines too, and found Linda's mother. Somehow they'll get all three—I mean all four—of them together."

"That's a relief," I said. "Remind me to send a note to Social Services complimenting their efforts."

"Hey, Rob, how are you doing?"

I looked up to see who was feeling so cheery. Charley and Irene were standing on the other side of the counter. Relieved to see some friendly faces, I thought maybe I had found Daniel's replacement. "Just ducky. Say, Charley, how'd you like to be the hospital spokesman? You don't have anything else to do now that you've cleared out the ER."

"Sorry. I already have a job," he said with phony regret. "I appointed myself Irene's assistant. It's a whole lot easier."

"He's good too. He makes phone calls and runs errands. But I haven't been able to get him to make coffee," joked Irene.

"Excuse me. Where's Congressman Hamilton?"

We turned to face a reporter I didn't recognize. How did he know about the congressman? I pointed down the hall. "The pressroom is—"

I didn't have a chance to say more. The reporter shoved a microphone between us, and his cameraman started rolling. Then, the tidal wave hit. The other reporters must have seen enough to think they were being scooped. They poured from their comfortable makeshift newsroom and charged over. Charley and Irene quickly found themselves trapped behind the counter with me. Connie had disappeared, and I didn't blame her.

I had seen these assaults on TV before. Microphones dangled like a swarm of mosquitoes, bright lights glared from the videocams, and cameras clicked like machine guns. It was one thing to view a scene like this from the comfort of your living room, and something entirely different to be on the receiving end. At least we had the reception counter to barricade us from them.

Charley, Irene, and I stood together, stoic but united, as if facing a firing squad. As long as we stayed calm—and kept breathing—we would get through this. We had worked enough crises over the years to handle just about anything. Even a journalist assault.

Irene was trying to silence the crowd when I saw Connie fast-talking a man who had been pointed out to me earlier as a police detective. I nudged Charley, who glanced quickly in that direction. The detective pushed his way through the shouting throng of reporters. He looked to be about fifty, physically trim, with more than a touch of gray to his dark hair, a firm jaw now softened by age, and brown eyes that had seen too much.

I stepped back as he moved into the spot where I'd been standing behind the counter. "Is there a problem, Detective?"

He looked at me as if I was the village idiot. "I'll handle it from here." He brushed by and inserted himself between Irene and the counter.

Incredulous, I looked at Charley. "I thought we were handling it," I muttered.

"Not anymore," Charley said with an amused glint in his eyes, amusement I didn't share.

Equally surprised, Irene had stepped back too, and the three of us watched the detective go into action. I had to admit, begrudgingly, that he seemed to know what he was doing.

He silenced the crowd of jabbering reporters with his

sharp look before he addressed them in a deep gravelly voice. "I'm Detective Matthew Pierce, Madrona Bay Police Department. As you already know from listening to the police and fire scanners," he said sardonically, "a major accident occurred this morning on Snoqualmie Pass. It involved multiple cars and semi-trucks. The most seriously injured were airlifted to Harborview. Some trauma cases were taken to Overlake, and the rest came here to Madrona Bay. The State Patrol has asked our department to help with the interviews. At this time, it appears the accident was an unfortunate chain reaction that occurred when a semi hit a patch of black ice and lost control."

"What about Congressman Hamilton?" The news was out. A rumble grew as the rest of the reporters realized they had almost missed the biggest part of the story.

The detective appeared unruffled by the questions thrown at him. He glanced at the three of us, then settled on Irene. "You prepared to talk about this?" he asked in a low voice.

She nodded once. I watched how he took her arm to ease her in front of him, a gentle gesture at odds with the rest of his brusqueness.

Irene blinked at the flashing lights before her and swallowed hard. Her voice quavered only slightly when she said, "Congressman Jake Hamilton has been admitted to our hospital. His condition is stable. HIPAA regulations prohibit me from saying anything more. His family will be the ones to release any information."

Matthew Pierce reinserted himself in front of her. "That's all for now."

"Ms. Kelly, tell us what it was like to deliver a baby in the middle of a disaster," a voice called from the back, a deep melodious voice that made me gasp.

I squinted to see past the bright lights, but even the faint profile was enough. At the sight, my stomach clenched.

It was Peter.

Peter Armstrong, ace reporter for a cable news service. First at every war and scene of mass destruction. Pulitzer Prize winner for his sensational exposés. What the hell was he doing in Seattle?

After the initial shock, I was suddenly, unreasonably angry. How like him to distort reality for the sake of a story. "That's a total exaggeration," I snapped. "The disaster was up on the pass, not in our ER. The baby was delivered by a qualified midwife who had the full resources of the hospital supporting her." Okay, so I had morphed the truth a little. I didn't think Linda Tucker would want the story sensationalized any more than it already was.

Detective Pierce stepped in front of me. "That's all for now, folks. The hospital has provided you with a comfortable place to wait. They will keep the coffee and donuts coming, and sandwiches?" He glanced at Irene. She nodded. "And sandwiches. All we ask is that you not bother the victims, their families, other patients, or the staff. We'll let them know you're here so they can come to you for their fifteen seconds of fame."

A couple more questions were thrown out amidst the chuckling, but the reporters started moving away. I turned my back on them, not wanting to know if one reporter in particular had chosen to linger.

"Guess that'll keep them happy for a while," Detective Pierce said in his throaty growl as he watched the crowd disperse.

Irene groaned. "Can't those reporters read?"

I turned around again to see what she was talking about. The television reporters had moved to different corners, their cameras turned on for live transmissions. Print journalists were standing in front of Radiology, talking rapidly on their cell phones.

"How many signs do we post saying do not use cell phones because they interfere with the equipment?" She went for the closest reporter and tapped his shoulder, gestured to the posted signs, then pointed at his cell phone. When he started to argue, she signaled for one of the security guards. She made her way down the hall, waylaying every reporter who was in a "no cell phone" area.

Detective Pierce watched her progress, a hint of amusement lifting the corners of his mouth. "We could use someone like her for crowd control during the Taste of Madrona Bay festival."

Charley looked at the now-empty space in front of the reception counter. "I'm going to the ER. Call me if something comes up." He squeezed my shoulder and left me standing there with the detective.

Detective Pierce grunted. "Well, that's over."

"For a while at least," I said, wishing I was alone and anywhere else, but here. Thinking about the complaint against me, I sighed. "They'll be back for all the gory details."

"About that baby?" He glanced at my chest where a nametag should be, and I realized I wasn't wearing it. "Are you a nurse?"

I winced at his mistake. "No. I manage the Patient Relations department."

"The what?"

"Unhappy patients come to my department and we try to sort it out."

He smirked. "Bet you're not very popular around here."

"What do you mean by that?"

"I mean, if you take the patient's side in an argument, the rest of the employees are probably leery of you, at best. At worst, they don't like you. You're like IA."

"No, Detective. It's not like Internal Affairs at all." I told myself not to be defensive. "You would be amazed how often the staff calls and asks us to contact an unhappy patient."

"If you say so." He wasn't a tall man, but he had a patronizing way that made me feel small and I didn't like it.

"Hey, Mom!"

I turned to see Josh loping across the lobby, his long rangy body still waiting to be filled out. A baseball cap covered his dark-brown hair and he grinned broadly as he took in the cameras and reporters loitering nearby. A coat hanger with a clean blouse and slacks hung over his shoulder and he held a plastic bag with shoes. The clothes didn't match, but at this point, I didn't care. I briskly introduced Josh to Detective Pierce.

"Call me Matt," Pierce said as they shook hands.

"Nice to meet you. Mom, I gotta go. I'm double-parked in a fire lane." He grinned at Pierce, who merely shook his head as Josh raced out the door.

"Good kid you have there."

"Thanks. I think so too," I said. Most of the time. "He's a sophomore in mechanical engineering at the U."

"His dad must be real proud of him."

"Yes, he would be. David died when Josh was five, in a car accident. A drunk driver crossed the center line." *He died in my arms.*

"I'm sorry."

I turned to look at him and shrugged, pushing the nightmare back into the memory box I usually kept tightly locked. "It was a long time ago, Detective."

"That kind of hurt never goes away completely."

A lump formed in my throat and I swallowed hard. He was right. David's death had been forever, while the driver had been released after only three years in jail to drink and drive and kill again. Pierce's compassion brought the pain back unexpectedly, pain I had thought was long past. I twisted the gold claddagh ring on my right hand, a gift from David that I still wore. The Irish symbol of a crowned heart embraced by hands represented love, loyalty, and friendship, everything David and I meant to each other.

Nodding, I looked at the clothes Josh had brought. "Guess I better change before the next media assault."

"Are you coming back?"

"Of course. This is my designated place."

"Your what?"

"The disaster plan says I'm supposed to be here and direct the flow of information to employees, victims' families, and the media."

"That's a big job."

Did I hear an underlying condescension in his bland statement? It was hard to tell. "It's nothing we can't handle, Detective. Well, I really do need to change."

I started to leave, then turned back, basic courtesy winning over my desire to escape from this man who saw too much. "Thank you for helping us with the reporters."

He nodded and remained to talk to Connie, who apparently liked the detective, if her easy chatter was any indication. I slipped down a back hallway to a restroom. The brown slacks were snug, reflecting the few extra pounds I had put on since last winter, and the variegated blue blouse would have looked better with my navy slacks and navy shoes, not the taupe pumps Josh had brought. He had been in a hurry, I knew, and even in the best of times, his sense of fashion was a minus two on a scale of one to ten. At least these clothes were clean and unwrinkled. I didn't tuck in the blouse, convincing myself it made me look taller. And thinner. Delusional maybe, but I felt better.

After wrapping the dirty clothes in the plastic bag, I tried to do something with my hair. If I ever made it back to my office, I'd fix my make-up, but for the time being, this was as good as it was going to get.

Impatient to get back to Connie, I came barreling out of the restroom. The sight of a man lounging against the wall, his arms crossed casually over his broad chest, brought me to a stop.

"Hello, Rob."

"Peter. It's been a long time." I hoped I sounded insouciant rather than the way I really felt, like a stammering adolescent with a pounding heart.

Peter pushed away from the wall. The fluid ease of his movement told me he still worked out, although his tapered waist and taut neck were also evidence of a disciplined lifestyle. His jaw was still square, his cheeks hollow, and his eagle-sharp brown eyes missed nothing.

"What's it been? Five years?"

I laughed, but there was no humor. "Try more than ten. It was right before your career-making exploits during the Balkans wars." I silently berated myself for letting my hurt and Irish temper show.

"You look great, just the same," he said. Amazing how sincere he sounded. I raised a skeptical brow. He had the honesty to laugh at himself. "Okay, not the same, but you do look great, Rob. That blue blouse you were wearing before looked real nice on you. Matched your eyes."

"Thanks." The compliment caught me off guard. I took a couple of steps toward him and noticed some gray mixed with his tawny hair. "You've aged well too."

He ignored the jab. "What are you doing here?"

"I work here. The Patient Relations department," I said,

beginning to feel like a broken record. He was close enough now that I picked up a hint of his aftershave. Stetson. What he wore ten years ago. I breathed in more deeply, then stopped myself as the fragrance brought back heady memories.

"Really? Patient relations. That sounds interesting. I bet you know where all the bodies are buried."

His attempt at humor irritated me, and snapped me back to the present. "So why're you here? A freeway pile-up is a little tame for you. Shouldn't you be in the Middle East or some other hot spot, bringing man's inhumanity to man into our living rooms every evening?"

"Actually, I was at Sea-Tac when the network beeped me. It's an interesting change of pace, navigating through traffic on I-405 instead of through a war zone."

He looked away for a moment, and his expression turned boyishly wistful. "I had no idea you were here. I'm glad I found you, Rob." He took a step towards me.

His voice was so soft, I almost missed the words. But the implication slammed home to me. I hesitated before saying, "I didn't know you were looking."

"In between assignments, when I'd get back to the States, I would make a few phone calls, but no one seemed to know where you'd gone." He stepped closer.

I didn't tell him that the few who knew wouldn't have told. They had stood by me when David had died, and, for years, they feared I'd never fall in love again. Then I met Peter. When he disappeared from my life, they'd had to stand by in silent support as I struggled to pull myself together again. No, they would not have told.

"I've missed you, Rob. I've missed this." He tilted my chin up, and, for a moment, time stood still. He bent to kiss me.

I froze. My breath caught in my throat and then, his lips

were on mine, warm and achingly familiar. Instinctively, I leaned into the kiss, hungrily tasted him, breathed in the smell of him as if I had been starved for it. The years slipped away, along with the anger at his rejection, replaced by the flames of the passion we had always fanned in each other.

Slowly we parted. Still confused by his sudden reappearance in my life, I searched his face for signs of what he had meant by kissing me. His gaze had softened and his mouth formed that quirky smile that always made my heart somersault.

A deep cough from behind startled me. I pulled away and turned to see that police detective. My face heated with embarrassment. I had never done anything like this before, never lost myself in a passionate embrace in a place where anyone could walk by, and, of all the people to see us, why did it have to be him? How long had I been standing here with Peter? How long had the detective been watching? How much had he heard?

"Can…can I help you, Detective?"

Detective Pierce eyed Peter with a cold stare, then turned a bland look at me. "Connie needs you to read some report."

"Thank you, Detective. I'll talk to you later, Peter." Not daring to glance at either one of them, my emotions in a complete tangle, I hurried to the reception desk.

THREE

SUPPRESSING MY EMBARRASSMENT, I returned to Connie and the front desk, but the next few hours were a blur. I know I approved the in-house communiqués only because I saw my initials on them later, and I must have acted in a reasonably coherent manner because Connie didn't ask if anything was wrong. To say I was distracted, though, would be a gross understatement. Even the congressman's complaint against me faded from my mind.

Peter is back. Peter is back. The words swirled around and around in my head.

For a moment, I'd felt as giddy as a schoolgirl, thrilled down to my toes that he was here, yet bemoaning that I had been caught at less than my best when we were finally reunited.

But only for a moment. Then reality settled in. We were not reunited. If I had been an inveterate romantic, I might declare it was synchronicity, a fateful, unplanned crossing of paths. The skeptical realist in me insisted that he'd been on his way to somewhere else in the world; this meeting was a fluke, an accident. He had not sought me out.

At some level, my subconscious wish all these years had been that he would come to understand how much he loved me, how much he needed me, that he was willing to give up all the fame and excitement. Just for me. No woman wants to believe a man would choose action and danger over her passionate embrace.

Unfortunately, I had never given much thought to what happened next if he did declare his love and begged me to take him back. That was one of the problems with fantasies; they left out the nitty-gritty details. So now what?

Ten years was a long time, but I still remembered every moment we spent together. It had been the beginning of summer. I had put Josh on a plane to spend the vacation with my parents on their Colorado ranch, then rushed to a press function at the New York City hospital where I worked. Peter represented a local news station. Even then, he radiated energy, driven to succeed. He wanted to be *the* reporter. Not the anchor, but the one in the field who recounted the news as it happened without benefit of script writers or make-up artists.

It was pure chemistry. We started talking and gradually realized that everyone else had left and the clean-up crew was almost finished. We found our way to an intimate little basement bistro, one with a patio that looked through a charming wrought-iron fence to the sidewalk above. We sipped cabernet and toyed with our linguine, each reluctant to release the other's gaze. The next two months had been a whirlwind. When we weren't at work, we were together, and if one of us had to work late, the other one came to help.

I was the happiest I'd been in years, since before David had died, and I'd never thought to find that kind of happiness again. Yet, it was different. With Peter, I felt an intensity I never experienced with David.

As quickly as our relationship had flamed, it was snuffed out. Josh was coming home at the end of the week, and I didn't feel right living with a man in front of my young son. I arrived home planning to talk seriously to Peter about the future. Instead of finding Peter preparing another exotic feast, I found a note. It seemed that several months before, he had applied for a position with a cable news organization. The call had come that day. He'd been hired and was being sent to the Middle East to cover a war. Just like that, he was gone.

While the rest of America listened to his voice-overs on nightly news reports from a secret location behind enemy lines, I turned the television off. I found myself restless in the big city; everywhere I went reminded me of him. Of us.

The position at Madrona Bay came open at the right time, near what was then touted as the most liveable city in the States. Nine-year-old Josh loved the idea of a house with a yard and playing ball in the cul-de-sac with other neighborhood kids. I escaped the memories of New York and made a fresh start for myself.

We had made a good life here, Josh and I. Now, I asked myself: did Peter want me back in his life? More to the point, did I want Peter back in mine? If that searing kiss we shared was any indication, I would have to say "I think so" to both questions.

BY MID-DAY, the storm continued unabated, but the hospital had settled into its usual routine. The ER was open again for business, and the O.R.'s were finishing up with the last of the accident victims. We still had a few empty beds available, but not many.

Connie had returned to our office, where a slew of voice-mail messages guaranteed we'd be swamped for days. I had remained at the registration desk, but one more E-mail update and I could get back to my office.

Everyone knew the congressman was being monitored closely in a private room near ICU that could be guarded and cordoned off from the curious public and relentless reporters determined to get the scoop on *"How did it feel, Con-*

gressman Hamilton, when you saw the jack-knifed semi looming in front of you?" and other such ridiculous questions.

No one had approached me for a good ten minutes, so I decided to take a look around. I slipped through a door that led to the now-quiet ER. I peeked out the ambulance entrance where I had a reasonably good view of the parking lot.

The spaces closest to the building had been reserved for victims' families so they could come and go without running the gauntlet of reporters. Two uniformed police officers patrolled the perimeter of the lot, which was marked off with bright yellow crime-scene tape to keep away reporters and the curious.

I didn't see Detective Pierce anywhere. In fact, I hadn't seen him since the embarrassing encounter in the hallway, and that was fine with me. The man grated on my nerves, which was unusual because I don't often have an immediate dislike of someone.

From behind the yellow police tape, a few reporters waited like vultures for victims or their families to depart. Peter stood off to the side, gesturing broadly as he talked on his cell phone. I shut the door before he saw me, although I was hard pressed to explain why I was avoiding contact. Maybe I needed more time to sort out my feelings.

I checked in on our makeshift pressroom, and the scene reminded me of those old black-and-white movies with all the foreign correspondents sitting around a dark bar sharing war stories. Only this time there was no Scotch-on-the-rocks and no thick layer of smoke in the air. Instead, it was coffee by the giant urn-full, soft drink cans and yogurt cups in huge ice-filled bowls, a portable sandwich bar cart, and small bags of chips and cookies under glaring lights. If nothing else, the reporters wouldn't leave hungry. Those who wanted to smoke went outside. Otherwise, they munched and hunched over their laptops.

Melanie Cole, the Channel Eight reporter, approached me. She didn't have a microphone or notepad in her hands, so I relaxed. She followed local politics and knew everybody who was anybody, including the behind-the-scenes movers and shakers. In her mid-thirties, she was smart, articulate, and had a reputation for telling the story straight, rather than hyping it up. The word "shocking" was not part of her vocabulary, and I respected her for not caving in to network demands to sensationalize the news.

"How's it going, Melanie?" I asked as if we were old friends.

"I've seen election night losers' parties livelier than this." A quick grin brought a twinkle to her hazel eyes. Then, she wrinkled her nose and nodded toward the food table. "You're feeding us too well. I won't need to eat for days."

She was much thinner than she appeared on TV, lending credence to the theory that the camera added ten to twenty pounds. Her heart-shaped face was free of wrinkles and her frosted brown hair was cut in a layered bob. A lightweight black sweater fitted softly over her curves, and black boots met her black wool skirt at mid-calf. The black-and-tan plaid jacket she wore on camera was draped over the back of her chair, ready to slip on at a moment's notice.

"We don't want you guys getting cranky from sugar or caffeine deprivation. Is there anything you need in here?"

The quick grin appeared again. "Yeah, you can make something happen."

"I'll see what I can do," I said with a laugh.

"When will you have a press conference?"

I handed her a copy of the latest update. "Will this do?"

She glanced at it. "Not really. We need a real person so we can ask questions about Congressman Hamilton."

I grimaced. "Like that mob scene we had earlier this morning?"

"Well, maybe not like that. But an interview would be great, especially since we're so close to the evening news lead-in commercials. It would be even better to talk with the congressman himself."

"Hmm. I'll see if I can arrange for something to happen and a press conference. Anything else?"

"That about does it. Thanks, Robyn. I know this hasn't been easy."

"You guys have been reasonable," I said. "Except for those tabloid reporters who brought their own lab coats and pretended to be doctors to sneak upstairs."

Melanie laughed and shook her head. "That took balls, all right. I'm glad you let the rest of us stay after Security threw them out."

I left her then, remembering how Tom had been apoplectic when he discovered two reporters had brazened their way past a rented security guard and were fast-talking the police officer guarding the congressman's door into letting them examine Hamilton. After that, anyone not wearing the hospital's picture ID was denied access upstairs.

I returned to the front desk to corral a doc to talk about Congressman Hamilton, and someone to talk about disaster preparedness in general. That should keep the reporters happy, and put in a good plug for all the planning we did throughout the year.

As I punched in the number for the ICU nurses' station, two people came roaring through the front door.

"Robyn, what the hell is going on?" Will Slater's voice ricocheted off the lobby and echoed down the hallway. I winced as everyone within earshot turned to look at us, including Melanie and several other reporters who came to the doorway of our makeshift pressroom.

Will must have noticed as well, because his bristliness subsided as he strode toward me. He was a tall, lean man in his late forties, with a shock of silver through his black hair. An accountant at heart, he was an excellent money manager, with little patience for the unanticipated or the exception. My department dealt mostly with the unanticipated and the exception, and so our working relationship was troublesome at best. We just did not speak the same language.

"Will, I'm so glad to see you," I said more warmly than I felt. "We've had quite a time here."

"I can't leave this place for a single day. We'll be lucky to get any new program funds," he fumed, referring to the allocations scheduled to be made at this corporate-wide retreat.

"What's the status, Robyn?" asked the woman who had followed him in, her kind tone a sharp contrast to Will's. Brenda Martin, the Director of Nursing Services, was only about ten years older than me, but it often felt more like a generation separated us. Her gray-streaked hair was wound into a tight bun every morning, and by the end of the day, not a strand had dared escape. Her business suits were functional and unimaginative, devoid of any softness or decoration except for a large silver cross on a chunky chain, while her shoes could only be described as "sensible." Short and square, she seemed better suited for a military operation with her no-nonsense approach. But she was a staunch advocate for her nurses, who loved her and would follow her into hell if she asked them. Underneath her all-business demeanor, I occasionally sensed a bit of the zealot, but she never shared any personal opinions.

In answer to her question, I handed both Brenda and Will copies of the in-house E-mail updates and gave them a quick verbal summary of the day's events, finishing with, "Did you hear that one of the victims was Jake Hamilton?"

Will's head shot up. "Who?"

"Congressman Hamilton?" Brenda asked. "My daughter, Cynthia, works for him."

I nodded. "That's him. He had a number of injuries, nothing critical, but serious enough that he was admitted." I decided now was not the time to mention that the congressman wasn't totally delighted with all aspects of his care. "I'm in the process of setting up a press conference so the reporters can ask questions."

Will frowned, as if he couldn't decide if a press conference would be a good thing or bad, for the hospital or for himself. He was not big on impromptu events, so I quickly added, "I'm trying to get a doc to summarize the victims and maybe Charley to talk about our disaster planning."

"That should be okay, Robyn." He straightened his already straight tie. "I'll be there too, of course. To address any questions that might be best for me to answer."

Remembering the assault Irene, Charley, and I had survived, I swallowed a smile and wondered how Will would have reacted to it. And, to Detective Pierce stepping in to take charge. Now that would have been worth the price of admission to watch. "I'll let you know when it's set up. Oh, and Brenda? Your daughter's here."

"Cynthia's here?" Brenda appeared flustered, as if surprised her daughter was even in Seattle. "Where is she?"

"She's probably in the cafeteria or upstairs with Congressman Hamilton."

Brenda's lips tightened—with disapproval? I wasn't

sure. "Thanks, Robyn. Will, maybe we can meet later this week with the CEO to discuss our budget requests before he flies back to L.A." Brenda headed in the direction of the back stairwell.

Will absently drummed his fingers on the laminated counter as he looked around the busy lobby, then he scowled. "I better take a look at these reports and figure out how much this fiasco cost us. Let me know when you have the press conference set up, Robyn."

I watched him leave, his eyes moving like a radar dish, scanning everything, missing nothing. I remembered Tom's comments about today's extra security costs and was relieved I hadn't spent any money. Or had I? Which department did Connie and Dietary settle on to pay for the reporters' food? I decided not to check on that. I'd hear from Will soon enough if it was my problem. Instead, I resumed my efforts to organize a press conference so I could get back to my real work.

IT WAS MID-AFTERNOON when I finally escaped my lobby post. After the press conference, most of the reporters had left the hospital to find more exciting stories. They had squeezed out all the human-interest bystander interviews that television viewers could tolerate. The congressman was stable, but unavailable for interviews. Not much news there.

I started toward the stairs to grab a roast beef sandwich in the cafeteria and order my afternoon tonic, a latté with a double shot of espresso and chocolate syrup. Instead, I decided to take a detour first to pay a courtesy call on Congressman Hamilton. I still couldn't believe he had filed a complaint against me. All I did was tell him I couldn't give him pain meds, and that the doctor probably wouldn't order any until after a thorough exam. I certainly had not mis-tagged him, deliberately or otherwise. Charley said yellow, and that was the tag I put on Hamilton's arm.

It must be something else. Maybe he was on the congressional committee hearing Louisa's testimony. Was this a ploy to discredit our profession and undermine the patient-rights legislation? That wasn't possible. It was too far-fetched for even a moderate conspiracy theorist.

Maybe I could smooth things over so the congressman wouldn't follow through with his complaint. I hoped he was ready to listen to reason. Some people were much more pleasant when they felt better and had not just gone through a horrific experience. And surely he'd had enough treatment by now that he was feeling properly attended to. If not, there was a part of me that was tempted to point out the possible press interpretation of the congressman's aggressive demands for drugs. Only as a last resort, mind you.

Of course, I knew full well that such a tactic, regardless of how satisfying in the short run, could backfire in a big way. Jake Hamilton was an up-and-coming congressman from our state, and he would vote on a lot of patient rights and health-insurance bills over the next two years. My professional association would appreciate my keeping good relations with him. Sometimes, I thought with a sigh, a person had to keep the big picture in mind and stifle justifiable human reactions.

I reached the double doors that marked the entrance to 3-West. Like the other patient wings at Madrona Bay Hospital, the unit had a U-shaped hallway, with patient rooms along the outside walls, and staff offices and supply rooms down the middle.

Congressman Hamilton's corner room was at the far end of 3-West. "Wet floor" triangles had been used to cordon off the area, funneling all who came and went past the uniformed police officer outside Hamilton's door. The officer was a tall young man, dark-haired with the requisite macho mustache. Probably because I wasn't wearing either of the hospital's uniforms, a white lab coat or scrubs, he shifted his position to stand taller. His huge belt creaked the way only stiff leather can.

I glanced at his nametag and extended my hand. "Hello, Officer Tomlin. I'm Robyn Kelly, manager of Patient Relations. How're you doing?"

"Ms. Kelly." Noting the picture ID on my blouse, he seemed to relax, even smiled a bit. I was probably the first person to talk to him as if he were a real person. He shook my hand and I found his hand damp to the touch. For a fleeting moment, that puzzled me because he didn't appear overly warm.

"I've never spent time in a hospital before," Officer Tomlin said, his hands resting on his belt. "It's like a three-ring circus. I'd hate to be a patient. You never get any rest."

I almost chuckled, but it was not a laughing matter for most patients. "People don't come to hospitals to rest anymore, Officer. These days, they're treated and discharged as soon as they can sit up. Has it been busy?"

"People with charts and trays of pills and needles have been going in and out all day. And then there's the accident investigation. Several people have talked to Mr. Hamilton about the crash."

So Irene hadn't been able to keep him sedated. I only hoped the congressman hadn't taken those opportunities to share his opinion of me with investigators.

"I was wondering if I could pop in for a moment to say hi and see if there's anything we can do to make him more comfortable." And see if I could settle his complaint before it made the news.

Officer Tomlin shrugged. "Don't see any reason why

not. No one's come by for at least fifteen minutes or so. He may be asleep."

"I'll check quietly," I promised.

The door to Hamilton's room was closed. Taking a deep, calming breath, I steeled myself for another unpleasant encounter with this man. I knocked softly, but didn't hear a response, so I slowly opened the door and peeked into the semi-darkened room. A cart rattled noisily down the hall. I ducked inside the room and shut the door quickly.

This time of year, there wasn't much sun in the Pacific Northwest, and even with the blinds tilted open, only a little light entered the room. The overhead fluorescents were turned off, but the bathroom door was ajar and a narrow stream of light escaped through the crack.

"Congressman Hamilton?" I said in a hushed voice. If he was asleep, I didn't want to wake him.

It was then that I was struck by how quiet it was, what could only be described as a chilling silence. I rubbed my arms as if to ward off the cold.

Shaking off my unease, I stepped farther into the room. The congressman lay in the bed, his face turned away from me. I raised myself on tiptoes to see. It seemed the congressman's eyes were open.

"Congressman?" I said in a conversational volume.

When he did not respond, I moved closer until I rounded the foot of the bed. A prickly feeling crawled up my spine as I leaned forward. Even in the dim light, I could see a glassiness in his eyes, and I realized he wasn't breathing.

FOUR

AN ICY-HOT WAVE OF nausea hit me. I backed away, then ran to the door and flung it open.

Officer Tomlin grabbed my arm as I lurched from the congressman's room. "What's wrong?" he asked.

I escaped his grasp and ran to the nurses' station. "Code Blue. Hamilton's room."

Susan Wong, the nurse manager, blanched and hit the intercom button. "Code Blue...Three-West...Code Blue...Three-West." She flipped off the intercom and ran into a supply room, reappearing with a crash cart. She raced with it toward the congressman's room, and two other nurses met her at the door.

I sank into Susan's chair and started deep breathing. Although I work in a hospital, my exposure to dead patients was limited. I held family members' hands while they made difficult decisions, or talked to them about their complaints. I spent time with patients who weren't happy. But I did not do dead people.

Some patient reps became very involved with patients and their families, and stayed with them during the final moments. Those reps usually worked for hospitals with large cancer or research units, and the patients were there so long they were more like family. But Madrona Bay replaced hips and delivered babies, and took out gall bladders, a general purpose in-and-out local hospital. And that was fine with me. Drained of emotion and over-whelmed, I buried my face in my hands.

As my shock at finding the dead congressman sub-sided, I began to worry. This should not be happening. He'd been listed in stable condition. A few broken bones and lacerations, and a possible concussion. He wasn't critical. He wasn't even connected to any monitors.

The door to Hamilton's room was half open, and the team inside was still trying desperately to revive him. Officer Tomlin was talking into his shoulder-mounted radio and from his grim expression, the response was not going well. Beyond the barriers already set up around the room, a crowd had gathered, staff and visitors, trying to see this latest installment of a very bizarre day.

At last, the team in Hamilton's room seemed to pull back from his bed as one. Several of them snapped off their latex gloves. A quick glance at the clock told me they had tried for half an hour.

But, this was not the end of it, not by a long shot. I didn't want to begin to contemplate the furor that was coming. At the very least, Will Slater would have an apo-plectic fit, and the press would go into another feeding frenzy. At the thought of it, my stomach flip-flopped.

And, as selfish as it sounded, I worried about the con-gressman's complaint against me. Where was it? If I was lucky, it was only in Charley's notes where it could easily be forgotten. After all, who would we follow up with? At worst, it was written up formally with copies floating through the inter-office mail system.

Hoping to escape before all hell broke loose, I slipped down the hallway to my office. Connie was just starting to make a telephone call. She looked up and must have seen something awful on my face, because she dropped the receiver and came to me at once.

"Rob, what happened? You look like you've seen a ghost." She guided me to the small couch in our waiting area and sat me down.

"That's so close to the truth, your psychic training must be working," I said ruefully. I told her about finding Hamilton's body and the unsuccessful efforts of the crash team to revive him. "So now, it's going to be worse than this morning. Call PR and tell them to get someone over here *now*."

I didn't care about excuses. Public Relations was handling the next round of press conferences. They were paid a lot more than me, and I wasn't letting them off the hook this time. With a groan, I sagged against the back of the couch and closed my eyes. "I don't even want to think about it."

At a knock on the door, my eyes popped open. "See," I said. "It's beginning already. Go away." The last was in a half-hearted whisper.

Connie frowned, at me or the interruption, I didn't care, and went to answer the door. As she reached for the knob, the door opened.

Detective Pierce stepped into the office. His rapid scrutiny of the room stopped when it landed on me. His eyebrow quirked, but his quick assessment must have told him that my supine position was not from terminal causes. Through half-open eyes, I saw his solid steadiness and felt a flash of calm. But that was ridiculous; he followed in the wake of trouble. I wrote off my momentary relief as a semi-hysterical reaction. If one can be semi-hysterical while leaning listlessly against a couch.

"Ms. Kelly?"

"Yes, Detective?"

"You look like hell," Pierce said.

"Detective, this has been a very difficult day," I said

with a scowl, and decided this man really was annoying. I struggled to sit up, but my bones felt like mush.

"Don't get up." When I sank onto the couch again and closed my eyes, he added, "Perhaps I should rephrase that. You don't have to get up, but don't go to sleep."

"What do you want?"

"I have to question you about Congressman Hamilton."

I opened my eyes to study him. "Why me? I don't know anything."

"An injured, but not seriously injured, congressman is unexpectedly found dead. A lot of people think that's a problem. You found him, so I'm starting with you."

"There's not much to tell. When I entered his room, he looked like he was dead. Not breathing. Glassy-eyed stare." I shuddered at the memory.

"Why did you go to Congressman Hamilton's room?"

This probably wasn't the time to mention that I visited the congressman because he had filed a complaint against me and I wanted to resolve it before it went any further.

"I decided to pay a courtesy call on Congressman Hamilton. Volunteers visit all the new patients. Part of our patient-relations thing. But, since he was a VIP, I thought it would be best if I did it myself."

I pushed myself to a full sitting position. "When I discovered he wasn't breathing, I ran out and called a Code Blue."

At that point, Connie came over and put a comforting hand on my shoulder.

"A Code Blue," Detective Pierce said.

"Yes." I sighed. "Code Blue means someone has stopped breathing, or their heart stops."

"I know what it means," Pierce mumbled to himself. He looked toward the window for a moment, and I had the oddest suspicion he was pulling himself together. When he turned to face me again, he appeared to be his usual brusque self.

"Tell me exactly what happened when you went into the congressman's room. Everything, no matter how trivial you think it might be." He sat down at the other end of the couch and slipped on a pair of half-glasses that magnified his weary brown eyes. He took out his notepad and pen, and looked at me.

"I introduced myself to Officer Tomlin and we chatted for a moment. He seems very nice. I hope you have a lot of officers like him."

"As opposed to crusty old farts like me?" Detective Pierce looked at me over the top of his glasses.

From the heat on my face, I figured I was blushing furiously. His attempt at humor surprised me. Maybe he wasn't as arrogant as I'd first thought. "That's not what I meant at all, Detective. Experience and maturity are also very necessary for a police department. Besides," I added with a placid smile, "you're not old, just well-seasoned."

"Like a good steak, huh?" He gave a tired chuckle. "I've been called a lot of things, Ms. Kelly, but never well-seasoned. Now, you were telling me about finding the congressman?"

"Where was I?"

"You chatted with Officer Tomlin."

"Oh, yes. Very nice young man. I said that already, didn't I? Okay, so I knocked on the congressman's door and started to open it when a cart came rattling down the hall. You know, Detective Pierce, we have these on-going debates about whether the floors should be carpeted or vinyl," I said earnestly, leaning forward. "Carpeting is so much quieter, but the carts are easier to push on vinyl and—"

"Ms. Kelly."

"Hmmm? Oh. Sorry. Guess I'm still a bit upset by the whole thing." I shifted my position and took a moment to gather my thoughts. I rested my hands on my lap in gentle fists and stared at a spot on the carpet. "The cart was making a lot of noise and I didn't want to wake the congressman if he was asleep, so I ducked into his room and shut the door."

A bone-chilling cold settled into my bones. I started to shake. Even my teeth chattered. Then came the tears, cascading down my cheeks like a waterfall.

"Get her a coat or a blanket," Detective Pierce snapped at Connie. She ducked into the storage area and returned with my Eddie Bauer jacket. Detective Pierce grabbed the jacket from her and slipped it over my shoulders, pulling it close and hugging me to him.

"It's okay, Ms. Kelly…may I call you Robyn?"

He patted my back as a parent would a child. I felt uncomfortable with his closeness, but not enough to pull away. I sniffed and nodded against his shoulder.

"Good. You'll be okay in a minute, Robyn. You're just having a delayed reaction." He held me for a moment until I stopped shaking, then set me back in my corner of the couch.

"Feel better?" he asked.

I nodded.

"Ready to continue?"

I nodded again and dug a handkerchief out of my coat pocket. He was being so nice, I thought maybe he wasn't so bad after all. After blowing my nose and swiping at my eyes, I reached for the steaming cup of coffee Connie held out for me. I took a sip and shuddered at the bitter taste. It had been sitting in the pot for several hours, but it was hot and that was most important.

"I'm sorry, Detective. I don't usually fall apart." I took another sip of coffee before setting the cup on the floor.

"You don't fall apart period, Rob," Connie chimed in. "She doesn't, Detective. She's always calm. No matter what."

She stood next to me, a worried look on her face and a box of tissues in her hand. I pulled one out and blew my nose again.

After taking a deep breath, I said, "Okay, I went into the room and shut the door. Then I felt the cold. It was like nothing I ever felt before. Do you know what I'm talking about?" I searched his face for confirmation.

He nodded. "I do. It's a feeling I get whenever I walk into a room where someone's recently died. It's as if the warmth of that person's soul has departed, leaving the body to face the chill of the grave alone."

His poetic description caught me by surprise. Some of the tension slipped away too; he understood.

"That's exactly what it felt like, but I didn't know it at the time. I called Congressman Hamilton's name quietly, but he didn't respond."

"Describe where he was."

"He was lying in bed." From Detective Pierce's glowering, he wanted more than that.

I closed my eyes and tried to recreate the scene in my head. "He was lying in the bed. On his back. Looking away from me toward the window. The covers were rumpled around his waist. His arms were bandaged from all the cuts and his left"—I shifted my shoulders—"no, his right arm was in a full cast. The left was all bandaged up, including his hand. Both arms were at his sides, but not straight. More of a forty-five-degree angle. Slightly bent at the elbows."

I opened my eyes, surprised but pleased I remembered so much.

"Then, what did you do?"

"I stepped toward him. Quietly, because I didn't want to disturb him if he was sleeping. I rounded the foot of the bed and leaned forward to see if he was awake. That's when I saw his eyes were open and it looked like he wasn't breathing. I ran from the room and called the code."

"Did you touch anything while you were in the room?"

"I don't think so. It all happened so fast."

He nodded. "That should do it for now. But—"

The office door opened and Peter stepped inside. He stopped for a moment as he took in the scene, then his expression hardened.

"Rob? Is everything okay?" He came to me and, when I stood up, threw a protective arm around my shoulder. "What are you doing here, Detective?"

Part of me was gratified by Peter's macho protectiveness, and part of me found it smothering. I eased away from him. "I'm fine, Peter. Really I am. Detective Pierce has been asking me to describe what I—"

"That's fine for now, Ms. Kelly."

Detective Pierce flipped his notepad closed and stood. The wary distaste I'd seen in his eyes earlier when he caught Peter and me kissing had returned. It irritated me that he didn't mask his personal opinion.

"I'll check back with you if I have any more questions. In the meantime, it would be best if you didn't talk about this. With anyone."

Although he gave Connie a passing glance, Detective Pierce glared at Peter, leaving little doubt exactly who he meant. Of course, Peter stiffened, but had the sense not to open his mouth. Under the circumstances, being allied with a reporter might not be a good thing. I felt caught in the professional crossfire between the press and the police.

"Mr. Armstrong, the third floor is off limits." Detective Pierce opened the door and I saw another uniformed officer standing outside. "I'm sure you know that. Officer Leeds here will escort you back to the first floor."

Peter scowled. "I need to talk to Robyn for a few minutes. Then, I'll come down." Peter glanced at me. "She'll see that I don't go where I'm not supposed to."

Detective Pierce frowned, his gaze shifting between me and Peter. Finally, he stared hard at me. "Five minutes. Then, I want him downstairs."

After I nodded my agreement, Detective Pierce and the officer left. Connie shuffled a stack of papers on her desk and glanced at Peter and me from downcast eyes. "I, uh, I remembered I have to go to the mail room."

Connie was barely out of the room when Peter turned his frown of concern toward me. "I was so worried about you." He rested his hands on my shoulders. "We heard about the congressman, and that you were involved."

Peter pulled me closer. He was still devastatingly attractive and the chemistry was still there, even after all these years. Then, I couldn't help but be annoyed for capitulating to his charms so easily. Determined to prove, if only to myself, that I wasn't a complete pushover, I asserted some willpower and pushed away before it went any further. I found his penitent expression almost amusing.

"I'm sorry, darling. I can't help myself when I'm around you. Never could, could I?" he said with a sheepish grin, one of his most endearing expressions.

"That's okay, Peter, except this isn't the time, and this certainly isn't the place."

His grin broadened and he ruffled my hair affectionately. "It didn't used to bother you."

I refrained from rolling my eyes. His playfulness and spontaneity were part of what I had loved about him. Instead of giving in, though, I chided him. "That was in a locked office late at night after everyone had gone home.

This office is open to the public, and that door is unlocked."

Now too warm, I took my coat to the storage room. When I returned, Peter was standing beside the couch. "We could always lock the door."

Was he testing me? Memories flooded back, memories stuffed into a dark corner where I did not have to see them. Memories of a time when I had been deliriously happy, so in love with Peter that any risk was worth it to be with him.

But that was then, and this was now, and I wasn't the same person anymore. Well, maybe I was the same person, but an older, wiser version, and I'd worked too hard to risk everything for a moment's pleasure. The jury remained out as to whether or not I was still in love with Peter. Or trusted him. I wanted to believe, but could I?

As quickly as his countenance turned serious, it changed back to frisky. He wiggled his eyebrows and leered blatantly at me. "Baby, when two people have that special something, time doesn't matter."

"Oh, for heaven's sake, Peter, you sound like a bad B movie." Smiling now, I wondered if maybe I was taking this all too seriously.

"I want to see you again, Rob. But not here. Someplace where we can talk."

He sounded sincere, which meant I had to reconsider my earlier worries. This time, I thought with my head and not my heart before saying quietly, "I don't know, Peter. I have to think about it. Come on, let's get you downstairs before Detective Pierce comes looking for you."

Peter frowned and touched my arm. "Is there something I should know about?"

Bewildered, I said, "What? What are you talking about?"

"You and the cop. Is there something going on? I saw the way he looked at you."

I laughed then, a hearty laugh, the first and only one in a long, difficult day. "Honestly, Peter. Don't be ridiculous. I just met the man this morning."

Shaking my head, and still laughing, I opened the door and ushered Peter from the office.

"Then, you don't owe him anything." Peter stared at me so intently his eyes could have burned holes through my skull to see into my brain. He gripped my arms. "Look, Rob, everyone knows Hamilton is dead. Do you know how it happened?"

I had forgotten the congressman's death was already common knowledge; the hospital grapevine can disseminate news faster than the Internet. I slipped from his grip and said, "You'll find out when everyone else does, Peter."

I didn't say anything more until I opened the stairwell door to the 1st floor and we stepped around the corner to the makeshift pressroom.

He leaned forward to kiss me, but this time I was prepared. I side-stepped as if unaware what he was attempting. He looked hurt, but he'd have to live with it. I wasn't about to provide another public spectacle.

"Ms. Kelly, I have some more questions."

With a silent groan of dismay, I recognized Detective Pierce's voice from behind me. I felt like a teenager caught sneaking a cigarette behind the gym. Peter cast a withering look at Pierce, but he moved away and entered the pressroom without saying another word.

"Yes, Detective, I'm ready." I noticed he had gone back to the more formal address. Maybe he only used first names when witnesses were hysterical.

Wordlessly, we crossed the waiting area to the west wing elevators. When we got in, Detective Pierce pushed

"Three." I expected to return to my office when we stepped off the elevator. Instead, he led me in the opposite direction. I shuddered as we walked down the 3-West hallway toward Congressman Hamilton's room.

Bright yellow crime-scene tape covered the door. "Why is that here?" I asked.

Pierce only shrugged. With the help of the officer standing guard, he pulled the tape aside and we passed through.

I held my breath as we entered the room, but the chilling cold I felt before wasn't there. I slowly started to breathe again and looked around to see an ordinary patient room waiting to be cleaned by housekeeping.

"Why are we here?" I asked.

"Procedure." Pierce shrugged again, but I wasn't buying it. An underlying current of energy ran through him. He wasn't as blasé as he wanted to appear.

Intrigued, I asked, "What do you think happened?"

Pierce ignored the question, which only heightened my curiosity. "Okay, Ms. Kelly, I want you to run through the scene again. You walked into the room and came around the end of the bed."

He signaled for me to retrace my steps. "Did you touch anything?"

I thought for a moment, before I reached out to put my hand on the bed. "Yes. I put my hand here. Only, I touched the pillow."

It wasn't there now, which wasn't surprising given the efforts of the crash team to revive Congressman Hamilton. I looked around and saw it lying on the floor in the corner, and bent to pick it up.

"Wait!" Detective Pierce grabbed my arm. "Don't touch it."

"Why not?"

"Think about it. Why was the pillow at the foot of the bed?"

Annoyed at this one-sided game of his, I snapped, "How should I know?"

"Are patients automatically given a pillow or is it an option?"

"I expect it's placed under their heads automatically. Congressman Hamilton was probably sedated when he was brought here, so, yes, it's safe to assume he was using one."

Detective Pierce stared at the empty bed as if willing it to confess. "Could he have moved the pillow himself if he had a seizure or something?"

"You mean thrashing around?" When he nodded, I approached the other side of the bed. "I don't think so. If he had thrashed around, it would have fallen on the floor next to his head." I tried to think of other scenarios. "His right arm was in a cast over the elbow, so he couldn't bend it. And his left hand was bandaged, making it difficult to hold onto anything. Either way, I can't see him grabbing the pillow and tossing it to the foot of the bed. If anything, he'd push it on the floor."

"What about a nurse, would she put the pillow there?"

"I don't think so," I said again. "She'd be more likely to toss it into a chair."

"Get me a large plastic bag to put this pillow in."

"Sure. I'll be right back."

I left Detective Pierce mumbling to himself while I tried to figure out why the pillow was such a big deal. I walked the short distance to the nurses' station. "Hi, Susan," I said to the nurse behind the counter.

Susan Wong, the manager for 3-West, looked up, and I saw her harassed expression. A petite bundle of energy, Susan always stood tall and wore a heavily starched, im-

maculate white lab coat over her street clothes. Now the
lab coat looked like my blue silk blouse, spotted and
wrinkled, and her shoulders were slumped with fatigue.
Usually her long black hair was neatly tied up, but strands
had slipped from the hair clip and she didn't seem to
notice, which worried me.

"Rob. Do you believe it? This morning was bad
enough, but this. I didn't like that man in the first place,"
she grumbled. "If I had known…."

"You didn't like him?"

"Oh, I don't know. Maybe like is too strong. I mean, he
was pretty much out of it when he transferred here. But
later…" She frowned. "I guess he just, well, I don't know.
Maybe I just dislike all politicians on general principle.
Even the good ones turn out to be smarmy on closer inspec-
tion."

"This whole thing is a nightmare. Important people
aren't supposed to die at little ol' Madrona Bay. It's crazy."
I wanted to ask her more, but Pierce was waiting for me,
so I said, "Listen, do you have those plastic bags we put
patients' things in?"

Nodding, she went to a supply closet and returned with
one. "Are you checking in?"

"Don't I wish," I said. "No, this is for the police. The
detective wants to take a pillow."

She looked unnerved. "A pillow? Why?"

"Who knows?" Shaking the bag open, I turned to leave,
then stopped. "Susan? Who's been here today?"

"Who?" She thought for a moment and shrugged.
"Only the whole western world. Let's see," Susan continued, counting on her fingers. "The police were here, of
course, investigating the accident. Brenda came, repre-
senting Admin. Will wouldn't want corporate to hear we
annoyed a congressman—"

I winced inside; what would corporate say if they learned a congressman had complained about me?

"—We had eight victims admitted to this unit, so all their families. And the staff. But everyone checked in with me about the clinical stuff, and then again with that darling officer standing guard at the door."

I smiled; so she wasn't too tired to notice him. Married with four kids, Susan was old enough to be Officer Tomlin's mother. "Okay, thanks." I started down the hall when Susan called after me.

"Wait, Rob. His assistant, that girl. She was here too. A real nuisance, crying and carrying on after she saw him." Susan shook her head. "I had to call a social worker to get her out of here."

"When was that?"

"Sometime this afternoon?" Susan shook her head. "I don't know. The whole day's been a blur."

Returning to Hamilton's room, I kept mulling over the list of "the whole western world." In a hospital, that covered a wide territory: lab and pharmacy techs, physical and respiratory therapists, doctors, nurses, housekeeping. I did not envy Detective Pierce his task.

In the room, I found Detective Pierce facing the bed, one hand fisted and resting on his hip, the other hand covering his mouth. He started when I entered.

"Penny for your thoughts, Detective."

He raised an eyebrow. "I don't think you really want to know."

"Try me."

He paced the room once, twice, then stopped again. "With someone as prominent as the congressman, a lot of people will be peering over our shoulders, telling us what we should have done."

He sighed and wiped his hand over his face. He

motioned for me to hold the plastic bag open while he pulled on a pair of latex gloves and picked the pillow up by the corners and very carefully set it into the bag. Then he marked the bag with an adhesive label he dug out of his pocket and sealed the bag with a tie from another pocket.

"What are you afraid you might have overlooked?"

"I don't know," he said thoughtfully. "We had a uniformed officer outside the door at all times."

"What do you mean?"

He gave me a quelling look, then started for the door, the bagged pillow in his hand. Stunned by his implication, I hesitated, then quickly followed, not eager to stay in the room alone.

It had finally sunk in: Detective Pierce believed Congressman Hamilton was murdered.

MURDER.

I couldn't get it out of my head. Detective Pierce thought Congressman Hamilton had been murdered. I reeled at the possibility, and I wanted nothing more to do with any of it. After all, I had withheld information from the police.

When questioned by Detective Pierce earlier, I had deliberately not mentioned that the real reason I went to Congressman Hamilton's room was because he'd filed a complaint against me, and I hoped to change his mind. Would that be considered a motive?

And I was the last person to enter the room. Would the police believe Congressman Hamilton was already dead when I went in? Surely they wouldn't suspect me. Or would they? I certainly hoped not!

When I left 3-West, Detective Pierce was on the phone. Again. What could he hope to find from a pillow tossed on the floor? The Code Team had made a mess of the room when they tried to revive the congressman. The Crime Scene Unit would have a nightmare sorting through the evidence left by all the people in and out of that room.

I figured an autopsy had been ordered, and it was a safe assumption that Congressman Hamilton was at the top of the medical examiner's waiting list.

It had already been a demanding day, but if I thought this morning had been challenging, it paled compared to what was coming. At least this time a corporate PR person was dealing with the media. I really hoped I would escape notice.

As I left 3-West and crossed the waiting area, I spotted Cynthia Martin standing near the window. Despite my plan to not be involved, I couldn't help but respond to Cynthia's obvious distress. Her shoulders were hunched and her face rested against the window while she gazed in the direction of the concrete wall that made 3-North.

"Cynthia? Are you okay?" I asked in a soft voice as I approached her.

At first, she didn't respond, but then she shuddered and turned to face me. Her face was blotchy and swollen from crying. "He's dead," she said in the most pitiful voice I had ever heard.

"I know, dear." I put my arm around her shoulder. "I'm really sorry."

She leaned into my shoulder and started to sob. "Why? Why did he…have to…die? He was…he was so wonderful," she sputtered.

"I don't know. But I'm sure we'll know when the autopsy's done."

She jerked away from me, her eyes wide with horror. "Autopsy? They're going to do an autopsy?"

"Well, yes," I said slowly. "Whenever someone dies unexpectedly, they usually do."

"No. Oh, no," she wailed, backing away from me. She turned and ran. At that moment, the elevator doors opened and she pushed past the elderly couple coming off and frantically hit buttons until the door closed.

I stood for a moment, stunned. Was it the volatile reaction of youth? Or was it something more? I sighed heavily. That was Pierce's problem, not mine.

Thinking it must be close to midnight, I glanced at a wall clock; it was only late afternoon. Not even quittin' time yet. All I wanted was to go home, take a long, hot shower, turn on the gas fireplace and sip a glass of Cab-Merlot.

Any thoughts of leaving early disappeared when I saw Connie's beleaguered expression as she talked on the phone, the flashing lights on the telephone that indicated people on hold, and my overflowing message box. I grabbed my messages and sifted through them as I hurried to my desk.

I picked up the phone and punched one of the flashing lights. "This is Robyn Kelly. I'm sorry you had to wait. How can I help you?" I grabbed a pad of paper and a pen.

"This is Myrna Flanders. I'm not sure what I should do."

I sighed and set aside all thoughts of murder. Mrs. Flanders sounded like an older lady, the kind who never complained, because she didn't want anyone to get in trouble. Most of the time, I only talk to patients on the phone, but I'd met a few women like Mrs. Flanders in person when they came to see Margie. They were always a bit fluttery, and soft and round, and smelled faintly of vanilla. On their next visit to the medical center, they brought home-baked cookies to the office to thank us for helping them.

"Why don't you tell me what the problem is, Mrs. Flanders?"

"Well, dear," she said with a hint of an English accent. "I had this surgery and I...oh, I don't want to make trouble."

"It's okay, Mrs. Flanders. You are not making any trouble. We want you to be happy with the care you received here. What kind of surgery was it?"

"It was for my gall bladder. Terrible gallstone attacks, you know." She tsk-tsked at the memory.

"I've heard gallstones can be very painful. When did you have the surgery?"

"Let's see, it was two weeks ago. On November third."

"And you're having problems now?"

"It seems very odd, dear. But since the surgery, I keep feeling this cool breeze across my pancreas, as if they left me open. I can't find a hole, but I must say, it's quite put me off my porridge. I don't know what to do."

I struggled not to laugh at her description. She sounded very sincere. I reassured her that Dr. Davisson would want to see her again and offered to call his office. She seemed so relieved that for the first time all day, I started to relax.

Then I shuddered, remembering how I'd been too late to help Congressman Hamilton. But if he was murdered, and if I had arrived earlier...I could have walked in on the murderer.

Snapping back to the problem at hand, I gathered some additional information from Mrs. Flanders, then called the surgeon's office. He wasn't in, so I talked to his nurse, who thought Mrs. Flanders was a sweetheart. Gladys assured me she would get the patient in right away to talk about her cool breeze.

When I finished, there were no more flashing "hold" lights, so I quickly documented my conversation with Mrs. Flanders, then sorted the telephone messages by urgency.

"Ms. Kelly?"

I looked up to see Detective Pierce standing in my doorway. He did not look happy. In fact, his expression was downright hostile.

"Detective. Come in." I gestured hesitantly for him to sit down.

"You left out something when I questioned you earlier. You want to remember it now?"

I winced inwardly. "And that would be?"

Detective Pierce scowled. "You forgot to mention a little detail, the one about Congressman Hamilton complaining about you. About how you tagged him wrong during triage."

"First of all, that's blatantly untrue. Charley said he was a yellow, and that's the tag I gave him." I sighed. "I was hoping it would go away. How'd you find out?"

"Back-tracking to follow the congressman's movement from the time he arrived until when you found him. So he was real angry with you?"

"Look, things like that happen all the time when patients are upset," I said. "As soon as the trauma is over and they calm down, they usually forget the whole thing."

"So, if he was supposed to forget the whole thing, why did you go to see him? And don't give me this business about him being a VIP so you went instead of a volunteer. Wouldn't an administrator go, not a middle manager? Even if she is in charge of patient relations, and especially if he had complained about her."

"We try to have the staff person involved in the complaint try to solve it first. It's standard procedure. In fact, I can show you the brochure we hand out to patients when they're admitted. But that's beside the point. Why do you think he was murdered?"

"You don't see dead bodies very often, do you?"

"Actually, Detective, I don't see dead bodies at all." I shivered. "Until today."

"Let's just say I saw some things that said the cause of death wasn't natural." From the way he crossed his arms over his chest, I gathered he wasn't going to share any details with me.

"Are you going to arrest me?"

FIVE

DETECTIVE PIERCE STARTED. "Am I—? For what? With-holding evidence? Obstruction of justice?"

His expression softened just a bit. "No. Of course not. Like I said before, this case is going to be scrutinized by everyone so I want all the t's crossed and the i's dotted. All the lines of questioning taken to their logical and accurate conclusions. You just wasted my time, is all, by not being up front from the beginning."

I leaned back, feeling like an overblown balloon that had released some of its extra air. "That's a relief."

"You really thought you were a suspect?"

"Didn't you?"

Detective Pierce shrugged. "Maybe. For a minute. Until I figured out there's no way you could have killed him in the length of time you were in the room."

So, he had considered me a suspect. A cold shiver ran down my spine at the thought of being fingerprinted and forced to wear a bright orange jumpsuit. "I guess I'm glad you calculated the timing."

"Now we only have two hundred ninety-nine other possible suspects to rule out." Pierce stood and flipped his notepad closed. "Don't leave town, in case I need to talk to you again."

I might have worried if I hadn't caught the hint of a smile as he turned to leave. As it was, I kept quiet, relieved that the truth was now out in the open. Hopefully it would go no further. The last thing I needed was for Will to hear about my problem with Congressman Hamilton.

After the detective left, I flipped through the phone messages and decided they were routine and could wait until tomorrow. I surveyed my office. Damn. On the desk, a teetering stack of case reports I needed to write up before I could no longer decipher my notes. On the table, a staggering mound of data waiting to be interpreted and summarized for my section of the Quality Committee Report. And, in the in-box, copies of E-mails from members of my professional association telling me what to include in the congressional testimony I was drafting on patient rights. No wonder a bottle of Excedrin had a permanent spot next to my phone. If the message light started flashing again, I planned to ignore it. It could only be more bad news.

Which pile to tackle first: Eeny, meeny, miney, mo— the Quality Committee would be understanding if the report was late, but the association's lobbyist needed that draft. And I really needed to do something with that Insurance Commissioner's complaint about Nancy Stone.

I pulled the Stone case file from the teetering stack of folders and medical records, the pile labeled "Urgent," and flipped it open. Some of the tension from Pierce's visit dissipated as I threw myself into the comfortingly normal task.

On top in the file was the Insurance Commissioner's office cover letter, then Mrs. Stone's complaint letter to him, followed by my acknowledgement letter to the IC, my letter to Mrs. Stone asking her to sign and return a medical-records release form for the non-plan physician, Dr. Chin, whom she had seen, a copy of the signed form she returned to me, and copies of Dr. Chin's and Mountain View Hospital's bills that Mrs. Stone wanted Health As-

surance to pay. I shook my head. A whole lot of paperwork and nothing had even happened yet.

The case log sheet showed we mailed the original
signed release to Dr. Chin's office two weeks ago, but the
records had not arrived. The deadline for my response
letter to the IC was next Monday.

Mrs. Stone was requesting an exception to the "no
coverage for non-plan physicians" clause in her insurance
contract because she felt one of our docs had given her
poor medical care. I had our records, but I needed Dr.
Chin's records before I could send the case to Dr. Weiser
to review.

Two phone books later, I called Dr. Chin's office and
asked to speak to the office manager.

"This is Nadine," the office manager said when she
picked up the phone.

"Hi, Nadine. This is Robyn Kelly. I'm the patient-
relations director at Madrona Bay Hospital. I'm calling
about your patient, Nancy Stone. We sent a records-release
form two weeks ago for the care Mrs. Stone received from
Dr. Chin last spring."

"Yes, I remember seeing it."

"Well, I'm calling to see if the records have been sent
yet." I try very hard not to say "you" in these conversations, having learned that "you" puts the other person on
the defensive. Hard to keep things neutral, but I've devel-
oped a repertoire of phrases for these kinds of calls.

"What did you say your name was?" Papers rustled on
her end of the line.

"Robyn Kelly. Patient relations at Madrona Bay."

"Hmm. Oh, here it is. We get to these requests when
we have a chance, but frankly, it's not a priority."

"I see. Well, Mrs. Stone is asking for Health Assurance
to pay Dr. Chin's bill, which was…" I flipped through the

file to the billing statement. "Which was about five thousand dollars. I'm ready to send the case out for review, but without Dr. Chin's records, I can't start."

"What's your fax number?"

I smiled and gave it to her. It was a sorry fact of health-care life that if a request did not generate income, it fell to the bottom of the pile.

While I waited for the faxed records, I sifted through our medical records, flagging the pages I needed to copy, then checked Mrs. Stone's insurance coverage to be sure her Health Assurance policy was in effect for both the care she received here and the care from Dr. Chin.

A few minutes later, Connie brought me the faxed records. I try to do a quick assessment before sending cases to Dr. Weiser, but today I didn't have time. Instead, I made the copies that Dr. Weiser needed, wrote a cover memo to him with the due-date for his response in bold, organized it, stuck it in an oversized envelope, and asked Connie to take it downstairs to the Medical Staff office in the Admin suite.

That done, I pulled out the stack of E-mails and tried to outline a coherent statement of our association's opinion for Louisa.

Before I knew it, Connie was standing at the door of my office. "It's almost six, boss. Okay if I turn the phones off?"

I nodded and took the opportunity to stretch. "Nothing we can do for someone who calls now anyway. How're you getting home?"

"Philip's picking me up at the teriyaki place across the street so he doesn't have to drive through all this mess."

I glanced out my window. In the summer, the view from my office sweeps west across a sailboat-filled Lake Washington to Seattle's skyscrapers. Not that I have much time to enjoy the view, but it wasn't summer or sunny. It was still November, and rain still pelted my windows. A few police cars remained in the circular drive, along with a horde of reporters with cameras and lights stationed around the perimeter, waiting for the next news release. They reminded me of vultures, lurking, waiting to pounce when their prey weakened. I stood up to see the hospital entrance and thought I spotted Detective Pierce. Sinking back into my chair, I considered the long day he'd had, and the even longer night facing him.

"I'll be leaving soon too, Connie. Do you think Louisa will forgive me for not sending a polished draft of this testimony if I explain a congressman's been murdered?" I tried to smile, but there was nothing funny about the day.

"It's been all over the news. She'd have to be in a monastery not to have heard. See you tomorrow."

She was right. I flipped from my word-processing program to E-mail. Maybe Louisa had sent me a message. While I waited for the download, I called out to Connie, "Any more messages I need to know about?"

She came back, shrugging into her coat, and wincing, which told me she didn't want to be here when I read one of the messages she'd taken.

"How bad is it?"

"Debbie called from Admin. Will scheduled a debriefing meeting for tomorrow."

"I expected that. If nothing else, this morning was a good test of our disaster preparedness."

"Bet you didn't expect the meeting to be at six a.m."

"You're kidding." I slumped back in my chair. "Please say this is a joke."

Connie shook her head. "Sorry. He wants the meeting over before he meets with the CEO."

A quick glance at my E-mail did not find the hoped-for reprieve. I threw up my hands. "Okay. I surrender. I'm sending this as-is to Louisa with my apologies and a referral to the eleven o'clock news. Then I'm going home."

"Good idea. I'll see you in the morning."

I waved her away, then spent another few minutes preparing my draft for E-mail.

I'd just clicked the "send" key when I heard the outer door open. Connie should have locked the door behind her. Nothing like a murderer running loose to keep the imagination in overdrive. Suspicious, I stepped out of my office, but relaxed when I saw it was Pham Nguyen from housekeeping.

"Pham, you're here early tonight."

He bowed slightly. "Sorry, Miss Kelly. I not disturb you. Three-West is closed by policemen, so I cannot clean."

"Yes. I imagine they don't want anyone in there for a while. Come on in. I'm just about to leave." I turned around and went into my office to start picking up.

"Miss Kelly?"

I looked up from my desk, surprised to see Pham standing in the doorway. He was older than me and well-educated, but when he first immigrated, he'd been unable to find a job that matched his training because of his limited English. We had talked on numerous occasions and he told me of escaping from Vietnam with his family, and living in refugee camps until finally obtaining a visa to come to the United States. He had put six children through college. Now he had a doctor and a lawyer in the family, as well as a stock broker and a teacher. He was fiercely proud of his children, including the one he least understood, the independent filmmaker.

"Yes, Pham. What is it? What cause are you raising

funds for now?" With a smile, I gestured for him to sit in the chair next to my desk.

Pham stepped inside my office, but didn't take the offered seat. "I hear about the murder, Miss Kelly."

"It was awful. I'm the one who found the body."

"I sorry you find him, Miss Kelly." Pham's face darkened. "But I am not sorry he dead."

Surprised, I asked, "What do you mean? Congressman Hamilton was considered by many to be a good man." So what if I wasn't one of them. No point in defaming the dead.

Pham shook his head violently. "No. No."

Before I could ask him why, I heard the outer office door open again. "Wait here, Pham."

I stepped from my office and saw Detective Pierce with yet another uniformed officer. "Detective?"

He glanced at the housekeeping cart, then back at me. "Is Mr. Nguyen here?"

"Yes," I said. "He hasn't touched Three-West, if that's what you're worried about."

Detective Pierce nodded. "I know. Where is he?"

Puzzled by Detective Pierce's grim expression, I pointed toward my office. "What's this about?" I asked, following behind him.

He turned and gestured for me to back up. "Wait over there, Ms. Kelly." He signaled for the policeman to come with him.

I didn't wait by Connie's desk, I followed him. The last thing I expected, though, was to hear Detective Pierce say, "Pham Nguyen? I'd like you to come with me for questioning about the murder of Jake Hamilton."

I stumbled back against Connie's desk. What was going on? Why Pham? What could he know?

The officer led Pham from the room. His eyes pleaded with me. "Miss Kelly? Help me. I not do this."

I grabbed Detective Pierce's arm as he tried to pass by. "This is crazy. You don't think Pham had anything to do with Congressman Hamilton, do you? This is a mistake. He's a highly respected member of the Southeast Asian community. He—he sponsors refugees and finds them housing and raises money for children's programs and—"

Detective Pierce looked at me with those sad brown eyes, then shook his head. And I knew what he suspected.

"But why?" I cried. "Why would Pham possibly do such a thing?"

"He had opportunity." Detective Pierce sighed heavily. "And he had motive."

My hand slipped from the detective's arm. "You're wrong. You've made a horrible mistake."

He patted my shoulder, and I sensed he wished I hadn't seen this. "Go home, Robyn. It's been a long day." He shut the door quietly.

Stunned, I stared at the closed door, unable to believe the cruel twist this nightmare had taken. Random thoughts. Detective Pierce was wrong. What motive? What opportunity? And how had Hamilton been murdered, anyway? The questions tumbled over themselves as I struggled to make sense of what I had just witnessed.

I don't know what it was that finally jolted me out of my daze, but I had to do something. At least there was one thing I could do to help Pham now. I used my security clearance to access his employment records in the Human Resources database and called his home. Fortunately, one of the kids answered rather than Mrs. Nguyen who spoke almost no English. I explained the situation and left it to him to find a lawyer.

I hung up the phone and plopped into my chair, fuming

at the injustice. No matter what the police thought, I could not, would not, believe that Pham murdered Congressman Hamilton. I had volunteered for some of Pham's projects. I had seen him work with people, pulling a diverse refugee community together. It just didn't make any sense.

THE STORM HAD RETURNED by the time I sprinted across the hospital parking lot with my useless umbrella and climbed into my Ford Explorer. I breathed in the cold fresh air and listened to the rain pounding its rhythmic tune on the top of my car. Then, I turned on the radio to check the traffic. The highways, bridges, and arterials were all moving at a crawl. At this rate, the Puget Sound area would redefine rush hour as five a.m. until ten p.m. There were simply too many people on too little asphalt, and with our topography, there was no room to build more.

I started the engine and began my trip home, following circuitous routes I had worked out in advance using my *Thomas Map Guide*. Maybe it's because I grew up in the wide open spaces of Colorado, but I refuse to be stuck in traffic. I probably knew every alternate route on the Eastside. My friend, Andrea, laughs at me, but my feeling is that moving steadily is far better than just sitting. Other people must have thought the same thing tonight because even some of my most secret routes had more than the usual amount of vehicles.

At last, I turned into my cul-de-sac. As I drove to the end of the street, I noticed few cars in the driveways, but lights on in almost every home. Except mine. It was totally dark.

Damn. Josh wasn't home. I wanted to hear about his day, all those ordinary things that would reassure me that what I'd been through had been an aberrant nightmare.

I pulled into the garage and, after hanging up my wet

coat to drip on the concrete floor, let myself into the house, anticipating the assault I knew was coming. "Oopf," I groaned as eighty pounds of golden retriever pounced on me. "Taffy. Down. Good girl."

I talked to her as I pushed past, left my damp shoes in the laundry room, and entered the kitchen. When I snapped on the lights, I was relieved to see signs that Josh had been home, even if it was dirty dishes in the sink. Taffy hadn't been waiting for me to let her out and feed her. I glanced at her and smiled. She was sitting now, doing her hungry dog imitation, looking at me, looking at her dish, looking at me.

"Oh, no, you're not conning me." Her ears drooped and I had to laugh as I rummaged in the cupboard for a biscuit. "Here you go, girl."

With her taken care of, I poured myself a small glass of wine. From the kitchen, I went through the dark dining room to the equally dark living room where I turned on some table lamps and sat down on the sofa. A collage of Irish landscapes and black-and-white photographs of people from bygone eras adorned the wall over the used-brick fireplace.

"Hello, ancestors." I lifted my glass in a toast. "Bet you never had the kind of day I had today."

The pictures had come from my paternal grandmother's home after she died. I wasn't sure who they all were, but my dad rattled off their names and relationships every time he visited. One of these times, I would write it all down.

The phone rang next to me and I glanced at caller ID before picking up the receiver. Speak of the devil. "Hi, Da."

"Robyn Anne, are you all right?"

"I'm fine, Da." Lying to a parent was allowed if it

reduced their anxiety over something they could do nothing about. "It's been a busy day, though."

"Hrmph. I keep telling you the city's not a safe place for a young girl—"

I grinned at his standard refrain to lure me home. It hadn't worked when I lived in New York City, and it certainly wasn't going to work now.

"—no place to bring up a child."

"Da, Josh is nineteen. He's not a child anymore. Besides, Colorado has crime too."

"Well, you stay away from those politicians. They's nothing but trouble and taxes."

"I'll stay away from them." As far away as I could get, especially if they were cranky or dead. "Listen, Da, I just got home and haven't even had time to change. Can I call you back later?"

"Naw. I just wanted to check on you."

"Thanks, Da. I love you."

Before he hung up, he mumbled something that might be interpreted as him loving me too, but he was not one to express emotion. In his mid-sixties, my father was still hale and hearty, capable of putting in a full day's work on the ranch. He was a charming fellow with twinkling blue eyes and believed family was the most important thing in the world. He called me once a week, and when he thought I was in trouble or danger, like tonight.

I worried about him being alone, but it was his choice. After my mother passed away, he was inundated with cakes, pies, and offers of home-cooked meals—and probably more—by ladies in a twenty-mile radius. He turned them all down, preferring to hire a housekeeper to cook and clean while he was gone all day, and have his evenings to sip beer and watch ball games on TV in peace.

He had his ranch hands and he had married friends to socialize with, so I didn't fuss with him about being lonely.

Now where was I? I finished my wine and turned to Taffy. "Let's get out of these clothes, and take a nice hot shower, shall we?" I wasn't sure if it was the too-tight waistband on these slacks or the obscene amount of coffee I'd consumed, or maybe it was just the events of the day, but I was getting a stomach ache.

A knock on the door scared the daylights out of me. Taffy went nuts, barking and wagging her tail as if she just knew her best friend was on the other side of the door.

I shoved her aside to look through the peephole. Peter. I groaned, leaning heavily in the direction of not answering the door.

"Rob? I know you're there. Please let me in."

I looked at Taffy, who was always ready to make new friends. With a sigh, I unlocked the door and glared at Peter. "It's been a long day. What do you want?"

He held up a bottle of wine, and I felt myself weaken. I stepped back and let him pass. "Wine glasses are in the cupboard to the left of the sink. Taffy will help you find them," I said, pointing him in the right direction. "Excuse me while I change."

He smiled that little smile that made my insides flip-flop. "Come on, Taffy. Maybe you'll even show me where the good silver is," he said, obviously referring to goldens' reputation for being extremely friendly toward strangers.

I watched him shed his jacket and disappear through the dining room before I went to the bedroom to slip out of my mismatched work clothes. I hesitated for only a moment before deciding to jump into a hot shower. After all, I had promised it to myself, and just because Peter had shown up, uninvited, didn't mean I had to alter my plans.

It didn't take me long. My hair dried quickly, and I

dabbed on only a touch of make-up before I slipped into my northwest casual uniform of well-worn jeans, an oxford shirt, and comfortable loafers.

I took a quick look in the mirror, then chided myself. I didn't care what Peter thought of me.

He was part of my past. True.

We were over. Probably.

Through. Maybe.

With a sigh, I realized the only thing I knew for certain was that a charming man had brought a bottle of wine at the end of a horrendous day. I would sip some wine, keep the conversation light, then graciously escort him to the door. No one was asking for a lifetime commitment, right?

My resolve was tested as soon as I entered the living room. He had settled comfortably on the couch, the gas fireplace was lit, the bottle of wine stood open on the coffee table. A familiar aroma drifted from the kitchen.

When he saw me sniff, he smiled. "I thought you might be hungry and I remembered you always kept nibbles in the freezer." The timer went off and he went to the kitchen, Taffy following close behind.

I raised an eyebrow. So, he had rummaged in my refrigerator and made himself at home. I felt invaded, but perhaps I was being churlish for not appreciating his efforts. Even my dog thought he was great. But then, she wasn't the most discriminating judge of character.

Rather than say something stupid, I poured two glasses of wine, took the half-filled one, and sank into my favorite overstuffed chair. Peter returned with a plate and napkins. I had to admit, the mushroom canapés were delicious after a long day, and the wine was excellent. I closed my eyes and enjoyed the silence.

"I meant what I said earlier today," Peter said.

With a start, I straightened in the chair. Had I dozed

off? Maybe I had. Vowing to keep my eyes open, I asked, "What was that?"

"When I said you look good. I meant it. The years have been good to you, Rob."

"So I have changed."

He was leaning forward, his elbows resting on his knees. He stared at the glass he held like a snifter and chuckled. "Yeah. In some ways, you look softer now. But you're more wary. Life teaches us that."

"You should know. You were one of my best teachers." I wished I could bite back the words as soon as I spoke them, but it was too late.

"I'm sorry about that, Rob. It was wrong. Arrogant. To think I could take off and you'd wait around for me to return in a couple of months for a brief visit before I was sent on another assignment."

"You expected me to wait?"

"Yes."

"But you never said anything."

"I know. That's the arrogant part. I didn't think I had to say it, that you would just know."

I laughed at his audacity, then drained my glass and held it out for a refill before I curled my feet under me. "What a time we had."

I took another sip before I cocked my head and said, "It's hard to believe that two people who spent two months practically inside each other's skin could have made such wrong assumptions."

"Guess communicatin' wasn't high on our list." The smoldering look in Peter's eyes reminded me of why we had not spent a lot of time talking. I looked away quickly; I wasn't sure I wanted to go down that path again.

"So, Peter, what are you working on these days?" Discussing work was much safer.

"That's the one thing that doesn't change, Rob." He shrugged. "Man's need for power and control. His willingness to do anything to get it. And the hatred. God, I get so tired of it." He slumped against the couch. "I'm so weary of trying to understand why what your grandfather-to-the-x-power did to my uncle-to-the-y-power over five hundred years ago to get some land makes any difference now. Why it means we can't live together peacefully today. So often it's based on something as ridiculous as that. And then you throw in some religion. Christians, Moslems, or Jews; they're all as bad. If they aren't fighting each other, they're fighting within. Just so long as they're fighting. They always need to have an enemy, someone they can hate."

He stopped, and looked sheepish. "Whoa. Where did that diatribe come from?"

I was surprised at his assessment of what he had seen, and the passion in his response. He sounded so…so mature, but then, even Peter would have changed in ten years. Hopefully we all were wiser than we were in our youth.

"Could be you've thought this for a long time, but haven't been anywhere safe to say it. If you told someone you were interviewing that they were at war for greedy or stupid reasons, I suspect you'd be the next casualty. And the networks don't want to hear it. They want more blood and gore to boost the ratings."

"You're right. But you left out something."

"What's that?"

"You're very easy to talk to. Something about you inspires confidences."

I had to laugh, thinking about the Mrs. Flanderses I had met over the years. "Peter, you'd be amazed, or maybe appalled, at the confidences I inspire at work. All day long I listen to people."

"Whatever you're doing, it must agree with you."

I didn't argue because I did enjoy my job. On most days. But right now, I needed to know why Peter was here. So, I asked him, "Peter, why are you here?"

"Why?" he asked as if the question surprised him. "I thought I told you. I was at Sea-Tac waiting to change planes when I heard about the crash. So I rented a car and headed to the hospital."

"I know that. I mean why are you here?" I asked, pointing to the floor.

"That should be obvious, Rob. I wanted to see you again. The hospital wasn't a good place. Too much going on, too many distractions." He shrugged again, a gesture he used a lot. "I guess I wanted to see if the old flame still burned."

Caught off guard, I choked on my wine. That was the last thing I expected him to say. "Wanted to see an old friend" or "catch up on old times," maybe. But not "see if the old flame still burned." Coughing and sputtering, I set the glass on the coffee table and tried to catch my breath.

Peter crossed the room and patted my back. "You okay?"

I nodded, and the pats turned into gentle rubbing. He perched on the arm of the chair, and I was acutely aware of his closeness. I shifted away from his touch. I took a deep breath, then wished I hadn't because his aftershave was another reminder of the past.

I stood up and crossed the room before turning to face him. "Look. Peter. I'm not sure this is a good idea." I gestured at the whole scene, the fireplace, the wine, the canapés.

He rose from the chair, a fluid sinewy movement that reminded me of one of the big cats. He approached, his intent gaze never leaving my face. Mesmerized, I let him almost reach me before I moved again, this time toward the door, scooping up his jacket on my way. I held it on my crooked finger.

He grimaced as he snagged the jacket and shrugged into it. "I can't believe you're throwing me out."

I sighed. "Peter, today was a very long day. So, quite frankly, I'm just not up to this right now."

I reached for the doorknob, but he caught my hand. I almost laughed. This whole thing really was becoming more and more like a bad B movie. I stopped laughing, though, when I saw the heated look in his eyes.

Then, Taffy pushed her way between us with a low growl, a sound so foreign for her that it broke the mood. Surprised at Taffy's behavior, I pulled away from Peter to see headlights flash through the side windows as a car pulled into the driveway.

Josh was home. Yup, good time for Peter to leave. I didn't want to explain him to Josh, especially not tonight.

"I'll see you tomorrow. I have a meeting at six, and I should be done by eight." I heard the garage door start to close, and I opened the front door. "Meet me in the cafeteria and I'll buy you a cup of coffee."

I practically shoved Peter out the door and closed it quietly as the door from the garage to the kitchen opened. Rolling my eyes at Taffy, I whispered, "Not a word to Josh, understand?"

She wagged her tail, so I took that as a good sign and reached for the bottle of wine. I saw Peter's glass on the coffee table just as Josh walked in. "Hi," I said brightly.

He took in the scene very quickly for a boy and grimaced the way teenagers do when they've caught their parents doing something disgustingly human.

I decided to ignore him, and scooped up the glasses, wine bottle, and plate of canapés as I breezed toward the kitchen. "How'd your day go?"

He followed me into the kitchen and leaned over my shoulder to grab the remaining canapés and shove them into his mouth. "Okay," he mumbled with his mouth full. He opened the refrigerator and took out a gallon of milk and makings for a sandwich, then gave me a hard look. "Heard your day got worse."

"You saw the evening news?"

"Naw, I was gone by then. Heard it on the radio while I was stuck in bridge traffic. Jeez, Mom. I can't believe you let a congressman die in your hospital. That's really going to look bad."

I draped an arm around his shoulder. "Josh, my boy, you have no idea how bad it's going to look."

He slathered mustard and mayo on two large pieces of sourdough French bread, then piled on the roast beef, provolone, sliced tomato, pickles and lettuce. He squeezed the whole thing together so he could get his mouth around it, with the mayo-mustard blend oozing out the sides. I poured him a large glass of milk and signaled for him to sit at the kitchen table.

"Did the radio give any details?"

Josh shook his head. After he swallowed, he said, "They just said he died."

"I was the one who found him." I let the words sink in, then reached under the counter and pulled out the Godiva Chocolates box, the one I kept for really bad days. To be sure, today had been the worst.

Josh shoved back his chair. "No way, Mom. Really? What was it like?"

If I wanted sympathy for the horrific experience I'd been through, it wasn't going to come from Josh. He had a ghoulish interest in every detail, and thought it was "so cool" that it had been murder. At least he showed some concern about Pham being taken in for questioning. Josh had met Pham while working at the hospital during summer vacations and school breaks.

"Why'd they suspect him?" Josh asked as he took his plate to the sink. I gestured for him to put it and his other dirty dishes in the dishwasher. "He wouldn't do anything like that."

"I don't think so either. But the police say he had motive and opportunity."

"If he didn't do it, then who did?" he asked.

I didn't have an answer for him. But, if I firmly believed Detective Pierce had arrested the wrong person tonight, I was left with only one choice. I had to find out who did murder Congressman Hamilton.

SIX

THE NEXT MORNING, I slogged through another Pacific Northwest commute, testing a new "shortcut" that turned out to be more trouble than it was worth. By the time I reached the hospital, I was ready to trade in dark, cold, and drippy for sunny, hot, and dry. Our senior snowbirds were already ensconced in Arizona for the winter, while the rest of us scanned the newspaper's travel section and dreamed of escapes to Hawaii. A few days of blue sky: was that too much to ask?

I swung into a parking space and gathered my stuff, including my latté. No wonder Starbucks was such a success here. We had substituted caffeine for serotonin. A number of my friends had invested in full spectrum lights to ward off the mid-winter blahs, or seasonal affective disorder.

Splashing my way across the parking lot, I wasn't surprised at the number of cars that I recognized. I was on time for Will's pre-dawn meeting, but I hated to be the last one to arrive. As it turned out, managers were still streaming past my office toward the conference room. I stopped by my office to drop off my coat, then joined Charley Anderson in the hallway outside the conference room.

He looked as if he had not slept or left the hospital in days. His eyes were bloodshot and worry lines seemed permanently etched into his forehead.

"I don't know how you did it," Charley said.

"Morning to you too." Knowing full well he was refer-

ring to my finding Congressman Hamilton, I changed the
subject. "How are things in the ER?"

"Quiet now. But the clinic administrators are insisting
on a cut of the billing because their docs were involved.
The docs don't care. They get paid for their services
wherever they work. But the clinics say this was on 'their'
time, and want the administrative overhead normally
included in their billings." Charley sighed. "I'm meeting
with them this afternoon."

I nodded. "With specialists like the orthopedists, that
could be expensive."

"Yeah. What a nightmare."

"And, we aren't done yet. Are you ready for this
meeting?" I asked.

"It's too much to hope that Will focuses on how well we
followed the disaster plan." Keeping a poker face, Charley
cast me a sidelong glance. "Of course, I'm not worried. I'm
not the one who found a dead congressman. Good luck,
Rob."

He patted my shoulder as we walked into the room.
Everyone fell silent, and I had this sudden churning sen-
sation that I was being served up as the main course.

Many of the twenty-odd people in the room had already
taken their seats; the rest clustered around the coffee urn.
They started talking again, but their gazes stayed on me
as I slid into a chair at the far end of the table from Will.
Maybe if Will had to look around others to see me, he
wouldn't skewer me with an unobstructed glare throughout the meeting. From the uneasy looks on the faces of
those lingering around the coffee, I had chosen well.

Will stood up and everyone took a seat. The room
quieted immediately. He towered over those around him,
and I didn't have to look up to know he had moved and was
staring at me. Damn. I'd counted on him staying seated.

"So, Rob," Will said, drawing out my name. "Do you want to tell us about your visit to Congressman Hamilton's room yesterday?"

I hated it when he used my nickname. He did it only when he had some point to make, or wanted to act like he was my best buddy—just before he lambasted me. And from the way he was starting the meeting, how well we implemented the disaster plan was low on his agenda.

Then, something inside me rebelled. I hadn't caused that accident on Snoqualmie Pass. It wasn't my fault a congressman was one of the victims. I did not mis-tag him. I did not plan to find him dead, and I did not purposely put Madrona Bay in the media spotlight. I hadn't caused any of these problems. I was involved only because I came in early to work on Will's report. I refused to bear the brunt of his frustration.

"As you know, Will," I said, drawing out his name just a tad, "volunteers visit every new patient. I felt that with a congressman, you would prefer a manager make that visit."

I figured now wasn't the time to mention Hamilton's complaint against me. If Will didn't know about it by now, then Charley and Irene had buried the ridiculous thing under a mountain of paperwork. No point in volunteering for a public flogging.

"I see. What happened when you went into his room?"

I wasn't sure where Will was going with this, unless he was looking for a scapegoat. Did he think I handled it wrong? Perhaps he thought I should have started CPR myself and rung for the nurse and waited for her to arrive, rather than go to the nurses' station and get an immediate response. Everyone hated how he set these landmines. We knew they were there, but we hadn't found a way to avoid being wounded. I glanced around the room and saw compassion mixed with relief on the faces of my co-workers.

"I went into the room. Congressman Hamilton wasn't breathing and I called for help." I don't know what perversity propelled me to open my mouth again. "It wasn't until later, when the police came to my office and took Pham Nguyen in for questioning, that I learned the police suspected the congressman was murdered."

There. I had broken the taboo and said the "m" word. Not only had I said that word, not only had I found the deceased congressman, but I had been on the scene when the suspect was taken in.

The silence was complete. No one shifted position. No one rustled a paper or scratched notes with their pen. From the furious look on Will's face, I knew he had wanted to be the one to make the official announcement, even though the morning news was already reporting it. I hadn't done myself any favors by upstaging him. Oh, well.

Ever since I learned that Hamilton was murdered, I had resisted the idea that someone I worked with was responsible for the congressman's death, but I had vowed to help Pham.

In spite of my belief that the murderer couldn't possibly be someone I knew, I took advantage of the awkward quiet around me to study the people in the room.

Darlene Skaggs, the midwife who calmly delivered a baby in a potentially dangerous situation. Susan Wong, who tried valiantly to revive Congressman Hamilton. She hadn't hesitated to respond, even though she didn't like him. The security chief, Tom Geralding, busy all day trying to keep the curious and the press from interfering with our work. Director of Nursing Brenda Martin had been everywhere, making sure her nurses had whatever supplies they needed to treat the victims. Danny Vincent, the warehouse manager, had worked his tush off to deliver those supplies. Engineering supervisor, Lee Hastings? No way. The man was a teddy bear with a tool belt. Will Slater was difficult to work with sometimes, but I could not see him as a murderer, and I definitely couldn't picture Charley or Irene doing someone in. I sighed with relief, knowing I didn't have to worry about these people.

There were others around the room I did not know as well, and hundreds of employees elsewhere in the building who had the opportunity. Then again, maybe it wasn't someone who worked at Madrona Bay. Dozens of people were here yesterday. Reporters. Congressman Hamilton's staff, including the semi-hysterical Cynthia Martin. Victims and their families. Cancelled surgery patients. People coming and going all day long. Many with opportunity. The task of figuring out who murdered Congressman Hamilton was growing to monumental proportions. What had I committed myself to when I vowed to help Pham?

Maybe if I concentrated on finding a motive it would be easier. Who, among all those hundreds of people, had a motive strong enough to kill? I knew that statistically, most people were murdered by someone they knew. Not a particularly comforting thought as I took another survey of the group seated around the table.

But how many at Madrona Bay would know Congressman Hamilton except by reputation? He wasn't from this area. So much for the obvious personal motive. He didn't represent us in Congress. There went the obvious political motive.

My eye caught Brenda's and she gave me an encouraging smile. I could almost hear her say, "There, there, it will be fine," and I wished I had a boss like her, a boss who cared about her staff and supported them unconditionally.

Then, I glanced at Will glaring at a blank space on the wall, lost in his own fury. He twisted the pencil in his hands. It broke, snapping him back to attention.

"Yes. Well," Will said. "Now that the police have a suspect in custody, we'll discuss the disaster, the accident. How well did our plan work?"

Part of me sighed with relief at being off the hot seat, while another part of me wanted to jump up and say, *No, no, you're wrong. They arrested the wrong man.* But, I kept quiet. It was unwise to advertise that I believed Pham was innocent, or that I intended to conduct my own investigation.

THE DEBRIEFING LASTED longer than I'd anticipated, even taking into account how much administrators love meetings. By the time it was over, I was more than ready to leave. No matter what the situation, Will had found opportunities to question my efforts during the disaster. No one came through unscathed, but I felt especially picked on. Will even vetoed my suggestion that we waive the co-pay for the cancelled surgery patients. What a Scrooge. I was fed up enough that for two cents I would've taken the rest of the day off. But with Margie on vacation, that wouldn't be fair to Connie. I glanced at my watch and realized I was late for my appointment with Peter in the cafeteria.

Wanting to escape from everyone, I took the stairs instead of waiting for the elevator.

Peter was seated at a window table that overlooked a patio. In spring and summer, the flowers and greenery were wonderful. Now, it was gloomy and woebegone, despite the landscaper's best efforts. I signaled to Peter and he flashed his Emmy award-winning smile in my direction as I entered the food service area. The pastry tray held one last apple fritter, so freshly made that the sugar glaze hadn't completely hardened. I gazed longingly at it, then breathed deeply, knowing the sugary-yeasty aroma alone was good for five pounds. Instead, I chose scrambled eggs with ham and hurried away before the temptation was too strong.

"Sorry I'm late." I slid into a chair across the small table. I tasted the eggs, then added some salt and pepper. Peter chuckled and I looked up from my plate. "What's so funny?"

"You haven't changed," he said, his mouth quirked with amusement. "You're still the only person I know who always tastes their food before adding stuff to it."

I shrugged and continued eating.

"How did the meeting go?"

I shrugged again, but stabbed viciously at a chunk of ham.

"That bad, huh?" Peter said. "The disaster was a disaster?"

I set the fork down and leaned back in my chair. "No. The disaster plan worked really well. We did everything we were supposed to do. There were no significant recommendations to change the plan except to schedule the next disaster when more employees are here to deal with it."

"So what's got you so hot under the collar? I could see the steam rising when you walked in."

I sighed and thought for a moment. Peter was a reporter; I couldn't forget that. But he was also someone I had cared a great deal for, and he had cared about me. I hoped. "Which are you now, the ace reporter or my friend?"

"Your friend." He smiled and reached for my hand, enveloping it in his large rough hand. "I'd like to be more."

I smiled at the idea, but I wasn't in the right frame of mind to analyze my feelings or the niggling questions about a relationship. Friend was all I would commit to. For now. "Since I was the one who found Congressman Hamilton and was present when the arrest was made, I took a bit of a hit."

"You were there when the police arrested the suspect?"

I glowered at Peter, who looked like a bloodhound on the scent. "You're supposed to be my friend right now, remember?"

He had the decency to look embarrassed. "You're right. So, why are you in trouble? You didn't do anything."

"My thought exactly, but my boss seems to think my visibility is too high right now. I should have gone to the lobby with Connie instead of helping in the ER. I should have stayed away from the congressman, and let only senior administrators pay him a visit. Can you imagine if my boss had found Hamilton?"

I stopped. My voice was no longer a conversational whisper and I was attracting some unwanted attention. I started again in a quieter tone. "You don't know Will. Trust me, he would've flipped out. He's an okay guy, but he's a bean counter, not a healthcare provider." The image of Will finding a dead body brought the first laugh I'd had all day.

"Didn't you help deliver a baby while you were in the ER?"

I looked thoughtfully at Peter. "Yes, I did. Darlene spoke up for me in the meeting, saying she could have done it alone, but it was safer having two of us. Risk is something Will understands because it translates into dollars."

"What're you going to do now?"

I slumped in my chair and sighed. "Go back to my

office and get some work done. I'm so far behind that if I work through Christmas, I might be caught up by New Year's."

"Can I meet you for lunch?"

The offer was appealing, but I hesitated. "Thanks, Peter, but I'll be eating at my desk today."

Peter pursed his lips, then said, "I don't know how long I'll be able to stay here."

My stomach clenched. Was he here only to disappear from my life again? "You mean…you're going back to the front? Wherever that is now?"

He nodded slowly. "I could take some time off. They owe me, and I can't think of a better way to spend it than with you."

"Oh, Peter," I said, shaking my head. "As much as I'd like to, I can't take off right now. I have a person on vacation, and I can't leave Connie by herself. Dinner tonight?"

"Good. I'll meet you in your office at five o'clock."

"Better make it six o'clock. I'll see you then." I hurried from the cafeteria. Being around Peter distracted me, and I sensed that if I wanted to keep my job, I needed to focus all my attention on the hospital.

I HUNG UP THE PHONE from what had to be the twenty-fifth patient calling to complain about the rescheduled date for his surgery. The accident had lost us only one full day of O.R. time, but it wasn't as if we had a lot of free time slots to plug those patients into. All the surgical specialties were involved, orthopedics, general surgery, GYN, head/neck, and, of course, anesthesia worked with every one of them, as did the surgical and recovery room nurses. Add to that the physicians' clinic schedules, which were also a mess. What we had was a scheduling challenge under the best of circumstances. And this was not the best of circumstances.

Somebody with absolutely no sense of customer service had decided to simply shift these non-urgent patients to the end of the line, which, with the holidays rapidly approaching, was extending their waits. A true recipe for a public-relations nightmare. We needed to make some extra effort to get those people in quicker, certainly before the holidays.

I glanced at my watch and saw I had twenty minutes before my regular meeting with Will. His secretary, Arlene, hadn't called to cancel or postpone it, so I assumed we were still on. Now was as good a time as any to discuss the O.R. backlog and my idea to write off the co-pays for yesterday's patients. He had vetoed the idea out of hand at the meeting. Maybe he'd be more amenable without an audience to impress.

I wanted to avoid talking about my section of the Quality Committee Report, the data still in haphazard piles on the floor waiting for me to make sense of it. I nudged one of the piles and it slid, threatening to merge with another pile.

I started to separate the stacks when the door opened. A man entered my office and sat down next to my small table. Connie had followed and now stood in the doorway with an exasperated frown. I nodded that it was okay, and she left, shaking her head.

"Hello, Stewart," I said. In an odd way, I was pleased to see him, the rare bit of normalcy in a bizarre week. I sank into my chair, prepared to spend a few minutes.

One of my regulars, Stewart Fromm was in his fifties, but the years had not been good to him. His graying hair was disheveled from constantly running his hands through it, his face deeply lined from myriad anxieties that had plagued him for decades. The polyester pants and jacket were leftovers from the seventies, a leprechaun-green plaid that jolted me every time I saw it. I had the same reaction to the sky-blue leisure suit he wore during the summer.

"It's all the fault of that doctor. If he'd of told my wife to stop smoking, none of this would of happened." Stewart didn't look me in the eye when he spoke, but somewhere off into the glazed distance.

I let him rattle on for a few minutes about all our transgressions over the last thirty years before I interrupted. "What can I do to help you today, Stewart?" My first attempt to focus him.

"If she hadn't of kept drinking, the girls wouldn't of started. It's all that doctor's fault. He told her to have a drink every day for her nerves. Said it was better'n Valium. And he got her started smoking too." He continued to rant about the evils of alcohol and about tobacco addicts.

"I understand, Stewart, but that was over thirty years ago. What can I do to help you today?" Second attempt.

It was as if he never heard me. "They went on to other things, you know. First it's alcohol and tobacco. Then, it's marijuana and who knows what all. Now they just sit around the house and smoke and drink all day."

"I know. Have you talked to your doctor?"

"Yeah. He won't do nothing. Says I can't force 'em to do something they don't wanna do."

"Have you talked to your wife?"

"Yeah, but it never does any good."

"When do you talk to her?"

"When I can't stand tripping over the beer cans no more."

"Can I make a quick phone call?" He nodded, and I punched in the number for the insurance desk. After a brief conversation, I hung up the phone, disappointed with the answers I was given.

"Your doctor's right, Stewart. No one can force someone into treatment." I slid a piece of paper across the desk. He eyed it suspiciously. "Here's the phone number for the alcohol-treatment program. Call them and see what they can offer you. Then talk to your wife before she starts drinking, say after breakfast."

He scowled. "Oughta be something you can do since it's your fault."

I knew better than to take the comment personally. "Call these people, Stewart. Give them a chance to help you."

After I handed him a paper with names and phone numbers, he got up without a word.

Connie came in as soon as he'd left. "He gives me the creeps." She shivered and rubbed her arms.

"He's okay." I smiled sadly. "Well, he's not okay. He's a very troubled man, but he's not dangerous."

"It's weird how he pops in here, then leaves." Her youthful lack of empathy was coming through loud and clear.

"We need compassion for people like him, Connie," I said kindly so as not to make her defensive. "Somewhere along the line, the wires got crossed, and he's never been able to straighten them out again. I don't know why. Maybe something in Vietnam; who knows? But the fact remains, he's a troubled soul who keeps coming to us because we listen and treat him with dignity."

"I suppose." Connie grimaced as she turned to leave. "I'm just glad I don't have to talk to him. I'm going to lunch now. It's Hannah's birthday, so we're taking her to TGIF's."

"Have a good time," I called after her. I was glad the

Admin secretaries included Connie in their fun. I picked up my notepad and pen, then followed Connie out the door, locking it behind me.

I was a few minutes early when I walked into the Administration suite for my meeting with Will. All the desks were empty; everyone had gone to the party.

It suddenly dawned on me that this was my first chance to investigate the murder. I could see who had an alibi at the time of the murder. The administrators each had their own secretary who kept their calendars. I approached the first secretary's desk and glanced at the open calendar lying face up, then made my way down the line. After years of reading physicians' scribbles, reading upside-down calendars was no problem.

Howard Knowles, the chief financial officer, was gone for the week. Lucky him. Brenda Martin had been in a meeting with Darlene Skaggs. That gave both of them an alibi. Larry Bridgeway was in a medical staff meeting. When I reached Arlene's desk, I saw that she had nothing written down for Will for that time period. He had no alibi? Too bad he didn't have a motive.

Will's door was open and I leaped away from Arlene's desk as he moved into view. He was walking around his office, talking on his cell phone.

"—with him gone, maybe I have a chance for that appointment now," Will said. He chuckled. "Yeah, couldn't happen to a nicer guy at a better time."

He turned and saw me, and his expression shifted from satisfied to annoyed. "I have to go now. My next appointment's here. The patient rep." He turned away from me again. "Yeah, mine too." The laugh that followed sounded false.

It wasn't hard to guess. He was talking to another hospital administrator who had a patient rep who did her job well. I knew better than to let on that I understood not only his words but the attitude behind them, as well.

I entered Will's office when he waved me in, feeling the usual chill from the sterile room. I found the various pieces of modern art jarring. The desk surface was clear and the bookshelves' contents were perfectly aligned. Aside from some framed diplomas and awards, the room reflected nothing of the person who occupied it. Or, perhaps it did.

We took our usual places, him behind a massive mahogany desk in a high-back leather chair, and me to the side of his desk in what had to be the most uncomfortable chair I had ever sat in.

"Let's make this short, Robyn." Will looked down on me. I wasn't sure if it was because of his height or the height of the chair. "I have a lot of other things on my plate right now."

"That's fine with me. In fact, I have only two urgent matters to discuss with you." I launched into a brief description of the previous day's scene at the check-in desk. "Those people showed up on time, fully prepared for their surgeries. Some came a long distance, and their family members took time off work. I think it would be excellent PR to give them a credit on their co-pays when they come back, say up to fifty dollars."

Will responded immediately. "Get me the exact numbers. Then I'll decide. Next item."

At least he hadn't said "no." It would take time, something I didn't have, but knowing what I did about the rescheduling fiasco, I had at least a week to work out the details.

"The next item also relates to the O.R., rescheduling the patients whose surgeries had to be cancelled."

"We have a joint Admin–Medical Staff meeting next

Monday. I'll make sure it's on the agenda." Will started to rise from his chair.

"I'm sorry, Will, but that's not acceptable," I said, letting him hear my disappointment. I kept my expression as bland as possible, holding his gaze, but not in a confrontational way. It was a technique I had perfected over the years dealing with recalcitrant patients, physicians, and administrators. It usually worked.

With an annoyed frown, Will sank back into his chair. "Why not?"

"The accident, our disaster preparedness, and this other situation," I said with a little brush-off wave to acknowledge the murder, "will continue to be in the news. Now, if word gets out that we are making these patients wait, think of the bad press."

"We don't have much choice," Will said.

We had lots of choices; he didn't want to spend the money. I knew it, and he had to know I knew it. "I think we have a couple of choices. We can send the patients to other hospitals."

"Absolutely not. We can't afford to lose the revenues. If that's the best you can come up with." He stood to again signify our meeting was over.

It wasn't. I swallowed the retort that he wanted to bring in as much revenue as possible before the end of the year because it would increase his annual bonus.

I tossed out option number two. "Look, Will, what if we get all the involved departments to agree to put in a couple of extra evening hours and maybe a Saturday shift or two. That way, we keep the revenues in-house and demonstrate that we're making a real effort to care for our patients despite this unexpected accident."

"Do you know how much overtime that'll cost?"

I wanted to beat my head against the wall. The man had

no vision, except for a narrow tunnel that went straight to the bottom line. I forced myself to remain calm. "So, you tack on a small surcharge for a month or two."

Will stared at me for a moment, and I could almost see the wheels turning. He was figuring how to make this work, and he was irritated I'd thought of it first. It didn't matter to me how it happened, I simply wanted the problem solved so angry people would stop yelling at me. Just because I worked in customer service did not mean I liked getting yelled at.

I knew he would figure out a way to take full credit for this solution. That was okay. Sort of. I'm not a Pollyanna. I like recognition for a job well done as much as the next person, but that isn't why I took this job. It was the intrigue that kept me coming back day after day, the problem-solving. Sometimes, I stuck around if only to see what happened next.

From the Cheshire cat grin crossing Will's face, he'd put the pieces of the puzzle together in his favor. "You may have something there, Robyn. I'll look into it and talk to Larry."

"That's great. Well, I know you're busy, and I am too. I'll see you next week."

I rose from the chair, pleased I could still move after sitting in the torture seat. Will was already flipping through his Rolodex. I made it as far as the door when Will said, "The Quality Report is due today, Robyn."

"It's almost finished," I lied. "I should have a draft on your desk before I leave."

If *I leave today,* I thought. If I started now and did nothing else, I might finish by midnight. My head filled with dark thoughts aimed at administrators who find legal ways to torture their subordinates. Report writing called for another caffeine hit, so I headed for the cafeteria.

I was surprised to find Detective Pierce standing in the espresso line. The first thing I thought of to say was "you've got the wrong man," but I forced myself to be politely friendly. "Why, Detective, I didn't know you indulged."

He nodded and said, "Even an old gumshoe like me enjoys a good cup of coffee."

"Good coffee in a hospital? Isn't that an oxymoron?"

"Yeah, like all cops love donuts." He chuckled. "I hate donuts."

He picked up his order, and I expected him to leave. Instead, he waited for me. "Have a moment?" He pointed toward a corner table with two chairs.

I hesitated, then figured the Quality Report wasn't going anywhere. I nodded and neither of us said anything until we were seated and had taken a few sips of our lattés. He shifted in his chair as if preparing to say something. Finally he did.

"Ms. Kelly." He sighed. "May I call you Robyn?"

I nodded. Given yesterday's events, we were beyond the formalities, but I had yet to bring myself to call him Matt.

"Robyn, I want to tell you how sorry I am you were there when we picked up Mr. Nguyen."

"Have you charged him?"

Pierce nodded. "Early this morning."

I turned the cup around and around in my hands, then looked at him thoughtfully before saying, "I'm sorry you arrested the wrong man."

Pierce grimaced at me. "You think we weren't careful? You think we don't know what we're doing?"

"What I think is that you're probably a very good detective. But I know there's tremendous pressure on you—"

Pierce snorted. "You can't even begin to imagine the pressure to make an arrest in this case."

"Oh, I bet I can. This wasn't just any murder, this was a congressman."

"Tell me about it." Pierce sank back in his chair and closed his eyes.

For a moment I saw the fatigue, the worry etched in his face. I regretted I had to make life more difficult for him, because he seemed like a decent person. But he made a big mistake when he arrested Pham, and I was going to do all I could to prove he was wrong.

"I guess now that you have the case all wrapped up, you'll be off to investigate some other crime."

"What's the matter? You trying to get rid of me?"

"Not at all, Detective Pierce."

"Matt," he corrected. "I still have hours of interviews to conduct. The prosecutor's office wants an airtight case before we proceed. No slipups on this one."

"I'm sure you'll be thorough. But please, keep an open mind. Pham couldn't have done it."

"You don't know what a man will do when pushed hard enough. Mr. Nguyen thought his family was threatened. Did you know Hamilton was sponsoring a bill that would deny visas for the rest of Mr. Nguyen's family to immigrate to this country? He was the last person Officer Tomlin let into the room before you came and found the body."

What could I say? Pierce had identified motive and opportunity, but I had to defend Pham. "Well, I reserve the right to disagree with your conclusions. Pham has spent hundreds of hours, thousands maybe, in support of refugees. A bill that denied visas to Pham's family would of course make him furious. But Pham was so sincere when he told me he was innocent. I think I'm a reasonably good judge of character, and I've known Pham for several years. He's a compassionate and caring person. To you, he's just an anonymous suspect."

I stood and collected my things. "I'll let you know what I find in my investigation."

Pierce caught my wrist. "Don't do that, Robyn. Don't get involved. It's dangerous. Leave it to the police."

"So you can send an innocent man to jail?" I shook my head and gently pulled my arm away from his grip. "I'll be discreet, Detective Pierce. Remember, I'm an investigator myself."

I left him scowling, and although I gave him a bright smile when I left, inside I was scowling too. I had to help Pham. And I had to write that damn report.

SEVEN

MERCIFULLY, MY PHONE was quiet for a few hours. Usually I was interrupted every ten minutes or so, which resulted in my having a ridiculously short attention span. If Connie didn't break in with a question or a phone call, I bounced out of my chair four or five times an hour to retrieve a file, connect with Connie and Margie, or get another cup of coffee.

This afternoon was different. Numb from the last two days' events, I concentrated on the Quality Committee Report without the usual mental distractions. My section of the report boiled down to two essential issues: what patients were complaining about, and how much money my department wrote off in charges. I was confident I could justify every penny.

To my amazement, the information came together faster than I'd expected. Maybe it was because this year we had installed an automated system so the computer crunched the numbers for me. Maybe it was because, after doing it three years in a row, there were few surprises. Maybe it was because I was too tired to be creative. Whatever the reason, I finished before closing time.

"Here it is, Connie." I set a disk on her desk. "I've tortured the data until it confessed."

Connie saved and printed the document on her computer before she hit the exit key and picked up the disk. "What does this year's Quality Report say?"

"Same as last year's," I said with a laugh. "And the year before that, and the year before that. If doctors and nurses are nice, the patient thinks the medical care is great. If the doctors and nurses are rude, the patient thinks the care was bad. Hospital food is terrible. And they don't want to wait for anything."

"Sounds reasonable to me. I suppose you want me to clean this up and make it pretty." Connie wagged the disk in her hand.

"That would be great. I'm supposed to have a copy of the report on Will's desk this afternoon, but I think he's in Seattle and won't be back tonight."

"We have plenty of time," Connie said. "If you have it on his desk by noon tomorrow, it will be fine."

I looked at her with skepticism. "Are you playing psychic again?"

She hesitated long enough for me to begin wondering. Then she gave me a "gotcha" smile. "Not this time. I had my afternoon break with Arlene and she was saying how relieved she was that Will's out of the building for a while. I guess he's on a tear, yelling at everyone. She said it's even worse than last week when he had a student intern in tears for misfiling a folder."

"Really? Well, I suppose he has reason to be upset. It's not every day an administrator can claim a congressman was murdered in his hospital."

"That goes for the rest of us too," Connie said. "I'm getting E-mails and instant messages from friends and relatives I haven't heard from in months, asking how things are. Real chummy. And then, wanting the scoop on what's really going on."

Knowing I would probably find the same thing when I checked my E-mail, I shook my head. "Don't you just love people?"

Leaning forward, Connie turned serious. "Rob, who do you think did it?"

Her question stopped me cold. "The police arrested Pham," I said, perching on the arm of the couch.

"Somehow I can't see him doing it. But who else could it be?"

"If Pham didn't do it, then maybe someone else in the hospital did. But I find that hard to believe. It was an outsider."

"So, how're we going to find out?"

"We?" I responded with raised eyebrows. I didn't want to lie to Connie, but there was no way I would involve her in this mess. I felt an almost parental urge to protect her, even if it was a case of do-as-I-say-not-do-as-I-do. "It's in police hands. Detective Pierce seems quite capable."

"But—"

"No buts, Connie. This might be the patient-relations nightmare of the decade, but it's outside our jurisdiction. Way outside."

"But—"

"Look, it's one thing for us to be involved when a patient dies because of some accident or oversight. But this was murder. And I don't think Admin or Risk Management or the Chief of Staff or the police or anyone else wants you sticking your nose in this." I smiled to soften my words. "Besides, with Margie on vacation, we have more than enough to do without adding a murder investigation to the list."

"Well, other work never stopped Dr. Mark Sloan or Jessica Fletcher," Connie grumbled as she handed me the document she'd just printed.

"And look at how they almost got killed at the end of every episode," I reminded her. "We're staying out of this, even if your psychic abilities combined with my investigative skills would be an awesome force. Okay?"

Connie pouted as she tugged the clip from her hair and redid her twist. "Okay. If you insist." She handed me a pen. "Sign this, please."

I scanned the printed page and added my signature.

Connie picked up the letter. "Want me to print you a copy of the report now?"

"Might as well. I want to review the numbers at home tonight to be sure I didn't forget anything or transpose some figures. You know some of those committee members. They'll take a fine-toothed comb to the report, looking for errors."

"I'll start formatting now. Philip's running late, so I won't be leaving until six or six-thirty."

"Are you sure you want to wait here?"

"I'd go shopping, but the weather's nasty out there, and, besides, working on this without the phone ringing every two minutes would be heavenly."

"Well, make a note of the extra time so you can take off early some afternoon."

"How about next Wednesday?"

"Next Wednesday? Sure," I said with a shrug. "That's an odd time."

"Rob," she said with a laugh. "It's the day before Thanksgiving."

I froze. "Thanksgiving's next week?" How could I have forgotten?

"Yeah. And dinner's at my house this year. In-laws and everything. Philip thinks I'm a crazy woman. I'm scouring places I've never cleaned before, and making him dig out his den."

"Uh-oh, that is serious. Talk to Larry Bridgeway. I'm sure he can find a prescription to cure you," I joked, glancing at the message slips in the holder on Connie's desk. "Anything I want to know about?"

"Nothing big. Mostly staff calling to report on cases. I noted the gist of their comments so you don't have to call them back."

"Thanks." I flipped quickly through the half dozen or so message forms. "Josh called?"

"That's right. He said to tell you not to worry—"

"Like that'll be the day," I said.

Connie laughed again. "You're not to worry about him tonight. He's going to Chuck's house to work on a project, but he promised to feed Taffy before he goes and he might be late so don't wait up. Who's Chuck?"

"Darned if I know," I said with a heavy sigh. "I used to know all his friends. From preschool on. I even knew the kids who were in his high-school classes. When did I fall so completely out of the loop? What kind of a mother am I?" I said with a sharp pang.

"It's okay, 'Mom,'" Connie reassured. "He's in college now. You can't expect to know everyone anymore."

"At least Chuck is in his engineering program. Someone who understands what he's talking about," I said, somewhat mollified. "Honestly, when Josh starts one of his long explanations, it's all I can do to keep from glazing over. It's as if he's speaking a foreign language."

"He is, just like you speak medicalese. Don't be so hard on yourself. The kid's growing up, that's all."

Mumbling that I wasn't reassured, I returned to my office and shut the door. Connie was right. How could I expect the same involvement in Josh's life at nineteen that I had at nine? Still, it hurt to realize that soon the center of my world would be gone. Of course I wanted him to grow up to be an independent adult, and to someday marry and have a family of his own. I just wished he wouldn't do it quite yet. I wasn't ready to think about life after Josh.

Except for resolving to have a home-cooked dinner with him this weekend, there was little I could do about Josh at the moment. I had no choice but to refocus my attention on work. Before I started, I took a deep breath and stretched. It felt really good to get that report off my to-do list.

The haphazard stack of handwritten notes perched on the corner of my desk was waiting. We documented all the compliments and complaints that came into the office, and sent copies to the department managers. Complaints about physicians went directly to the Chief of Staff's office.

It was a cumbersome system, but we hadn't come up with anything simpler, at least not without spending a gazillion dollars on a customized database management system. And that was not likely to happen anytime soon.

That pile of incoherent notes should be translated to one of our forms soon. I thumbed through the pile, relieved that none of them needed urgent attention.

Now that I had rationalized my way out of writing the case reports, I logged on to the Internet. Despite what I said to Connie about all the reasons why *she* should stay out of the investigation, I still planned to find something to prove Pham Nguyen's innocence. Somehow I convinced myself I was not a hypocrite.

An oddity in Microsoftland, I seldom used the Internet. I have friends who spend hours clicking from one site to another, finding all sorts of incredible things. Me? I have a couple of favorite sites for shopping. It's nice to come home to a "present" on the front porch. But I usually go on the Internet with a specific destination in mind. The concept of blindly "surfing the Net" was a bit intimidating.

Today was different. I had a specific purpose, but would

have to search to find what I wanted. I figured I needed to start with motive. Who had a motive to murder Congressman Hamilton? And where should I look? As I reached for the Excedrin bottle, it came to me.

In a hugely popular historical mystery, the detectives figured out who the murderer was by studying the victims. That's what I could do: investigate Congressman Hamilton to find out why someone might want to kill him.

Since he was from eastern Washington, he probably knew few people from around here, so the odds were high that the motive wasn't personal. My best bet was to find information about his congressional activities.

I typed in "Jake Hamilton" and clicked on the "Search" button.

Bingo! Hamilton's Web site was the first site listed, so I clicked on it. His homepage was impressive, with red, white, and blue flashing stars, and a picture of him looking quite the hunk in a white shirt, bolo tie, tan corduroy jacket, and snug jeans while he leaned against a fence post with rolling hills of Palouse wheat country flowing behind him.

Clicking around the site, I learned that I could receive an informational packet about the congressman, including an autographed picture, by keying in my home address. That would keep me on the contributions mailing list forever, I thought.

Or, I could give my E-mail address and receive regular updates from Congressman Hamilton, who would also respond personally to any queries sent to him. My perverse sense of humor wondered how he would respond to "who murdered you?"

The site even had a video of a recent town meeting with his constituents. I watched, so fascinated by the technology that I had to replay the segment. Hamilton was a charismatic politician, no doubt about it. He knew the right words, the right inflections, the right gestures, without seeming the least bit phony. I found it an amazing performance.

I clicked it to replay one more time. That's when it struck me. Whenever Hamilton started to say something that would make him look good, he lifted his chin ever so slightly. It was a mannerism he repeated each time he talked about what he had done for his district. Someone else I knew did that, but who? It probably didn't matter.

It might not be long before the Web master shut down the site, so I decided to print some of the pages for future reference. For the most part, it was a lot of razzle-dazzle and not much substance.

The bio was short, the bare essentials. Born and raised in Walden, Montana, he went to Montana State in Butte and graduated with a degree in public administration. Then, he moved to Spokane, where he became involved in party politics and rose quickly to the top, and was now serving his second term in Congress. Until yesterday, I thought gloomily.

As I read through the Web site, Hamilton's skill at marketing himself fascinated me. He was absolutely committed to saving Social Security, improving education, protecting the environment, promoting business, improving transportation, and, last but not least, cutting taxes. Yet, nowhere did the Web site discuss specifics of how he would do any of this.

Hamilton had more loopholes in his position statements than a medical insurance contract. I'd been around long enough to know that "improve education" could mean anything from a massive federal program to returning all control and monies to local school districts. Save

Social Security? For those over sixty? Assumed. But what about us tail-end boomers? What about Josh and his generation?

I realized this site told me nothing as far as why someone would want Hamilton dead, but it certainly gave me a better idea of how polished and professional this man had been.

Were all congressmen this way? I took a few minutes to check on other Washington state representatives. They all had their own Web sites, but most were pretty basic and straightforward compared to Hamilton's.

If the other congressmen failed to use their Web sites' full capabilities to connect electronically with their constituents, why was Congressman Hamilton's Web site so sophisticated? Was the representative from the eastern part of the state actively cultivating supporters from outside his district? It certainly appeared that he was not targeting his farmer, rancher, or logger constituency with this site.

Intrigued, I looked for another Web site that would tell me more about Hamilton's position on some issues. After some false steps, including one that took me to a porno site—oh, I hoped no one monitored this—I found a government site that had the Congressional Record online.

I typed Jake Hamilton's name into the query box, defined a time frame of the last six months and clicked the search button. The number of results astounded me. This wasn't going to be quick. I clicked on the first item and started scrolling my way through the text.

SOMETIME LATER, I leaned back in my chair, stunned by what I had read. Last week, a debate had involved a large healthcare funding bill, and in it was a small budget for a new department within Health and Human Services. Congressman Hamilton had spoken adamantly to have the allocation dropped. We did not need another government oversight program, he declared, regardless of what Will Slater, the speculated soon-to-be-appointed head of that new department, had testified.

Will? Testifying in Washington, D.C.? How had I missed that? It made sense, though. Will was an ambitious man, and still fairly young. He made a perfect bureaucrat. Despite our different perspectives of the world, I had to acknowledge Will was an excellent financial manager. However, if he received an appointment such as this, I could only hope there would be people around him who remembered that patients were people, not machines. Healthcare had become so cost-conscious and so high-tech that the personalized high-touch component was too often forgotten.

However, if Hamilton had spoken out against funding a new department, and Will missed a promotion to work in D.C., well, that certainly sounded like a motive to me.

The words I'd heard while standing outside Will's door suddenly flashed into my mind: *maybe I have a chance for that appointment now…it couldn't happen to a nicer guy at a better time.*

Then I remembered Connie's comments about Will's anger last week. If he followed the budget debate, he would've known that Hamilton wanted to kill the funding. But would Will murder Hamilton in return? The idea was staggering, and I wasn't much more comfortable with Will being the murderer than I was with Pham.

Did the police know about this motive? Had they bothered to investigate anyone besides Pham? I doubted it. If they knew about Will, they might not have been so hasty to arrest Pham. If Will had a motive this strong, who else around here had an undiscovered reason to dislike Congressman Hamilton?

Still unnerved by the implications of what I had read, I prepared to move on to the next set of congressional testimony when muffled voices filtered through from the front office, Connie's and a man's. I heard them laugh, so I didn't get up. A quick glance at my watch told me it was six o'clock. Realizing whom Connie was probably talking to, I felt a rush of pleasure as I opened the door and stepped from my office.

"Hi, Peter," I said. His dark-brown sweater did wonderful things for his tawny hair and eyes. So did the warm smile that touched his lips.

"How's my timing?"

"I'm impressed." Realizing I probably hadn't done it when Peter had come to the office the previous afternoon, I made quick introductions, then said, "You know, Connie, when I first met Peter, he was always very punctual. He consistently arrived ten minutes after he was supposed to."

"Ah, come on, I wasn't that bad," Peter protested.

"You were too," I responded. "Do you remember the time—"

"Rob," Connie interrupted. "I'll see you tomorrow. Nice to see you again, Mr. Armstrong." Her lingering smile would have raised her husband's jealous hackles if he'd seen it.

Peter nodded while I said, "Good night, Connie. I'll see you in the morning."

The door clicked softly behind her, and I struggled not to laugh out loud. "I see you haven't lost your charm, Mr. Armstrong."

He winced. "She makes me sound so old when she calls me mister."

"Well, you are old to a twenty-five-year-old. You're old enough to be her father." From the pained expression on his face, I'd struck a raw nerve.

"Watch it, Rob. You're old enough to be a grandma."

"Ouch! You really play hardball, don't you?"

His expression softened, and I felt that old shiver run down my spine.

"We better get out of here." His voice was husky.

"Right." I hurried to the storage room to get my coat. Slipping it on, I noticed that Peter already had the door open. As I stepped into the hall, I asked, "What're you in the mood for?"

"How about a candlelit Italian dinner?" He flipped off the light switch and pulled the door closed.

In the bright hallway, I searched his eyes for a reason for his choice. Ah, so he too, remembered. I wasn't sure I wanted to repeat our first date, but my mind was so rattled by his closeness that I couldn't think straight. "I know just the place. I'll drive."

"This once, I'll let you. But only because I don't know my way around."

We didn't talk as we hurried across the parking lot in the pouring rain.

"Don't you people believe in umbrellas?" Peter asked as he jumped into the car.

"Waste of money, most of the time. If you don't forget it someplace, a gust of wind blows it inside out." I turned on the ignition and blasted the heater, then noticed Peter wasn't putting his seatbelt on. "Seatbelt, please," I said.

Peter looked at me with surprise. "I never wear a seatbelt. Never know when I'll have to bail out into a ditch to avoid getting shot."

"This isn't the Middle East; it's Seattle. You won't get shot at here," I said. That wasn't completely true, but the chances of a drive-by shooting in the suburbs were close to nil. "Besides, it's a minimum seventy-five-dollar ticket if you get caught without one."

Peter rolled his eyes, but complied. Once we were on the road, I had to concentrate on my driving. The convoluted routes I used between work and home failed me. Gully-washing rain had turned all the roads into hydroplaning opportunities.

"Good God," Peter said as I braked for the umpteenth time and he braced himself against the door. "Now I understand why you made me wear the seatbelt. Where did these people learn to drive?"

"That's just it, they didn't." I gritted my teeth to keep from railing about the idiots who whipped in and out of lanes without signaling, and other drivers who inched along as if they didn't have a clue where they were going.

I took him to Giuseppe's, a small neighborhood restaurant halfway between the hospital and my home. The parking lot was almost full, but I hoped we were arriving as the early diners started to leave. We walked in and I sighed with relief; only three other groups waited ahead of us. Giuseppe's didn't take reservations, and so a forty-five-minute wait for a table was not uncommon.

Peter slipped out of his jacket, then helped me with my coat. He whispered in my ear, "If the food's half as good as it smells—"

"It's even better," I whispered back.

We stood quietly for the ten minutes or so it took before a cozy booth was available. A waitress quickly brought a basket of breadsticks and left with our order for a half carafe of Chianti.

I scanned the menu and said, "I haven't had Chianti since…" For two cents I would have taken back the words.

"Since Olivia's?" Peter filled in.

"The clam linguini is great," I said to quickly change the subject. "So's the chicken marsala."

Peter snapped the menu closed and laid it on the table. "I'm in the mood for old-fashioned spaghetti and meat-balls."

I nodded. "Good choice." A big plate of pasta, my favorite comfort food, sounded wonderful. But the slacks I was wearing today were snug too. Not as bad as yesterday's, but I had to do something.

The waitress returned and I ordered a chop-chop salad with strips of grilled chicken, figuring I could probably get a bite or two of Peter's spaghetti if I wanted. Realizing I was about to eat my fourth breadstick, I set it gently on the bread plate.

"Tell me about your day." Peter's request was so casual, so…so normal, as if we were an ordinary couple with a past. And a future.

I felt a panicky flutter, and took a sip of wine to buy some time. What was I doing here with this man? Why was he trying so hard to be part of my life? True, we had a history, but that had been a long time ago. As for a future? It was too sudden, and too many other things were going on right now. Relationships were not noted for being convenient, but I hesitated, unsure of where I wanted to go with this whole thing.

"Rob? Are you there? It wasn't meant to be a trick question."

I snapped back, unable to believe that I had mentally drifted off for a few moments. I smiled lamely. "Sorry. I guess the last two days have been a little much." That was the understatement of the year. I took another sip of wine.

"Well, how was your day?" Peter asked again.

"Oh, fine. Finished my report, handled a few problems." *Found a motive for murder.* "Just an ordinary day at the hospital," I said with a benign smile.

Peter leaned against the booth and started to drape his

arm across the top when he realized it was too high. Annoyance darted across his face, and then he started fiddling with his silverware. "I find that hard to believe. Ordinary and hospital don't seem like they should be in the same sentence."

"To an outsider, probably not. But for those of us who work there, it becomes a routine, just like anywhere else. Cut 'em, stitch 'em, send 'em home." Peter laughed at the description and I remembered how much I'd loved that hearty sound. "Tell me about your day."

"It wasn't my normal aftermath of shoot 'em, stab 'em, leave 'em for dead kind of day," he said, but the bleakness in his eyes betrayed his attempt at humor.

Before I could stop myself, I reached across the table and took his hand, squeezing it gently. "I could never do what you do and stay sane."

His mouth twisted in a crooked smile. "Who says I'm sane?" He looked across the room, but from the pain in his eyes, I sensed he saw not the wall twenty feet away, but one of a hundred battlefields thousands of miles from Seattle.

"I watched some of it on the evening news."

"That didn't even begin to describe it."

He started talking about his experiences, not the gory details, but the conditions and the issues and the participants and the aftermath, so that by the time we finished eating, I had a greater understanding of the rest of the world, and a much deeper appreciation for why some of those issues were spilling over into our own lives.

"Guess I talked your ear off," he said with a deprecating smile as he swirled the last of his wine around the glass.

"Not really." I shook my head. "So much suffering by the innocents. I'm glad you told me about it, though."

Peter nodded as he snagged the bill. After glancing at

it, he tossed a credit card on the table. Then he frowned and retrieved it, replacing it with another.

"Guess you can't put me on your expense account."

"What?" He looked startled.

"The credit card, the one you picked up. It had the news service's logo on it."

"Oh, yeah. They're clamping down on expenses, just like everyone else." He slid out of the booth and shoved his wallet into his pants pocket. "I'll pay for this up front."

"I'll leave the tip," I offered. It was the only way I could make a contribution without making a big deal about splitting the bill.

"Fine."

I rummaged through my wallet until I put together the right amount, then went to meet Peter at the front door. We stepped outside to a brisk wind. The rain had died down and the clouds had lifted. We approached my SUV and I clicked the locks. Peter went around to the passenger side.

Decision time. "I still have to work on that report tonight, so I'll take you back to your car," I said to forestall any suggestion that the evening continue.

Peter cast me a sardonic look across the hood of the Explorer. "In a hurry to get rid of me?"

"No." Although that wasn't entirely true. "But I do need some time to sort everything out."

As we climbed into the car, he nodded his understanding. "You've dealt with a lot the last couple of days."

"That's an understatement," I mumbled, shifting into reverse.

Traffic had diminished considerably since we'd entered the restaurant, but the streets were still busy. Didn't anyone stay home anymore? After we reached the hospital parking lot, Peter directed me to his rental car. I stopped behind it and shifted into park.

"Thanks for dinner." I couldn't think of anything more witty to say.

Peter smiled, his teeth gleaming as he moved closer to kiss me. In the limited light, the smile appeared almost feral, but I shook off the absurd notion and leaned into the kiss. It wasn't overpowering like our first one, but there was a poignancy to it that made me look questioningly at him when we parted.

"I'll see you later, okay?" His voice was husky as he slid from the Explorer.

"Sure." I waved as he swung the door closed, and out of habit waited until his car had started before I drove away.

What a night.

What a couple of days.

I exhaled heavily as I rolled my hands over the steering wheel. What I needed was some time off and a trip to a resort where there were sunshine and masseuses, frosty margaritas and good food. And nobody calling with problems for me to solve. What I was going to get was a short night of sleep because of that nagging report and a lot of headaches while I tried to solve Congressman Hamilton's murder.

I was a mile from the hospital when I remembered that I left my briefcase, with the report and all my notes, sitting in my office.

"Well, hell," I muttered. I glanced at my watch. Only eight-thirty. No choice, but to turn around at the next intersection and go back.

Alternately haranguing and forgiving myself for being forgetful, I returned to the hospital. I parked near the front and went in through the main entrance, since the other doors were locked by now.

There's something very soothing about a hospital at

night. Many of the lights are dimmed. Carts that rattle through the building all day carrying meals, linens, and supplies are parked for the night. Most of the staff have gone home, leaving a few nurses at each nursing station to monitor patients and complete charts. The ancillary departments such as Radiology and the lab have token crews in case an emergency comes up, but for the most part, the building slumbers.

I walked the silent halls and thought about Jake Hamilton in that final sleep. A part of me believed he wasn't yet at rest, at least not his soul. How could it be after being murdered and after the indignities done to his body in the name of justice? I had never been to an autopsy, but I read enough police procedural mysteries and saw enough episodes of *CSI* to know it was something I could live without. Maybe Hamilton's soul would rest when his murderer was found.

The elevator doors opened on my floor. I stepped out and wondered at myself: choosing to work on a report over spending a long evening with a gorgeous guy. A guy I knew could knock my socks off. It was scary to think I was too tired to consider a night of romance and passion. These days, a good dinner and a couple of glasses of wine, and I was ready for a long night's sleep. With a sigh, I pulled my keys from my coat pocket. Life had a way of catching up with you, I thought as I started to stick the office key in the lock.

But I didn't need my key. At the slight pressure, the door eased open.

EIGHT

I STARED AT THE DOOR. Adrenaline surged through me and my weariness disappeared, replaced by an overwhelming sense of danger. Something was very wrong. Tensed for fight or flight, I considered my next move.

The door is kept unlocked during the day when Connie, Margie, or I are in the office; otherwise, it's secured. Normally, I would've charged right in, indignant that housekeeping had left the door open. But that was before Jake Hamilton's murder in broad daylight. Finding a dead body had turned me more cautious than usual.

Carefully, silently, I reached for the knob and tried to turn it. It didn't move; the door was locked, but for some reason, the latch hadn't caught.

When I let go, the door opened a little more. I listened, my heart pounding in my chest. Nothing. I hesitated, not sure I wanted to know what, or who, might be inside. But I had to find out. I slipped into the dimly lit front office. Everything was as it should be. Standing in the middle of the reception area, I heard a muffled noise.

Hospitals have myriad subdued sounds, even at night, but this sound was distinctive, the muffled clickety-click of a keyboard. Puzzled, I wondered if thieves tested computer equipment before they stole it. I stepped to the left and saw the reflected glow of a computer screen from under my closed office door. My office. Somebody was messing with my computer. Forgetting the need for caution, I stormed forward and slammed open the door.

I stopped, totally off-kilter. "Peter?"

Of all the people I might have expected, he wasn't one of them. "What're you doing?" I looked from him to the computer screen and what I saw left a deep pit of dismay in my stomach the size of the Grand Canyon.

Peter jumped from the chair and tried to hit the Escape key, but it was too late. I had already seen too much.

"Rob." With a dazzling smile, he put his arms out as if to embrace me, then let them fall to his sides as the smile vanished. "I thought you'd gone home." His accusatory tone implied that somehow I was the one in the wrong.

"Obviously. Do you want to explain why you're reading Jake Hamilton's medical records on my computer? Records that are supposed to be confidential?"

"I, ah, I needed something for tomorrow morning's headline and I didn't want to bother you."

His excuse was so outrageous that it took me a moment to respond.

"I've been out of media relations for a long time, Peter, but I know your service has an above-board reputation. They wouldn't report something they had to know was obtained illegally."

The oddest expression crossed Peter's face. If I had blinked, I would have missed it, but now my mind started running through the possibilities. That was easier, less painful, than confronting how I felt about his betrayal of me. Of us. Again.

"This isn't for the cable news, is it, Peter?" I finally asked in a quiet voice.

He hesitated, then pursed his lips and shook his head.

"Want to tell me about it?" I pretended to be calm, belying the fact that I wanted to rip his head off with my bare hands. His accessing records on my computer could cost me my job, destroy my life. The murderous rage welling up inside me frightened the daylights out of me.

"I don't work for them anymore." His stance shifted, his jaw jutted out slightly, and he crossed his arms over his chest. His whole body language screamed defensiveness.

I was afraid to ask, but I did anyway. "What happened?"

"They found out an interview with some Islamic terrorists was…" He swallowed as if he had a huge lump in his throat and he started breathing hard. He radiated frustration and resentment. "It wasn't a lie. I'd spent enough time there to know that if I'd been able to arrange an interview, what I wrote was what they would've said."

I gasped. "You faked an interview? I, I can't believe— why on earth would you do something stupid like that?" I knew I sounded more like a parent than a lover, former lover, but he'd broken one of the first rules of journalism, to always tell the truth.

"My editor was making noises about bringing me in from the field, that some new guys, young kids, wanted their chance. He said I was…" He wiped his hand over his face, then glared at me. "He said I was getting too old to dodge bullets. I had to prove I still had what it took to be out there, that my age was irrelevant. My experience and my contacts were what really counted."

"So what was this all about?" I waved vaguely at my computer.

"I was at Sea-Tac waiting for a flight to New York when I heard about the car crash. I thought maybe I could scoop the majors. Seems I'm *persona non grata* in the serious news industry. Only the tabloids would take my calls." He laughed humorlessly. "All those years I spent out there, risking my neck to get stories everyone else was too afraid to go for."

"You could've come back and had a fine career with the network. You didn't have to spend your whole life living an adventure."

"And live your idea of a real life? The kind you wanted to trap me into ten years ago? The nine-to-five and Sunday afternoon trips to the zoo with the kids?"

The rancor behind his words was just another blow. I swallowed hard. "So, you didn't want that. Fine. Surely there were other options."

Peter sneered. "You always were so conventional, Rob. Good-hearted, but a little slow. You haven't even asked how I gained access to your computer. Your password's the same as it was ten years ago in New York. Misty. After the cat you had as a child. So predictable, Rob."

The callousness of what he'd done jolted me. I started to shake, angry with him for betraying me, angry with myself for playing the love-struck fool. Again. "Get out of my office," I said. All the hurt and rage bubbled up inside me and spilled out. I screamed at him, "Get out of my office. Now!"

I followed him to the door. He turned to say something. I didn't give him a chance to tell another lie. In a surge of fury, I shoved him hard. It caught him off guard and he stumbled against the doorjamb, then sprawled onto the hall floor.

I slammed the door in his face, but it swung open again. Before I could slam it again, a deep voice from the hallway outside stopped me. "Having a problem, Ms. Kelly?"

I put my fist against my forehead and closed my eyes. My worst nightmare was compounding itself. I opened them again as Detective Pierce stepped into view. A uniformed officer stood behind him, the same officer who'd been guarding Congressman Hamilton's door the day of the murder.

Pierce glanced at Peter, then at me. "What's going on?"

"I found this man in my office accessing confidential medical records," I said dispassionately. The man lying on the floor in front of me was a stranger. Maybe he always had been a stranger and I'd never realized it. The whole time I had known him, he'd been wearing a mask to cover his ambition.

"Did you let him in?" Pierce asked.

I shook my head. "I found the door ajar when I came upstairs a few minutes ago."

By now, Peter was standing up and Officer Tomlin held his arm, blocking his retreat.

Pierce crossed in front of me and ran his hand down the side of the door. "Hmmm," he murmured, then hunkered down to take a closer look. "Tomlin, what do you think?"

The uniformed officer gave Peter a warning look before moving next to Pierce. "Appears the door was taped open, sir."

At his words, I leaned over to see what they were talking about. A piece of silver duct tape covered the latch bolt, which would keep the door from closing and locking. No wonder it had bounced open when I slammed it. No wonder it had pushed open when I started to insert my key. Images flashed in my mind: Peter standing by the open door, Peter closing the door when we left to go to dinner.

Slowly, I straightened and turned to him. His cold-blooded actions of the last two days were more than I could comprehend. "You planned this ahead of time, didn't you?"

He shrugged and looked away as if bored by the whole thing.

"Did he get anything from your computer?" Detective Pierce asked me.

"I don't know. He had maybe fifteen minutes before I caught him."

Pierce looked at me for a moment, and I wasn't sure if it was compassion or pity I saw in his eyes. He went to stand toe-to-toe with Peter. "If it wasn't for the fact that it could get Ms. Kelly in a lot of trouble, I'd haul your sorry ass to jail and charge you with B&E and anything else I could come up with. Instead, I'm going to have Officer Tomlin take you to the jail and hold you as long as we can legally. Then we'll escort you to the airport and see that you get on the first plane to nowhere with an available seat. And if you reveal what you learned from breaking into her computer to anyone, I'll come after you myself. Got that?"

Peter nodded, and when Officer Tomlin tapped his arm, he started down the hall. Before they rounded the corner, he hesitated and turned to look at me. "If you let them do this, I won't be back, Rob. You'll never find someone like me again."

"I certainly hope not," I spat out as Peter disappeared from sight.

Detective Pierce touched my elbow and I started. I had forgotten he was there. "Here," he said, handing me a linen handkerchief. "You look like you need this."

I didn't know what to say. Or what to think. Or what to feel. I was numb all over, my mind, my body, my heart. He left, and it was then that I realized tears were streaming down my face.

Somehow I found my way into my office, and after sinking into my chair, I did the only thing any normal woman would do under the circumstances. I had a good cry. I cried for Peter's betrayal. I cried for the years I'd lost while waiting for his return. I cried for David's senseless death.

By the time I worked my way down the list and reached the tears for putting on five pounds since the first of the year and Josh having friends I didn't know, I decided the pity party was about over. In addition to Detective Pierce's handkerchief, I'd gone through half a box of tissues usually reserved for distraught patients.

After patting my eyes and blowing my nose one more time, I took a deep breath. It was a ragged breath, but I felt better.

"Are you okay?"

I jumped, startled to find Detective Pierce standing in my doorway. "How long've you been standing there?"

"Two seconds. I've been out there." He nodded toward the reception area. "Figured you could use some time alone."

"Thanks." I held up his handkerchief. "I'll get this back to you after I wash it."

He grimaced. "You still haven't answered my question."

"Which was?"

"Are you okay?"

"Oh." I had to think about that one for a minute. "I think so. At least I will be later."

"Can you tell if he found anything that could create a problem?"

I'd been so wrapped up in my feelings, I'd forgotten about the computer. I gestured for Pierce to sit down, then I moved the mouse to remove the screensaver from my computer screen. Peter had accessed a system with the best security money could buy. A staff member had to log onto the computer using a department security code, then use their personal password to access the medical records. Employees in most departments could look at only their portion of the records, the lab techs could view lab records, nurses could see records for only their unit.

Because of the nature of my job, I was one of the few people who could access everything about everybody. Even Will didn't have this level of security clearance. My mistake had been to forget to turn my computer off, and to not close and lock my office door myself when I left for dinner with Peter. He hadn't needed the department code to gain access to medical records, just my password. I chided myself for my laxness.

Scrolling up to see what Peter had been looking at, I scanned Jake Hamilton's records for something unusual. Lab reports. Physician notes. Nursing notes. Radiology reports. Finally, I turned to Detective Pierce and said, "Nothing special. Just the usual injuries you'd expect from being in a serious car accident."

Pierce smiled. "Glad to see you haven't lost your sense of humor."

"That's about all I have left, isn't it?" I exited from the medical records. "I can't believe I was such a fool."

"Don't be hard on yourself. You had no way of knowing he wasn't sincere."

I looked sharply at the detective. "Did you know?"

"Not really. You obviously knew each other from a long time ago. He just seemed to be coming on a bit strong. Let's just say my antenna was up." Pierce stared at the bookshelves over my desk, but I could tell he wasn't reading the titles. He was considering very carefully what he was about to say. He looked at his watch, then, from the slight nod, I could tell he had reached a decision.

"I'm off duty now, and it's been a long day. I think we could both use some fresh air. Join me for a walk on the promenade?"

His tone of voice told me this wasn't official business. But he was too good a cop to let his expression reveal what he was thinking. After what had happened with Peter, I wasn't feeling particularly social, but then, I didn't want to be alone either. Josh was at Chuck's, and I wouldn't want Josh to see me like this anyway.

I glanced out the window. "It looks like the rain has stopped."

"Are you afraid you'll melt?"

"No," I said with a chagrined smile. I touched my face. "I must look a fright."

"You look fine, considering all that's happened," he said.

"That bad, huh?"

He smiled and shrugged. "What do I know? I'm just a well-seasoned cop."

I flushed that he remembered my comparison of him to Officer Tomlin. Was that only yesterday? It felt more like a lifetime ago. "Tell you what, give me a few minutes to do something with this face of mine, then we'll go."

He stood to let me pass, and I went down the hall to the restroom. I took one look in the mirror and scared myself. The fluorescent light was most unforgiving, and I doubted I could make myself presentable. Some cold water and a fresh coat of lipstick later, I felt ready to face the world. My eyes weren't quite so puffy, and no one would see my red nose in the dark.

Detective Pierce was standing in the hall when I returned. I went to my office and made sure the computer was off. I glanced at the Quality Report that was supposed to be on Will's desk in the morning. Screw it, I thought. I'd dealt with enough already today. He would simply have to wait.

Feeling better after that minor act of defiance, I strode toward the door and ran my fingers over the latch bolt before shutting the door.

As we walked down the hall, Pierce chuckled at my

action. "Don't worry. I removed the tape. We can't have
people traipsing in and out of here at all hours of the
night."

"That's all I need." I shook my head and pushed the
elevator button. "It's bad enough during the daytime."

We didn't talk much, sort of like earlier when I left
with Peter. But I felt none of the tension with Detective
Pierce that I had with Peter. What I'd thought was
sexual awareness sizzling between us had turned out to
be the tension of deception. I felt neither with Pierce,
and that was okay.

"I'll take my car and meet you there," I said when we
reached the front door.

He looked at me for a moment, as if gauging whether
I had changed my mind and was looking for a way to
escape. He must have decided I wasn't, because he finally
nodded. "Good idea. Even though I'm off duty, there's
always a chance I'll be paged."

I hesitated to add that this also gave me control of how
long I stayed. I hurried to the car, buffeted by the wind
every step of the way. Was walking the promenade such
a good idea? High above the ground, tree branches
cracked, unable to withstand the stress. The trees were a
wonderful part of living in the Northwest, but they also
meant downed power lines whenever there was a windstorm. The place would be littered with limbs by morning.
I hoped I still had power at home.

After navigating my way through the branch-strewn
parking lot, I quickly drove to the promenade. The wide,
paved path along the edge of Lake Washington was a
popular place for joggers, bicyclists, inline skaters, and
moms pushing strollers. I'd given up walking there in the
summer because of the congestion. It's not relaxing or en-
joyable to be constantly on guard for someone running

into you from the front or the rear. I was surprised to see how full the parking lot was, even at this hour.

I pulled my athletic shoes and socks from the back seat and opened the car door, relieved to find the wind had died down and it still wasn't raining. I had slipped off my pumps and was tugging on the socks when Pierce approached my car.

"Prepared for anything, are we?"

I caught the teasing in his voice and smiled at him. "You bet. I even have a disaster kit in the back."

He raised an eyebrow. "I'm impressed. Do you change out the food and water every six months?"

I nodded. "Of course." Jerking the last bow tight, I slid from the car and locked it. As we walked across the lot, he quizzed me on the contents of my emergency supplies.

Here I was, on my second date of the evening, one with a deceitful jerk and one with a police detective. Did this mean my social life was picking up? Then I remembered an old saying of my grandmother's: a rogue and a decent man shouldn't be mentioned in the same day. That was out, but I would at least try not to think of them at the same time.

The promenade was well lit, and both directions were busy with lone joggers and walking couples, as if everyone was taking advantage of the momentary lull in the stormy weather. We waited a moment before we could merge into the stream of people. The brisk wind coming off the lake made a susurrous sound through the trees. I pulled my wool neck scarf a little tighter and tucked my hands into my coat pockets.

After we had walked a few minutes in silence, Pierce glanced at me. "You look better."

Tears started to well up, but I took a deep breath and vowed I would not cry. Not here. Not in front of God and everyone. Not again in front of Detective Pierce.

"I guess I am." I thought for a moment, then shook my head. "I feel like such a fool. I mean, how stupid could I be? The man walked out on me ten years ago for a job. He's a world-renowned reporter. And suddenly, he reappears. At the exact moment the biggest news story of the year hits my hospital."

I looked at him before turning my attention back to the asphalt path. "I'm supposed to be a reasonably smart person. A good judge of character. I do it all day long, figuring out who's being straight with me and who's twisting the facts to get something they aren't entitled to. Shouldn't I have seen what was going on from the very beginning?"

In spite of concentrating on where I was going, I stumbled. Pierce caught my arm, then tucked my hand around his arm. I told myself he was trying to avoid the embarrassment of my falling flat on my face.

"Don't beat yourself up, Robyn. It happens to the best of us. He was smooth. Very smooth. It wasn't as if he was a complete stranger pulling a con on you. Obviously you'd had dealings with him before, and they'd been mostly good. You had no way of knowing."

"I don't know." I shuddered to think how close I came to giving in to the yearning for intimacy. "At least he didn't get away with it. I guess I should be grateful for that report I was supposed to turn in today."

"A report?"

As briefly as possible, I explained.

Pierce said, "I'm surprised you put all that in writing. It's discoverable, you know. All that stuff in your office is."

"Always the cop?" I asked.

He looked embarrassed. "Yeah, I guess so. Sorry."

"Don't be. You're right, someone could subpoena our

records, but it hasn't happened. If we can't get the patient what they want, we explain everything so clearly, they understand why they aren't getting it. By the time we've worked with them, hardly anyone goes further."

"I bet you're really good at what you do."

The compliment caught me off guard. I smiled, warmed by the recognition. "I guess overall I do okay."

"I wonder if things would have been different if I'd had someone like you working for me a few years ago."

"What do you mean?"

"When my wife was sick." He hesitated, as if considering how much to reveal. Finally, he said, "She had cancer, but no one would do anything. She'd go to the doctor and he'd say nothing was wrong. She wouldn't consider seeing someone else because he'd been her doctor for so long, she felt it would be disloyal. I just watched. Didn't do anything. One night, she collapsed. I brought her to the hospital and a doctor in the Emergency Room…the look on his face when he felt her abdomen, it was awful. I knew then it was over. Didn't need X rays or blood tests to tell me it was too late. I've never felt so helpless."

"I'm sorry." Instinctively, I squeezed his arm gently, but I don't think he was aware of my presence. He was staring at the lake, reliving his nightmare.

"She lasted a week, hooked up to tubes and I.V.'s. They wanted to put her on a respirator, but I said no. What was the point? Then she arrested, and they called a Code Blue because she hadn't signed a Living Will. I couldn't believe it. They pounded on her, shocked her, abused her body in ways that were horrible. I kept yelling at them to stop, but they called Security to take me away. Can you imagine that?"

He looked over at me, and I nodded. I had seen it happen before and had never reconciled myself to it.

Pierce shuddered. "It was an awful way to go."

"I'm really sorry," I said again.

"Ah, hell, it wasn't your fault. Wasn't even your hospital."

"I mean, I'm sorry you had to go through all that," I said.

We came to a wagon selling hot drinks. Pierce ordered hot chocolates and we scooted across the promenade to a stone wall overlooking the lake. The drinks were very hot and we stood in silence, waiting for them to cool enough to drink.

Pierce set his cup down on the wall, his face so full of emotion that I watched him with concern as I took a hesitant sip.

"Did you sue the doctor?" I asked.

"Didn't see the point. Would have cost a lot of money, and a lot of time. And it wouldn't have brought Barbara back. I filed a complaint with the county medical society. Heard he retired six months later."

"So you didn't just let it go, you did something."

He picked up the cup again and heaved a heavy sigh. "I did it because everyone expected me to do something, and that was the fastest way to put it behind me."

Baffled by his abrupt response, I slowly sipped the chocolate, feeling it warm me all over. "I guess it would help the grieving process if you don't start something long and involved like a lawsuit."

Pierce laughed, but there was no humor in the sound. "I wanted to put everything behind me. Barbara, my marriage, everything. I sold the house and moved into a condominium."

At his vehemence, I stopped and looked at him in surprise. "But why? Why would you want to erase your life like that?"

"Because," Pierce said quietly, "when I started going through her things, I found cards. Letters. Sexy clothing I'd never seen before. She'd been having an affair. Some guy she met in a night class."

"Oh, I'm so sorry." I had to stop saying that, but I didn't know what else to say.

He shook his head. "Mostly my fault, I guess. I'd been working swing shift for a long time, and she got bored being alone every evening. After I found out, I started to wonder if perhaps she saw the cancer as her punishment for adultery, or maybe she was too tired to keep up the pretenses any longer and so she didn't fight it. I don't know."

I didn't know either. I never would have expected such a story from Pierce. He seemed like a nice guy, someone who would take all his responsibilities seriously. But then, my ability to judge character was rather suspect at the moment.

Lost in thought, we stared at the lake in silence. Clouds scudded towards us from the west bringing the next storm with them. Across the lake, the tops of Seattle's sky-scrapers shone like beacons. Homes and apartments dotted the hills and shoreline. In a few weeks, people would be lined up in this very spot to watch the Christ-mas ships parade.

I dragged my thoughts back to the present and tried to figure out how I could have been so wrong about Peter. Was it because David had been so incredible that I assumed the next important man in my life would be won-derful? Or had I seen what Peter wanted me to see, and hadn't bothered to look further? Or maybe, deep down, I had known that Peter would leave me.

Eventually my meandering mental processes wound around to the events that had led me to be standing next to a stone wall with a police detective. I glanced up and saw him looking sheepishly at me.

"Guess I made a fool of myself," he said.

"Not at all. You went through a horrendous ordeal. Two actually. The loss of your wife to illness, and then…the other thing," I finished lamely.

"Never told anyone before." He finished his drink in a few gulps and tossed the cup into the trash. "It was a long time ago."

"It's not something you easily forget."

"No, it's not. At least I don't think about it all day like I did at first."

It was time to change this morbid subject, and I knew just what I wanted to talk about instead. "So, Detective Pierce—"

"Matt."

"Pierce. What's the latest with the investigation?"

"Now, Ms. Kelly—"

"Robyn." I smiled sweetly and secured my scarf against a freshening wind.

"Ms. Kelly, that's confidential information. Our investigation is still underway, and we don't want to say or do anything that would—"

"—compromise the investigation," I finished for him.

He chuckled. "You watch too many cop shows."

"No, I watch too much local news and that's what your spokespeople are always saying. It's as much a part of the vernacular as 'you have the right to remain silent.'"

With a shrug, he said, "I guess it's okay to say that we know the accident on Snoqualmie Pass was simply that, an accident. The congressman just happened to be in the wrong place at the wrong time."

"And?"

He eyed me for a moment before turning back to face

the lake. "The M.E.'s report came back. Hamilton was definitely murdered. Smothered, in fact. There's not much
more I can tell you. He was alive when that nursing director
left his room, and he was dead when you went in. Pham
Nguyen was the only person who entered the room in
between you. We've officially arrested him and the case is
building."

"He wouldn't do something like that," I insisted. "Have
you looked at his activities? All the work he's done for the
Southeast Asian refugee community? I've known him for
years, and he's the gentlest man I've ever met."

"Gentle men can be pushed too far, like anyone else."

"But he's worked so hard and he's fiercely proud of
his family. All the kids did well in school, and they're
all successes."

"It's that family loyalty that pushed him over the edge."

"So he didn't like Congressman Hamilton's bill. A lot
of people hate legislation that's pushed through. But that
doesn't mean they murder the sponsors. A man like Pham
would work through the system."

"Robyn, we have him dead to rights," Pierce said in an
exasperated tone. He held up his hand and raised his index
finger. "He had motive. Hamilton sponsored legislation
that would prevent any more of Nguyen's family from im-
migrating to this country."

He raised a second finger. "He had opportunity. He
was the last person allowed in the room before you found
Hamilton's body."

He raised a third finger. "And he had the means. Given
Hamilton's weakened condition, it was easy for a small
but sinewy man like Nguyen to suffocate the congressman
with a pillow, especially if he was enraged."

Weighing each of those factors, I tried to find a hole
in Pierce's logic, and kept coming back to opportunity.

It was too obvious. Something must have happened between Nguyen leaving and my arrival. Someone else went into that room.

In my mind, I repeated what had transpired when I went to Hamilton's room. Something flitted through my memory, something that did not fit. It had to do with... Officer Tomlin. That was it.

Trying hard not to smile smugly, I said, "I think I've found a gaping hole in your case, Detective Pierce."

He scowled, whether at my use of his formal title or at my insistence in trying to prove he arrested the wrong man, I wasn't sure. It didn't matter. I knew I was onto something important.

"And are you planning to enlighten me?"

"First, tell me if Officer Tomlin has a problem with sweaty palms."

"A problem with what?" Pierce looked at me like I'd lost my mind.

"Does he have a problem with sweaty palms?" I repeated. "It's a treatable medical condition for those who have a serious problem."

"How the hell would I know? And even if he did, what difference would it make?"

I leaned against the stone wall and stared hard at Pierce. "When I went to see Congressman Hamilton, I introduced myself to Officer Tomlin, and I remember being surprised that his hand was damp. Now, if he doesn't have hyperhidrosis, sweaty palms, then that means he'd just washed his hands. And he couldn't have done it without leaving his post in front of Hamilton's door. Someone could have snuck into the room without anyone seeing. And whoever it was didn't come in to say hello. They came in to commit murder."

Pierce opened his mouth, then snapped it shut. His expression may have been frozen, but the mental gears turned and shifted as he considered the ramifications of what I had just told him. Then, he swore quietly under his breath. Taking my arm, he swung me onto the path and we double-timed it back to our cars.

NINE

PIERCE LOOKED MAD enough to chew nails. Choosing discretion, I said nothing as he gripped my arm and hustled me to my car. But as I climbed into the Explorer, I gave him another expression I had worked on over the years, this one a combination of expectancy and encouragement to share information.

He didn't disappointment me. "I'll call dispatch to track down Tomlin."

"Will you let me know what happens?"

Pierce scowled at me. "Don't push your luck, Robyn." He slammed the car door to cut off further probing. By the time I had the key turned in the ignition and the window lowered, he was halfway across the parking lot, talking on his cell phone and gesturing with his free hand.

I watched him thoughtfully. Here was a man who wasn't afraid to admit he had made a mistake. For a moment, I considered Pierce-the-man, not Pierce-the-cop. We had both lost spouses we loved, but how different our responses and the way we had led our lives since then. How sad that he felt driven to rid himself of everything that reminded him of his wife, her deception overriding any good memories. All he had now was his work.

I considered his initial gruffness, and how annoyed I was when I first met him. Then I reflected on his kindness, his gentleness when I fell apart. Like everyone else, he was a complex person. Yet, if I had to define him in only one word, it would have to be "honorable." I decided that perhaps I was fortunate to know someone like him.

A sudden gust of wind reminded me the window was still open. I started the engine and headed for home.

It wasn't every day a girl discovered her former lover was really a cad, capable of deliberately ruining her life for his own gain. I felt better now than I had a couple of hours earlier when I first discovered Peter's duplicity. Taping the door latch. Remembering my old password. Those were the kinds of tricks one read about or saw in movies. I'd never expected to experience them in real life.

At some level, I suppose I always knew Peter wasn't right for me. But then, probably no one was. No one could live up to the memories of my six years with David. Maybe if he had lived longer, if he had refused to help around the house, or left his wet towels and dirty under-wear on the bathroom floor, or insisted on spending weekends in front of the television watching game after game instead of going on family outings. Maybe then the sterling silver image would have been tarnished and pitted. As it was, we'd been idyllically happy and deeply in love, and no one could take his place.

I looked at the gold claddagh ring I still wore. The crowned heart between two hands was an Irish symbol for love, friendship, and loyalty. It had been David's mother's, and her mother's before her. He had given it to me as an engagement ring, and I moved it to my right hand when he replaced it with a wedding band. Even after all these years, I hadn't been able to bring myself to turn it crown inwards, signifying my heart was available.

Maybe that was why I'd been attracted to Peter. Maybe I had known, deep down inside, it wouldn't work out. In the last day and a half, I had held back, reluctant to believe this reunion was for real. Now I knew my gut instincts had been correct. My little voice had warned me, protected me from a second broken heart. It did hurt, a lot, that he played me for a fool, even if it hadn't been a total disaster.

But, it was over. Really over. Perhaps I was coming to a better understanding of myself and my self-imposed single status and I was comfortable with it. Like so many others, I wore different masks, pretending, even if only to myself, to be something I wasn't. It didn't mean I would change my life, just that I was aware of the whys.

With the distraction of Peter gone, I could concentrate on my efforts to clear Pham as a murder suspect. I sighed as I contemplated the direction that was taking me. It wasn't every day I learned my boss had a motive for murder. Tracking Will's activities or interests had never been high on my list. The image of us discussing hospital problems over a drink after work was laughable. We weren't likely to become friends. Even though his predecessor had hired me, Will had more important things to worry about than replacing me with someone he could control better.

But simply because we weren't simpatico didn't mean I could readily point an accusatory finger at him. That was a big leap in logic, from disagreeing with Will over killing programs for financial reasons to judging him capable of killing people. Still, with what I'd learned from my search on the Internet about Will's possible federal appointment and Congressman Hamilton's opposition, and the tail end of Will's telephone conversation I overheard, it, well, it was definitely enough to make me wonder.

I turned the Explorer into the driveway and pulled into the garage. I could hear Taffy jumping against the door in greeting. I'd had enough excitement and disappointment for one day. A glass of wine and a little cuddle time with my dog—that was all I wanted for the rest of the evening.

I entered the house determined not to worry about anything more until morning.

DISTRACTED AND A BIT overwhelmed by the events of the last two days, I forgot to set the alarm when I went to bed. Given the hours I'd been putting in lately, I rationalized oversleeping and my late arrival to work. However, I wasn't prepared for the furor that greeted me.

Reporters hovered around the front door and the employee entrances. As I ran the gauntlet, three of them pounced on me, demanding to know if I had an opinion as to who murdered Congressman Hamilton. I was relieved that Peter was nowhere to be seen. Detective Pierce must have followed through with the threat to hold him as long as legally possible.

When I finally made it to my office, I said, "Quick, Connie. Bolt the doors. They're coming to get us."

"Do you believe it? The police are interviewing everyone all over again. Do you think it means they decided Pham isn't guilty?"

I hoped that was exactly what it meant, but it was too soon to say anything.

"Tom is probably going nuts," Connie said, wide-eyed. "Do you think the police will let Pham go? I wonder what changed their minds?"

"Must have picked up some new information." I walked past her desk toward my office.

"Rob. You know something." Connie was out from behind her desk in a flash, following me like a hound on a fox scent.

"I've always believed Pham was innocent," I said.

"You know something," Connie repeated.

"Using your psychic abilities again?"

"No. I see that little twinkle in your eyes. The one that says, 'I know something you don't know.'"

"Well, perhaps I was able to point out some little detail that the police missed."

"When?" Connie threw up her hands in exasperation. "How did you have time? Last I saw, you were leaving for dinner with Peter."

I sat in my chair and flipped on the computer with a grimace. "Yes, well. That's over and done with. We won't be seeing him anymore."

Connie sank into the extra chair. "Rob, what happened?"

My plan had been to not say a word about the fiasco with Peter. But that plan went out the window when Connie put her hand on my shoulder and looked at me with apprehension in her eyes. I told her what had happened. It was either that, or start to bawl all over again, and I was finished with tears.

I gave her a highly sanitized overview, however, with just enough details so she understood. I held back the fact that Peter had actually accessed Hamilton's medical records. I liked Connie a lot, but she was young and new, and I shuddered to think of the whole story inadvertently becoming fodder during the secretaries' coffee-break conversation, and then filtering its way to my boss. Especially the part about Peter accessing the records because I forgot to turn my computer off and he remembered my old password. It was one thing for the story to spread of how the famous reporter had been caught trying to pull a fast one; it was another for anyone to know he'd partially succeeded.

"Oh, Rob, I'm so sorry." Connie gave me a hug. "He seemed so nice and acted like he was really pleased to see you again."

I forced myself to smile. "That's why he was very successful at what he did. He could charm anyone into telling him anything he wanted to know."

The outer door opened and closed. "Hello, anybody here?" a familiar voice called out.

Connie and I both stepped from my office. I remained in the doorway while Connie scooted back to her desk.

"Melanie. What brings you here?" As if I couldn't guess. It had to be only a matter of time before all the reporters found my office.

Looking sharp and sophisticated in another plaid jacket, this one red and black, over a silky black top and slacks, Melanie Cole smiled in a friendly way. After my experience with Peter, I was more suspicious than I'd been two days before, and had no interest in becoming any reporter's buddy.

"I wondered if you have a few minutes. With the new developments, I need some help with today's story."

"What happened?"

"The police released Pham Nguyen and are interviewing everyone again."

"PR should have what you need. Can I call them to check for you?" Even though I was stonewalling, I could at least appear helpful.

Melanie waved some papers. "I've got that already. There's nothing really useful, just generic stuff about the hospital and the parent corporation. I was hoping you could tell me something that would give this story more of a human-interest twist."

I had yet to prove that Pham was, in fact, innocent, but at least he was no longer the sole focus of the police investigation. We still had a murderer on the loose, and there was always the possibility that Melanie knew something that might help.

Deciding it might not hurt to talk, I said, "I don't know if there's anything I can add, but come on in." I signaled for Connie to bring her some coffee, then gestured for Melanie to come into my office and take a seat.

After we were settled, Melanie glanced quickly around my office. Her gaze hesitated at the collage of pictures of Josh, the association awards, the picture postcards of Ireland. Then she took out her notepad and flipped it open to a blank page.

"So, tell me a little about you," she started.

I obliged, giving my name, rank, and serial number, and a brief overview of the Patient Relations department, adding that most hospitals had something similar.

"Hmmm. I had no idea hospitals paid that much attention to complaints. Mind if I mention this to our consumer-affairs person? She might want to do a segment on you."

"Only if she agrees to include my counterparts from other hospitals."

Melanie nodded as she scribbled on her pad. Now was the time for me to ask a few questions.

"I've always been intrigued how someone ends up in front of the camera. Did you plan this or did it happen by accident?"

The question seemed to catch her by surprise. Maybe she wasn't accustomed to having the interview tables turned, or maybe it was the question itself that caught her off guard. Whichever it was, when she looked up, I caught a ferocity in her eyes that she quickly banked.

"I've wanted to do this for as long as I can remember." It sounded like a throw-away answer. Too automatic. Too pat.

"I grew up in Colorado, outside a small town, and didn't have a clue what I wanted to be when I grew up," I offered. "All I wanted was to move to a big city where things were happening."

"Ranch girl, huh? Me too, except I'm from Montana."

"Really? What a coincidence," I said, surprised that she was responding so easily to my prompts. "I started in media relations for a New York City hospital, then moved out here. New York wasn't the best place to raise a child." I shuddered. "Too much crime. We never had any problems when I was growing up in Colorado."

"I can't say the same for Montana." That ferocity flashed in her eyes again. "I've seen it everywhere, Robyn, and it's been happening forever. It's just that now we talk about it. People need to know what really goes on."

I didn't think she had any idea how revealing she was. Something had happened in her small town, something that no one talked about. Something had set a fire in her belly that still burned.

"You're right," I said.

Suddenly, Melanie smiled, her intensity softening so quickly it was as if she flipped an internal switch. "We're getting off the track here. Let's see…" She flipped through her pad. "What do you know about the suspect, Pham Nguyen?"

"I'm glad the police seem to be considering other possibilities."

"Really? Why?" The question had a sharpness, a biting edge that surprised me. This woman's moods changed as rapidly as a chameleon's colors. Did she have a personality disorder?

"I've known Pham for years. He's always been a kind, gentle man and very proud of his family." I told her about the last time he'd shown me pictures of his son's college graduation. "I just can't reconcile the man I know with a murderer."

"Sometimes people snap," Melanie said. Her words reminded me of Detective Pierce's assumption.

I shook my head. "Not Pham. He's come too far, and he's such a hard worker. I can't imagine him jeopardizing his family's honor by murdering someone."

"What can you tell me about Congressman Hamilton?" she asked quickly, as if by rushing me on to the next topic she could get me to say something I shouldn't.

"Such as?" I asked.

"Oh, what kind of treatment he was getting, test results, that sort of thing."

"I think PR put all that in the press release." I knew full well what she was fishing for; she was simply more straightforward than Peter in her attempts to acquire confidential medical information.

She looked resigned and flipped her notepad closed. "Well, I didn't think I could get you to slip, but it was worth a try. Guess I'll see if someone in Administration is available." She stood up, then hesitated. "I don't suppose you have any ideas about why the police are re-interviewing everyone?"

I reminded myself that she was a reporter, not my friend. This wasn't the time to share confidences and theories. "Haven't a clue."

"Didn't think so. Here's my card." She pulled a business card from her jacket pocket and handed it to me. "It's got everything on there, cell phone, pager, E-mail. If you find out something, call me, okay?"

"Sure thing." I stuck the card into my Rolodex.

I followed her to the hall and said good-bye, then shut the door and turned to face Connie.

"Well? What'd she say?" Connie asked.

"Nothing. She wanted to find out what I knew."

"Did you tell her anything?" She reminded me of Josh. Her excited eagerness somehow overlooked the fact that this wasn't fantasy, it was reality. A real person had died, murdered by another real person who might well be still walking the halls of this hospital.

"There wasn't anything to tell."

"Not even why the police are back?"

I laughed. "What makes you think I know?"

"Because of the way you sidetracked me before Melanie Cole came in. So, what gives?"

"I really don't know anything, Connie. I simply observed something that gives the situation a different twist than the police considered before. I shouldn't say anything until they finish their investigation."

Before Connie could badger me anymore, I returned to my office and shut the door. I wanted to avoid Connie's questions, and I also wanted to avoid interruptions for a few minutes because I needed to think. Melanie Cole was a driven woman. It might not be an obsession, but it was more than a passion for journalistic truth. Something she'd said kept ricocheting around my brain like a pinball looking to fall into a high-scoring hole. What was it…?

Bingo! It hit me. Well, okay, I mixed my metaphors, but I thought just maybe I had something. Clicking the computer to the Internet, I waited impatiently to check my theory. Before the connection was completed, someone knocked on my door.

"What?" I called impatiently.

Connie opened the door and whispered, "Mrs. Flanders is here."

My mind went blank. "Who?"

"Mrs. Flanders. The surgery patient."

It came to me then. The cool breeze lady. "What does she want?"

"She wants to see you."

"Now?" I couldn't believe this was happening, right when I was so close to proving, well, I wasn't sure what I was close to proving. Nevertheless, the patient came first. With a sigh, I clicked to end the Internet connection and followed Connie to the front.

"Mrs. Flanders? I'm Robyn Kelly." I extended my hand. She was what I had pictured during our phone call. Soft and pink and round. "And this is my assistant, Connie Wagner."

Mrs. Flanders nodded at us both. "Oh, my, Miss Kelly. Thank you for helping me yesterday," she said in a breathy voice.

I gestured for her to take a seat on the couch. Normally, I take a patient into my office to talk, but I didn't think privacy was an issue if she'd come by to thank me. "It was my pleasure. I hope everything went well with Dr. Davisson."

"Oh, my, yes. He was so nice, so reassuring, even though I'm quite certain he thought I was a bit dotty," she said ruefully.

I swallowed a smile and glanced at Connie. That was probably an accurate assessment on Mrs. Flanders' part. "So, what brings you here?"

"Why to see Dr. Davisson, of course." She looked momentarily puzzled, then brightened. "Oh, my, yes. And I wanted to say thank you in person and bring you something."

She reached into her oversized purse and I winced, then relaxed when she pulled out a flat, round tin and popped it open. Fresh baked cookies.

So my first assessment of her had been right again. "Mrs. Flanders, you shouldn't have," I said as Connie approached to accept the tissue-lined tin.

Connie held the cookies close and took a deep sniff. "They smell divine. Thank you."

Mrs. Flanders made a fluttery gesture. "Oh, my, it was no trouble. When I'm off my porridge, I bake. And then I don't know what to do with it all. I'm trying to keep my girlish figure, you know."

This time I smiled openly. "I know what you mean, Mrs. Flanders." I started to stand up, expecting her to follow suit. She didn't, and so I sank back down. "Is there something else I can help you with?"

"Oh, my, I don't know how to ask this." She looked so helpless. Then her eyes sharpened and she said, "What was it like to find the body?"

Caught off guard, I said, "Excuse me?"

"The body," she snapped. "Congressman Hamilton's body. What happened when you found him?"

I almost laughed out loud at her audacity. "I'm sorry, Mrs. Flanders. I'm not allowed to talk about it." Leaning forward, I whispered, "Police orders, you know," then pulled away and raised my eyebrows knowingly. I stood up again.

"Oh, I see." She pursed her lips as if annoyed that her ploy hadn't worked. "Well, I won't take up any more of your time."

She hefted herself from the couch and eyed the cookie tin in Connie's hands. I could almost see the wheels turning: should she or shouldn't she take them back? She must have decided she might need our services in the future, because she sailed out the door without another word.

Connie stared at me. "Do you believe—"

"Oh, my," I mimicked. "Believe it. I keep telling you, after you've been here awhile, nothing will surprise you anymore. Now, I have things to do." I started toward my office.

"Don't you want a cookie first?"

I thought about it for a moment. With a sigh, I capitulated. "Sure. Let's see what she brought."

We were delighted to find iced raisin oatmeal, rationalizing that the nutritional value of the raisins and oatmeal offset the sugar and butter. After sharing a cookie and fresh cup of coffee with Connie, I took one more cookie into my office and shut the door, determined to finish what I'd started before Mrs. Flanders came to call.

Drumming my fingers with impatience, I waited for the Internet connection to go through, then I typed in Channel Eight's Web address. As I'd hoped, they featured profiles of the key reporters. A couple of clicks later and I was opening Melanie Cole's bio.

Montana isn't a heavily populated state, with a whole lot fewer people than greater Seattle, and miles of wide open space in between. The chances of Melanie Cole and Congressman Hamilton knowing each other were pretty slim, but it was still a possibility.

The screen changed and I started reading. There it was. Born and raised in Walden, Montana. Stunned, I slumped in my chair. They had grown up together. Not just the same county, but the very same small town. And something had happened there that still drove Melanie. Could it have involved Jake Hamilton? If so, was it a motive for murder some fifteen years later?

I groaned at the leaps my imagination was taking and clicked off the Web site. Not for the first time, I wished Margie was back from vacation. She was the closest thing I had to a best friend at work. My outside-of-work best friend, Andrea, was out of town this week on business. We talked about everything. I sighed with frustration. They weren't here and so I had to muddle through by myself.

Finding a link between Melanie and Congressman Hamilton was more than I'd ever thought possible. Of course, what was the probability that Will and Hamilton would have a connection, or Pham and Hamilton either, for that matter? If Will and Pham had bad experiences with Hamilton, what were the odds that Melanie's were positive? The whole thing was giving me a headache. It seemed that everyone had a history with Hamilton.

The plaguing question was what I should do with this information. After the fiasco with Peter, I still didn't trust my judgment, and I didn't want to implicate either my boss or a highly respected local reporter simply because I was eager to give the police someone else to focus on.

From what I had learned about Pham and Will, Congressman Hamilton had not been the wholesome all-American boy he pretended to be. He seemed to have had a mean streak, something that usually appeared long before adulthood. It may well have been visible when he was growing up.

Which put me right back where I started, wondering what to do with all this unearthed information. My original goal had been to prove Pham innocent. If I failed to prove that, then at least I could help the police keep an open mind. I wouldn't come right out and tell Pierce I suspected Melanie. Instead, I would suggest he check the police records in Walden about the time Hamilton would have been there.

Pierce could draw his own conclusions.

TEN

IF I HURRIED, which seemed to be the only way I functioned anymore, I could grab a sandwich in the cafeteria and take a fresh latté upstairs with me to the nurse managers' meeting. As I paid for the sandwich, I noticed Darlene Skaggs and Kate Connolly sitting at a large corner table, surrounded by notebooks and laughing at a paper in Kate's hand. In need of a good chuckle, I started toward them.

"Rob," Darlene said. "Have you seen the new Bloomingdale's?" Still laughing, Kate waved for me to sit down.

Two years before, someone inside the organization had created the Bloomingdale family as a way to zap Admin and the physician leadership. Every now and then, a "Bloomingdale" wrote a letter and circulated copies throughout the building so the letters couldn't be kept a secret. Despite everyone's best efforts, the identity of the real writer hadn't been uncovered.

"I didn't know there was one." I slid into an empty chair as Kate handed me the letter.

"I don't know who's behind these, but they really know how to make a point," Kate said.

The first thing I did was check the sender, and breathed a sigh of relief. Sometimes, the letters were from "Patti R. Bloomingdale, Patient Relations", another source of friction with Will, even though he knew it wasn't really from me.

This one was addressed to Will from "Ena G. Bloomingdale," Madrona Bay Public Utility Department, chastising Will for disregarding the district-wide effort to reduce power consumption.

Last summer, we did a major remodel of the maternity unit on the fourth floor. The solid concrete north wall and part of the roof had been removed and replaced with green glass to create a spacious solarium, complete with a garden, benches for resting, and a small waterfall. Instead of the traditional labor/delivery rooms, with separate postpartum rooms, we'd put in deluxe suites, complete with whirlpool tubs.

The remodel was a marketing success, and the OB department was inundated with new patients. But despite the energy-efficiency claims, the new unit had increased our use of electricity and water.

In her letter to Will, "Ena G." went on to describe several very creative ways he could reclaim and recycle the whirlpool tub water, and suggested window coverings for the solarium to reduce heat loss through the glass.

The letter was funny, and guaranteed to give Will fits, especially since he'd made such a big deal about being one of the first community leaders to sign the "We Will Reduce" pledge.

"Has everyone seen this?" I asked.

"Just about. Even my docs are laughing," Kate said, referring to the physicians in the OB/GYN clinic. "And they are the biggest beneficiaries of the remodel."

"It's been wild." Darlene shook her head. "I don't know what happened last February, but we have a bumper crop of new babies this month."

"It was that big windstorm," Kate said. "Remember? The power was out for three days on the Sammamish Plateau."

"That's it." Darlene nodded toward Kate. "This is the

first meeting I've made it to since you and I delivered that baby in the ER, Rob, and that's only because Kate dragged me down here. Everyone was so busy absorbing that surge of patients from the accident that we cancelled everything on our calendars that day."

"Speaking of the new mom, how are Linda and her baby?" I asked.

Darlene beamed. "She's fine. They both are. She came to the clinic this morning so we could see the baby again before her husband took them home to Ellensburg." She rolled her eyes. "Boy, that could've been a real mess."

"We were so lucky," I said, glancing at the wall clock. "Uh-oh. I'm due at Brenda's meeting. See you guys later." Darlene and Kate were part of the OB/GYN clinic, not the hospital, so they didn't have to attend Brenda's meeting.

I didn't have time to get a latté, so I hurried to my office and grabbed what I needed for my presentation. Dropping papers and overhead projector transparencies into a box, I sprinted to the conference room. The weekly hospital nurse managers' meeting was already in progress with Charley leading a discussion about a new system to track patients' belongings from the ER to the inpatient unit. Charley was running overtime, as usual, so I winked at him and quietly took a seat off to the side to wait my turn.

The routineness of this meeting was at such odds with the chaos that had filled the hospital the last couple of days. I sat back, prepared to concentrate on the discussion, but my mind soon drifted to the realities outside this room.

The first, of course, was finding Congressman Hamilton's body. I would never forget that eerie, chilled silence until the day I died. And I never wanted to repeat the experience.

Mentally, I listed the possible murder suspects I had

identified so far. It was all very puzzling. I planned to call Detective Pierce after I finished this meeting. He was probably still annoyed with me for spoiling his case against Pham. Giving him some other leads would annoy him even more.

"Robyn? Are you ready?" Brenda's crisp voice broke through my thoughts.

I looked around. Charley was gone and the women seated around the table were looking at me with some amusement.

"Go easy on her, Brenda. She's had a rough week. It isn't every day our patient rep delivers a baby," quipped Nancy Mancuso, the postpartum manager. The twenty or so other nurse managers laughed.

"It's not every day she finds a dead body, either," added Irene, who had faced the reporters with me the morning the accident victims inundated the hospital. "At least it wasn't our fault." The murmured agreement was more subdued.

Picking up my box, I carted it to the head of the table and plopped it down, then sighed heavily. "I really wish they'd sent more of those accident victims to somebody else's hospital." There was another, louder, murmur of agreement.

"I'll say," said Judy Francis, the new O.R. manager. "It'll be weeks before our schedule's back on track. My satisfaction numbers for this year are ruined." She had a good point.

"We'll figure out something, Judy," I said. "Now, let's talk about the numbers."

I handed out copies of the report that included the overall hospital nursing data and the data for each manager's respective unit. Turning on the overhead projector, I laid the first transparency on the lighted screen and started talking. It pleased me to report that the number of compliments to the staff continued to far outweigh the complaints.

When I finished the formal presentation, Brenda turned to me. "Robyn, thank you for coming. We appreciate the information."

She led the discussion for another half hour, then asked, "Do I have some volunteers to look at the noise issue?" She nodded as three hands were raised. "Good. I'd like to see us make some improvement on this."

She glanced at the institutional wall clock and stood up. "Time to go. If anyone has something to add to next week's agenda, call me."

I put leftover copies of my report into the box and chatted with the managers as they slowly filed from the room. When I finished, I turned to see Brenda collecting her papers.

"I hope that went as you planned," I said.

She nodded. "Sometimes it's hard to hear that some of the patients aren't happy, but we need to know. And I value the fact that you present it in a way that doesn't cast blame."

Brenda thumbed through her copy of the report. "I'm not looking forward to discussing this with Will. He wants to identify the precise nurse who's responsible for the complaints and fire her." She glowered with indignation.

Alarmed, I said, "The report's not supposed to be used like that."

"Of course not. It's a learning tool. But he keeps cutting our budgets, which means I don't have the staff I used to, and then he wonders why it takes longer for the nurses to respond to call lights. Sometimes I'd like to make him a nurse, or at least have him spend a half day on each unit to see how busy we are. It's a wonder we get any compliments at all."

"From what I hear from patient reps at other hospitals, we're not unique," I said.

"I know. I hear the same thing from my colleagues too. But that doesn't make it easier."

I didn't have an answer for her. Many of us in the business were concerned about the dwindling resources to care for patients. It wasn't a problem that was going to be solved soon.

"I was thinking about what Judy said. She's right," I said. "The way we track this data over time, we'll be explaining this O.R. backlog for several years."

"Absolutely not," Brenda said, her mouth drawn in a hard line. "I am not about to have to justify the O.R. every year for something we had no control of. I don't want any more reminders of that…accident."

I sensed she'd been about to say something else, but had no idea what. "I agree."

Brenda's commitment to her nurses was commendable. She was a mother bear protecting her cubs. But I didn't envy her having to explain a spike in complaints over and over and over again for the next five years.

A solution suddenly occurred to me. "Brenda, how about this? I'll keep a separate manual tally of the O.R.'s complaints that are directly attributable to the accident victims bumping scheduled patients, and include them as a footnote. They won't show up at all after this quarter."

Brenda's expression relaxed. "That would be perfect. This whole thing's been such a nightmare. By the way, I heard that Pham is no longer the primary suspect."

I was relieved that Brenda had brought up the subject. She was a good administrator, one of the few who really cared about the people she worked with. I could talk to her, and know that whatever I said would go no further.

"That's right." I smiled. "Before I went into Hamilton's

room, I introduced myself to the police officer and we shook hands. I noticed his hands were damp, and I mentioned that to the police detective investigating the murder. It turns out the officer left his post for a few minutes to use the bathroom so someone else could have slipped into the room and murdered Hamilton without anyone seeing him."

Brenda's eyes widened. "That's very clever of you, Rob. Are you adding murder investigations to your repertoire of skills?"

I laughed. "No, not really. I have learned some interesting things about Congressman Hamilton. He wasn't always what he seemed to be."

"Really?" she said, straightening the chairs around the table. "He seemed very pleasant when I visited with him."

"You must have caught him at a good time."

"He wasn't in pain, but he was uncomfortable. I think he appreciated the extra attention. When I left, I told him to be sure to call me if he needed anything." She failed to mention Hamilton's complaint against me, for which I was grateful. Maybe she hadn't heard about it.

I realized I probably shouldn't say anything more until I talked to Detective Pierce. Changing the subject, I asked, "How's your daughter doing?"

Brenda looked startled and clutched the silver cross she wore every day. "Cynthia? She's upset, of course. But, she's doing better."

"I'm glad to hear that. When I saw her yesterday, she was still so distressed. Is she planning to return to D.C.?"

Brenda's mouth softened with maternal pride. "No. She's decided to move home. She'll work for my husband's furniture company. He always needs good sales people. It was hard on the family, having her so far away. I don't think we'll let her do something like that again."

I nodded, understanding that after losing her boss, Cynthia would need all her family's support, especially since she'd been so distraught after the accident and Hamilton's death. But, she struck me as being old enough to decide for herself what she wanted to do with her life. Maybe I had misjudged her age. "Was she working for Congressman Hamilton as a college intern?"

"Oh, no. She graduated from the University of Washington two years ago and finished her master's in public administration last spring."

I didn't want to say anything, but Cynthia seemed qualified to be much more than a sales rep for the family furniture business. But then, it wasn't my place to comment. I certainly didn't know how I would react when the time came for Josh to launch out on his own. The thought was troubling. "You have a son too, don't you?"

"Yes. Curtis. He's still at the university. In business. He'll take over the company when my husband's ready to retire."

"Sounds like you're keeping it all in the family."

"A family business is the best way to show your children what your true values are. Honesty, integrity, family. It's God's plan."

"Mmmm," I said as noncommittally as I could. This wasn't the time to point out that she herself worked for a huge organization, or that small businesses were struggling to compete against megastores and Internet sales.

She glanced at her wristwatch and scooped up her coat. Slipping into it, she said dryly, "I'm supposed to be in Seattle for a meeting in thirty minutes. Do you think I can make it in time?"

Her question surprised me. It was the nearest thing to humor I had ever heard from her. "Only if the 520 Bridge is wide open and you find a parking place right out front."

I followed her from the room as she flipped off the lights. "I'll see you later, Brenda."

Walking toward my office, I wasn't sure what God's plan was these days. Maybe Brenda had a reason to be worried enough about Cynthia to want to keep her close to home for a while. The girl had obviously been an emotional wreck when she arrived at the hospital, on the verge of a breakdown right there in the lobby.

She wouldn't be the first young woman to fall in love with her employer, but from what I'd been learning about Jake Hamilton, I doubted he would have risked his political future for a fling with a subordinate. He seemed too calculating for a misstep like that.

How would I feel if I were in Brenda's shoes, and Josh was the one involved with a sophisticated older woman? I wouldn't like it one bit. I'd haul him home for his own protection too. Or send him to my dad's Colorado ranch where he could mend his broken heart in splendid solitude. I smiled, thinking how that kind of banishment would appeal to an adolescent prone to occasional theatrics. Josh might be studying engineering, but he had the typical young man's mood swings and could be as dramatic as the next when it came to expressing his wounded feelings.

Counting my blessings that I wasn't the consoling parent in Cynthia's case, I fumbled to open my office door. As I stepped in, Detective Pierce turned around. He was standing in front of Connie's desk, eating one of Mrs. Flanders' cookies and looking very pleased with himself.

"Hello, Detective," I said and shut the door with my foot.

He looked at the box in my arms. "Need some help?"

"Where were you an hour ago when I couldn't see over the top of this thing?"

"Trying to put my case back together and explain to my

superiors and the DA that I wasn't a complete screw-up," he said with only a hint of sarcasm.

I winced. "Sorry." I proceeded to my office where I dropped the box onto the desk.

Pierce followed me. "It's not your fault," he said heavily. "I made the mistake of going with the obvious suspect."

"It's not like there was no pressure on you," I said. "Everyone was screaming for an arrest."

"Tell me about it." Pierce slumped into my extra chair. He was wearing the same tweed jacket he'd worn the night before, and judging from the wrinkles, probably the same white shirt. His brown eyes were so weary I wouldn't have been surprised if he fell asleep sitting there.

"I haven't released Mr. Nguyen yet," he said. "But his family hired a bulldog attorney. Nguyen still swears Hamilton was asleep when he went in to clean the room. He claims he only cleaned the bathroom so he wouldn't disturb the congressman. My case against him isn't strong enough for an indictment anymore."

He didn't add "thanks to you," for which I was grateful. "I hear you've been interviewing everyone again." I sat down in my chair and kicked off my shoes.

Pierce shook his head. "It's a nightmare. Do you know how many people were on and off that unit?"

"A lot?"

"More than a lot," he said with a grimace. "Why can't this place be like the tech companies where you need a security card every time you go in and out of an area? Then we could prove beyond a doubt who was there when."

"It'd be a nightmare for us. Besides, what would we be securing ourselves from? There's nothing of real value to steal on the units. Except for the drug cabinet, and only a few people have access to that."

"I suppose from your perspective it makes perfect sense to have everything wide open. For me to prove who dunnit? A nightmare."

I smiled and said, "How did you like the cookies?"

"Those were great. Connie told me how you came by them." He shook his head again and chuckled. "People. I suppose you see all kinds too."

"That's for sure. Most are only brief telephone encounters, and others we get so involved with, it seems like we should be spending holidays together. If they were all like Mrs. Flanders, I'd be a complete cynic by now."

"As it is, you're only a partial cynic?"

I grinned at him. "Yeah, only a partial cynic." I turned serious, but couldn't look him in the eye. I wasn't sure if I was about to do the right thing or not. Guilt over messing up his case swung the decision to confessing all. Still, it wasn't going to be easy. I fidgeted with my pen and said, "I might've found something interesting for you."

His eyes narrowed. "What do you mean?"

"I've been checking a few things, and—"

"Dammit, Robyn, this is a police matter." Pierce was no longer slumped in the chair. He was sitting upright, alert with an eagle sharpness in his eyes. "You're not to get involved."

"And I suppose I wasn't to get involved when I told you about Officer Tomlin's wet hands?" I said indignantly.

"That's different."

"How?"

"You were conveying information as a witness, not playing detective."

"Was I right?" I asked. "Did Officer Tomlin leave his post to use the bathroom?"

"Yes, you were right," he snapped.

I crossed my arms over my chest. "So. I guess you don't want to know what I've learned."

Pierce glowered at me. Finally, he said, "Okay, spill it."

"Well, since you asked so politely," I said to needle him. When he looked away and scowled as he shifted in his seat, I almost laughed.

"Ms. Kelly, would you be so kind as to share with this overworked and underpaid civil servant what you've learned, please, ma'am," he said finally, still scowling.

"Why, thank you, Detective. I thought you'd never ask." I shared what I had discovered about Congressman Hamilton's efforts to keep Will from a federal job and how Melanie must have known Hamilton, growing up in the same town.

At first, Pierce tried to appear disinterested, but after a few moments, he took out his notepad and jotted down everything I said. When I finished, he pursed his lips and tapped the notebook with the end of his pen.

"You found all this on the Internet?"

I nodded. "I just wanted to show that Nguyen couldn't have murdered Hamilton. I had no way to prove it, so I tried to find other people who had a motive and opportunity. I can't imagine my boss or a respected reporter like Melanie Cole killing Congressman Hamilton any more than I believed Pham did. But, I had no idea it would be so easy to find other suspects."

"Neither did I." Pierce sighed heavily. "Damn. The guy doesn't even live here or represent this district, and there's three possible suspects. Now we have to check out the background of every single person who had access to that room during the two or three minutes Officer Tomlin left it unguarded."

"Surely some people can vouch for each other that they were together."

"During that narrow a window?" Pierce snorted. "Not likely. Take the nurses. They can say they were together from one o'clock until two o'clock, after one returned from lunch and before the other went on break, but if one of them ducked into a supply room for even a few minutes, that left the other unaccounted for."

"Hmmm. I see what you mean." When he said it like that, even Susan Wong, one of my favorite nurse managers, had the opportunity. Fortunately, I couldn't imagine her killing anyone unless he was threatening one of her four kids. But even she had complained about the congressman. Should I add her to my growing list?

I didn't know what else to suggest to Pierce. I'd dealt with a lot of complicated "he said, she said" investigations in the past, but nothing on this scale, and certainly not involving a murder. I didn't envy Detective Pierce his job.

"By the way, we put Armstrong on a plane to Juneau this morning," he said with a wide grin.

I felt the heatwave surge through my body, and I hoped my face wasn't flushed a beet red. "I see."

Pierce chuckled softly and his eyes were lit up as if he was quite proud of himself. "Yeah, he was one unhappy camper." He must have seen my embarrassment, because he sobered immediately. "Sorry, Robyn."

I brushed aside his apology. "You have nothing to be sorry about. I'm the one who fell for his line."

"Not completely," Pierce asserted. "You're too smart for that. He was a really good reporter at one time, though. I checked him out through some of my sources. He really blew it with that faked interview, didn't he?"

"I can't believe he was that stupid. Or desperate." I looked at Pierce. "I guess some of us accept the fact that we're no longer twenty-five better than others do."

"Hell, I don't think I was ever twenty-five," Pierce said with a shrug. "I've always been a crusty old fart."

"Oh, I don't know," I said, relieved that the topic of Peter was now over. "I imagine you were quite the dashing street cop at one time."

Pierce rolled his eyes. "I live in constant fear I'll have to attend some official function that requires my uniform. I don't think they make them in my size anymore."

This was a side of Pierce I hadn't seen before, the dry sense of humor. He had shown me the tough-cop, the compassionate-cop, and the efficient-cop aspects of his personality, but not this one. I found it very appealing.

"They must make uniforms your size."

"Yeah, they do," he said wiping his hand over his face. "And then, they report the purchase to a commanding officer who makes you have a physical, and you know what happens then."

"No more cookies?"

He shook his head. "No more cookies."

"Almost not worth living anymore," I said with a mock sigh.

"My sentiments exactly."

"Would you like another of Mrs. Flanders' homemade, loaded with butter and sugar, cookies?"

"Absolutely."

We both laughed as I brushed past him and went to Connie's desk.

"Make it two," he called from my office. "One for the road."

"Having fun?" The gleam in Connie's eyes said she thought there was more than official business going on in my office.

"I'm trying to distract him from how much extra work I've created for him." I plucked a handful of cookies from the tin. At Connie's dropped jaw, I patted my hip and said, "Better him than us."

"You're right." But her gaze lingered hungrily on the cookies.

I popped the top back on the tin and returned to my office where I pulled a tissue from the box and laid it on the table for the cookies.

"Is this the best you can do?" Pierce asked. "Where's the good china? The linen napkins?"

"I wasn't expecting company," I quipped.

After we'd munched silently for a few minutes, I asked, "So where do we go from here?"

"*We? We* don't go anywhere."

"But, I helped you. I gave you information you didn't have," I protested.

"I know, Robyn. I appreciate what you've done, but this is a police matter."

I heard the exasperation in his voice, but I didn't like being brushed off. "You're just annoyed because I found some other possible suspects," I grumbled.

"Suspects you don't think could have done it any more than you think Pham did it. You can't keep coming up with people and motives, and think none of them could possibly have murdered Hamilton." Pierce's voice rose.

"Sorry," I said, my voice rising too. "Next time I find a viable suspect with a strong motive and opportunity, I won't bother telling you so you won't have your case muddled up."

"There won't be a next time," he said, his voice louder, "because you're not poking your nose into this any further."

"What are you going to do, arrest me?" I said, louder still.

"Don't be ridiculous." He picked up a cookie and waved it at me. "I'll say it again. I appreciate what you've done. But this is a high-profile case. I have to be very careful about how I get each piece of evidence. I have to build my case, brick by brick. I'll get to the truth, but I have to do it my way. In accordance with the law. *Comprendez?*"

I nodded. When he put it that way, I understood. Still, it seemed a shame to reject my help. I did my own form of investigation in this hospital every day. Everyone knew me and would talk to me a lot more freely than they would talk to a police detective.

At my nod, Pierce visibly relaxed. "Good. I'm glad we've got that settled." He took a big bite from his cookie.

"So, what are you going to do next?"

He scowled at me, but after he swallowed, he said, "I'm going to call Walden, Montana, and see what I can find out. It's a long shot, but you never know."

"I'd hate to think Melanie's mixed up in something like this."

Pierce shot me a patronizing look. "Robyn, you don't want anyone to be guilty. But someone has to be. Congressman Hamilton is dead, and he didn't die from natural causes."

"I know. It's just that I find it hard to believe anyone I know would do something like that."

"Anyone is capable of murder if the motive is strong enough. Trust me, Robyn. Anyone. And that means the guilty person will take whatever steps are necessary to keep from being revealed." He paused for a moment, then gave me a hard look. "Do you understand what I'm saying?"

He meant the murderer would be willing to murder again if it meant protecting himself.

A shiver raced down my spine. Pierce was warning me that I could become the next victim.

ELEVEN

WHILE I DROVE TO WORK the next day, I tried to take Detective Pierce's warning to heart. With Margie on vacation, we were short-handed, so I really had no time to investigate a murder. But as I worked, scenarios of who might have killed Congressman Hamilton drifted through my mind. Some possible, some ridiculous. None that I could prove.

The first thing I did when I reached my office, though, was sequester myself for half an hour to proofread my section of the Quality Report. I had given it back to Connie to print and deliver to Will when the phone rang. "Robyn Kelly."

"My office. Now." Click.

I had to laugh. Dr. Weiser always assumed I knew it was him. His deep voice with a hint of accent made him easy to identify, still even a brief comment about what I was dropping everything for would be nice.

The only case I had pending with him was the Stone case from the Insurance Commissioner, so I grabbed the file, a pad of paper, and a pen. "I'm going to Weiser's office," I told Connie as I sailed out the door.

When I reached OB/GYN, the receptionist nodded as I passed her desk on my way to the back. I saw Darlene and gave her a quick wave before knocking on Dr. Weiser's office door.

"Enter." A tall, wiry man, Gunther Weiser exuded

energy. With his salt-and-pepper hair, still thick and wavy, and his pewter-gray eyes keen with interest, he had earned the nickname, "the gray fox." Impatient with administrators and purposeless meetings, he listened attentively when it was important, picking up what was spoken and what was left unsaid. No wonder his patients fell in love with him. "Ah, good. I like that you are prompt."

I took my usual seat across from his desk, but didn't open my file.

Dr. Weiser handed me a stack of pictures. "These are from my trip to Indonesia." He proceeded to entertain me with anecdotes about a pirate ambush, hiking through the rain forests, and delivering a village chieftain's son, a breech birth that would have left the child brain-damaged and the mother hemorrhaging to death if he had not happened by at the right time. The chieftain, in his gratitude, offered Dr. Weiser a choice between three goats or his twelve-year-old daughter.

"I did not, of course, want either," he said. "But it is not wise to anger the tribal leader, so I chose the goats."

I looked up from the picture of him holding the animals on tethers and laughed. "How did you explain them to Customs when you came home?"

"Do not be silly. I sold them at the next market and put the money in an account for the child."

How like him, I thought as I handed the pictures back.

"Now, this case. What do we know?" He was all business, this time in his teacher role.

I wasn't prepared for a case review, and silently wished that for today, he would just give me the answer. Opening the file, I glanced at him and saw kindness in his eyes.

"This has been a difficult week for you."

It was not a question. "Yes, it has."

"Okay, we will walk through it together."

"I'd like that."

Fortunately, the case turned out to be very straightforward. Mrs. Stone had enrolled with Health Assurance through her job, and the medical-insurance coverage began April first. She saw our Dr. Kyler the end of April for menopausal problems. He prescribed hormone replacement and told her to return in six weeks. Instead, she saw Dr. Chin, who was not affiliated with Health Assurance, the first week of May and had a hysterectomy a week later.

Dr. Weiser tsked. "The uterus is the most maligned and abused organ in the body."

I didn't contradict him, but from flipping through Dr. Chin's records prior to Mrs. Stone seeing Dr. Kyler, it appeared she'd had problems for a long time.

"I think if you check, you will find she failed to fill Dr. Kyler's prescription," Dr. Weiser said.

"It looks like she changed insurances without checking first to see if Dr. Chin was on the provider list."

"Can you read that first line on the May appointment?"

I squinted and turned the page at an angle. "I think it says 'pre-surg exam'."

"Ah! How did you do that? I could not make sense of it."

A physician complaining about the legibility of another physician's handwriting? I didn't laugh. "It comes from reading so many different records."

"Good. Okay. So what does this tell us?"

"It sounds to me that she had already discussed the hyst with Dr. Chin." I looked at his notes from the previous appointment. "Yes, here it is, from March twenty-second. 'Discussed options with patient. She is changing insurance for lower deductible and will schedule surgery after April first.'"

Dr. Weiser leaned back in his chair. "So the doctor knows she is changing insurance, but he fails to mention his services are not covered by the new insurance." He tsked again. "From our perspective, this is not a question of medical care, Robyn. It is strictly insurance coverage. Now, Dr. Chin was negligent by not informing her, but that is not something we can affect."

"It looks that way to me too. She probably realized what happened when she received the letter rejecting the bills. Blaming Stan Kyler is a ruse. I'll write the letter, but since she stated her complaint as quality of care, I have to run it by you before sending it out."

"That is fine." Dr. Weiser scribbled on his pink sheet that there was no physician error and that it was an insurance coverage disagreement, and signed it.

I returned to my office and started organizing the case to write the letter after calling the pharmacy to confirm Mrs. Stone had not, in fact, filled Dr. Kyler's prescription. I had all of five minutes, just long enough to be totally immersed. I jumped when the phone rang. "Robyn Kelly."

"Hi, Mom."

"Josh." I glanced at my watch. "Is everything okay? Shouldn't you be at school?"

Josh laughed. "Everything's fine. I'm on my way to physics. But I was wondering, can I invite Chuck for Thanksgiving?"

Thanksgiving?

I flipped open my calendar. Oh, lordy, that's right. It was next week. Even with Connie's prompt, I'd forgotten to give a thought to my own dinner plans. I hesitated. "Sure. That would be fine," I said more positively than I felt.

"I knew you wouldn't mind. And Mom? Do you know how to fix baked yams?"

"Baked yams."

"Yeah, you know, the kind with marshmallows melted on top."

I pulled the receiver away from my ear and stared at it. This couldn't be my son. Some alien had taken over his body.

"Mom? You still there?"

I set the receiver back against my ear. "I'm here. You want baked yams this year."

"Uh-huh."

"I probably have a recipe for it somewhere."

"That'd be great. Chuck's from the south and it's kind of a tradition there."

"Okay. I'll see what I can do." I started jotting a shopping list. Yams and marshmallows. Turkey, bread, celery. After all these years, I had it pretty well memorized, but if I didn't write it down, I'd forget something small, but critical, like cranberries.

"What time?"

"Dinner at two with plenty of things to nibble during the football games?"

"Thanks, Mom. You're terrific."

Definitely an alien takeover. "I'm glad you noticed."

Josh laughed. "Gotta go. See you tonight."

"Bye." By then I was speaking into a dead connection.

I hung up the phone and sighed. Thanksgiving had always been quiet for Josh and me. That was the day David had died, and since then, we'd always spent the day alone together. We watched football, played games, and ate turkey, but it was a day we saved for each other.

With mixed feelings, I acknowledged that this year marked the change of that tradition. I had known it would come someday, and I was pleased Josh had reached out to a classmate who otherwise would be alone. At least Josh would be home and not going off to someone else's house. That was something. But what about next year?

He was growing up and soon he'd leave home. I had to start thinking seriously about that. Most of my life had been focused on Josh and work. I had other interests, of course, but I'd wanted to be there for Josh, and I had been. The reality was, he didn't have ball games for me to attend anymore. I hadn't been able to help him with his homework for a long time. All that physics and math numbed my brain.

But, he still needed me to buy his clothes. I smiled smugly. On that happy note, I set the Thanksgiving grocery list aside and went back to the letter.

Five minutes later, I became aware of the smell of fresh coffee. Looking up, I saw Connie standing in the doorway with a fresh latté in each hand.

"Here, Boss. Thought you might need this."

After clicking to save the letter I was working on, I reached for the steaming cup. "Thanks." I took a sip and sighed with contentment.

Connie nodded and slipped into the extra chair. A worried frown replaced her usual cheery expression.

Setting my cup down, I turned to face her. "Connie? What's wrong?"

She pursed her lips as if not sure what to say. Finally, she took a deep breath, then burst out, "I'm worried about you."

That was the last thing I expected her to say. I gave a short laugh. "Me? Why on earth would you be worried about me?"

"I overheard your discussion with Detective Pierce. I wasn't eavesdropping, but I couldn't help overhearing. And now… It's…it's this feeling I have. That something's going to happen to you."

I gave her a reassuring pat on the shoulder. "After the last couple of days, I'm sure it won't be anything I can't handle."

"No, Rob. This is different." She grabbed my hand. "I'm afraid something bad's going to happen to you because you're trying to solve Congressman Hamilton's murder."

I smiled and eased my hand from her grip. "Are you practicing your psychic abilities again?"

She looked at me, then her gaze shifted over my shoulder to the window, but not before I caught the haunted look in her eyes. "I don't understand it, Rob," she whispered. She glanced at me, then back to the window. "Just before I reached your door, I felt this overwhelming sense of something bad. This…this invisible cloud, menacing. The hairs on the back of my neck stood straight up. Then the feeling was gone. But I know it was intended for you."

Now, I'm not a superstitious person, but that gave me pause. I'd heard other people describe similar experiences, and found it disturbing to find it applied to me. Leaning back in my chair, I considered her words before I said slowly, "I suppose there's always an element of risk in a situation like this, but I'm being very careful."

"I know, but someone's going to figure out you're the one feeding the police information."

"Oh, I think Detective Pierce is more subtle than that. I'm sure he's doing his own research. He wouldn't act on my say-so alone."

Connie still looked worried and skeptical, so I added, "But if it makes you feel any better, I'll be extra careful from now on."

She nodded and returned to her desk. What else could she do? She was in no position to forbid me to continue looking for suspects any more than Detective Pierce was.

I tried to pick up the letter where I'd left off, but I was distracted. I kept thinking about what Connie had said, and was more unnerved than I wanted to admit. First Detective Pierce, and now Connie warning me.

There was a murderer out there, someone with a strong interest in staying undiscovered. Was that motive enough to kill again? I had to admit it was, yet I still found it difficult to accept that someone I knew, someone I worked with every day, could do something that cold-blooded. Will Slater? I couldn't see it. Melanie Cole? I couldn't see that either. Susan Wong? She didn't even make the list.

Rather than work myself into an emotional frenzy, I forced everything else from my mind and returned to the letter. That worked for about five more minutes, when Connie approached my office again and rapped lightly on the doorjamb.

"Melanie Cole's here," she said.

"She is?" I felt a twinge of dread and guilt. "What does she want?"

"She says it's about the patient-rep group you mentioned to her."

It took me a moment, but then I remembered our earlier conversation. "Send her in," I said, then grumbled to myself as I saved and closed the computer file, "I didn't want to finish this letter before Christmas anyway."

When Melanie appeared, I gestured for her to sit down. "How's the news business today?"

She bobbed her head from side to side. "So-so. No new big stories and nothing breaking on the old ones." She raised one eyebrow. "You don't have anything new on the Hamilton murder, do you?"

"I'm sure I know less than you do," I said, although I suspected that wasn't completely true. And what I knew would probably surprise the daylights out of her, especially that she was on my list of possible suspects. "What brings you here?"

"I told Ashley Volstrom, our consumer-affairs reporter, about you, or rather, your program, and that other hospitals have the same kind of thing. She's thinking about doing a feature and wanted to know if there's an organization."

Nodding, I pulled open a desk drawer and reached for a file folder. "Here's the current roster. I'll make a copy for you."

"Thanks. I'll give it to Ashley when I get back to the station."

I walked Melanie to the outer office and quickly made the copy. "Here you go." I handed the roster to her. "The current president is Sharon Forbes at Hillsbrook Memorial. She's probably the best person to start with."

Melanie made a small checkmark by Sharon's name and dropped the paper into her bag. "You never know when one of these consumer-affairs stories will turn into something big and be transferred to a news reporter." She grinned. "I want to be the reporter Ashley thinks of first."

"Cooperation is the name of most games," I said.

"Well, thanks again, Robyn." She gathered her coat and bag and headed out the door.

"Drop in anytime," I said.

After she left, I wondered why Melanie had come by personally when a phone call from this Ashley would have sufficed. Was it paranoia from Connie's warning? I finally brushed it off as guilt over mentioning Melanie's name to Detective Pierce.

Speaking of the detective, I realized it had been twenty-four hours since I'd seen him. That wasn't a bad thing, but he'd become a fixture in my life the last couple of days, and it seemed odd for him not to be there. I was sure he would show up again to harass me about something, so I shrugged it off and reviewed where I had left off with the letter.

"Rob!" Connie called from the front.

"What?" I couldn't keep exasperation from my voice.

"You have that meeting!"

"I got it. I got it." Thoroughly frustrated at my inability to get anything done, I scooped up a pad, a pen I wouldn't feel bad about losing, and my coffee, which was now cool enough to slurp with abandon.

"I'll be back," I said as I left the office and hurried down the hall. I wasn't looking forward to this. Corporate had a bee in its bonnet about the latest "new way" to do business, and the consultant was here to give us the sales pitch on how this would change our lives, improve everything, and reduce costs. I am not a total cynic, but yeah, right.

I hurried into the conference room and set my notepad and coffee on the table between Judy Francis and Susan Wong.

"Hello, ladies," I said as I sat down.

"Hi, Rob," Susan said, while Judy only gave a token wave, her attention focused on a report.

Will and Brenda were huddled in a corner talking to a man I didn't recognize, but I assumed he was our guest speaker. Melanie stood off to the side as if waiting to catch Will's eye. What was that about? She was holding a pocket calendar, so maybe she wanted to schedule an interview with him.

Most of the other people were still talking and helping themselves to the giant cookies and the cans of pop on the cart delivered by Dietary. It's a little known fact that hospitals run on caffeine in the morning and sugar in the afternoon.

I started to say something to Susan when I saw Cynthia

Martin standing in the doorway. The young woman didn't look well as she scanned the crowded room. Her agitated gaze rested on me for a moment, her eyes narrowed in recognition, and her whole body stiffened. Then, with a subtle lift of her chin, she continued her search, calm crossing her face when she spotted her mother.

I watched as Cynthia made her way to Brenda, who broke away from Will and the consultant to talk to her daughter. I wondered for a moment why Cynthia had appeared wary when she saw me. I'd only met her twice and had been nice to her both times. Maybe it was because I'd been the one who found her precious employer, or maybe because I told her about the autopsy. Whatever her anxiety was about, it wasn't my problem.

Melanie was now talking to Will, and from his expression, Will wasn't happy. But then, he seldom was.

With a few minutes left before the meeting was scheduled to start, I scanned the agenda. "I'm glad I don't have to perform this time," I said to Judy.

"This consultant better have the best idea since sliced bread," she replied. "I left a scheduling nightmare to come to this thing, and it better not be a waste of time."

"Tell me about it." Susan leaned forward to look around me at Nancy. "Do you know how hard it is to explain to patients and their families that it's perfectly safe to be here, even if a guarded congressman was murdered just a few rooms away?"

"You must both be doing a good job, because no one's called my office to complain," I said.

"I'm thinking about hypnotizing them to think it happened at Hillsbrook Memorial," Susan said with a sigh.

"Hey, if hypnosis works, let me know," Judy said. "I have some things I'd like my staff to forget."

As we laughed, I looked around the room again and

spotted Connie in the doorway. She beckoned for me to join her.

"What's up?" I asked as we stepped into the hall.

"Dr. Lieffer's on the phone. He needs to talk to you now."

I followed her to our office. The chief of the Kenmore clinic wouldn't be calling unless it was important. As it turned out, it wasn't serious, just a procedural question he needed answered while he had a patient in his office.

By the time I returned to the conference room, Brenda had called the meeting to order and had darkened the room for the slide projector. Will must have already given his two cents' worth because he was gone. But the chairs and tables had been rearranged classroom-style.

After my eyes adjusted, I spotted my things on an extra chair against the wall. I slipped into my seat and started taking notes. I took a big swallow from my latté and grimaced. After all this time, it was barely lukewarm, and bitter. I took only a few more sips.

I had been right. The consultant was here to give a detailed presentation on how his version of the "new way" was better than anyone else's. He went into minute detail, quickly flipping through slides. After a while, I started to feel woozy.

I stopped looking at the screen and tried to concentrate on his words, but that didn't make me feel any better. Then my heart started pounding. Slowly at first, then faster. I'd never felt anything like this before. The nausea worsened and my head pounded as if a dozen jackhammers were working inside my brain.

Panic set in.

I had to get out of there.

Fumbling, I gripped my notepad and cup and stood. I

fought the dizziness as I walked toward the door. One step. Then another. I concentrated on reaching the door.

I had to escape.

I groped for the doorknob and opened the door just enough to stagger into the hall. I squinted as the bright lights hurt my eyes. Everything looked yellow. What was wrong with me?

Leaning against the wall for balance, I made my way toward my office. I had to get there before…before… Everything was worse, the pounding in my head, the nausea. Something was terribly wrong.

At last, I reached my office. I pushed the door open and stumbled in. Connie was at her desk. She looked up. I opened my mouth to speak, but nothing came out.

Blackness.

"Where is she?"

Josh's voice filtered through the heavy blanket of unconsciousness. Shrill. Filled with fear. I pushed myself to concentrate.

I had to reach him, had to comfort him. But I could not get beyond…beyond… I did not know what it was I had to get beyond.

Then I heard another voice. Deep, familiar. Soothing.

"It's okay, son. She's going to be okay," Larry Bridgeway said with a physician's practiced reassurance.

"You're sure?" The panic in Josh's voice changed to wariness.

"I wouldn't lie to you."

"Okay. If you're sure." Josh was calm again. He did not need my help.

Tired from the effort, I let go and sank into peaceful oblivion.

"ROBYN. WAKE UP."

I stirred at the sharp command. Tired. Still so very, very tired.

"Come on, girl. Look at me."

With a groan, I slowly opened my eyes, then closed them again. "Too bright," I croaked.

Fingers snapped and the light dimmed. I opened my eyes again and blinked several times. Larry Bridgeway's ebony face hovered over me. An ICU nurse stood on the other side of the bed, her gaze focused on the monitors stationed behind me.

I wanted to sit up, but my body wouldn't cooperate. My mouth tasted gritty. "Water," I whispered.

Larry held my head up so I could drink from a straw. "Just a few sips now," he cautioned.

That was fine with me. The effort exhausted me and I was happy to sink against the pillow again. He handed the cup back to the nurse, then took my pulse and blood pressure.

While he did that, I tried to make sense of what was happening. Gradually, I remembered the meeting and not feeling well. Trying to make it back to my office.

"What happened?"

Larry glanced at the nurse, then back at me. His expression revealed nothing. He took my hand. "Don't you worry about a thing, Rob. You're going to be fine."

"Why am I in ICU?"

"You're getting the VIP treatment, of course. Only the best for our favorite patient rep." Larry smiled, but it didn't reach his eyes, and his jocular tone sounded false.

I felt myself growing more alert, and more concerned.

"Level with me, Larry," I said in a stronger voice. "What's going on?"

He sighed before nodding to the nurse. She stepped across the room, opened the door partway, and spoke quietly to someone on the other side. Then she stepped back, opening the door wider. Josh, his face pinched with fear, and Detective Pierce, whose expression was as masked as Larry's, stepped in.

"Mom." Josh stumbled toward me and buried his face in my shoulder. I laid my arm across his back and patted him gently. His sobbing broke my heart.

"It's okay, Josh. I'm going to be fine. Right, Larry?"

Larry nodded once, curtly. I wanted to ask more questions, but right now, Josh needed my attention. I spoke quietly to him and finally he lifted his head. He sat up, but held my hand tightly.

"What happened?" I asked again, glancing from Larry to Detective Pierce.

Larry signaled for the nurse to take Josh out and she moved toward him.

"I'm not leaving my mother." His jaw jutted out and he looked so much like his father. He held my hand all the more fiercely.

Larry glanced at Pierce, who shrugged. "You're very lucky, Rob."

I sighed. "No clinical mumbo-jumbo, Larry. Just give me the bottom line."

Larry glanced at Pierce again. The detective stepped forward.

"The bottom line is you were poisoned."

"Poisoned! But how?"

Larry and Pierce exchanged looks again.

"Someone tried to kill you." Pierce's words were flat, unemotional, but the effect on me was electrifying.

"Someone tried to what—?" I fumbled for the bed controls and pushed the button to raise the top. When I was finally sitting up, I tried to laugh it off. "You've been watching too much television, Detective Pierce."

"He's not kidding, Rob," Larry said. "You got a dose of digoxin. Not enough to be lethal, but enough to make you very sick."

Now I was more confused than ever. "Digoxin! That's a heart medication. I don't take that," I said.

Detective Pierce moved closer. "We found the remains of several capsules in the bottom of your coffee cup. It's lucky you didn't finish that latté. That's probably what saved you."

Stunned by his revelation, I slumped against the pillow. "After it got cold, it didn't taste good," I murmured.

By this time, Josh was squeezing my hand so tight that it hurt. I wriggled my fingers and he loosened his grip, but his expression was still an intense frown. I didn't like him hearing that someone had almost left him an orphan. I wasn't particularly happy about it, either.

"Dr. Bridgeway, would you mind if I spoke with Robyn alone?"

Larry gave me a visual once-over, then nodded. "But only for a few minutes, Detective. I don't want her tired out."

"You too, son," Pierce said gently to Josh. "I need to ask you to leave."

"But—"

"It's okay, Josh. I'll be fine," I said with more spirit than I really felt. "You go with Dr. Bridgeway and find out when I can come home."

Reluctantly, Josh nodded and followed Larry from the room. Pierce and I watched the door swing shut behind them, then turned to face each other.

"Who—"

"Who—"

Detective Pierce and I obviously had the same question. "I haven't a clue who could have done it," I said.

"Let's start with who had opportunity."

Despite the seriousness of the situation, I couldn't help but quirk a grim smile. Opportunity was what attracted the police to arrest Pham, and that had led to my looking for other possible suspects.

"Connie brought me the coffee, but—"

"She's the one who found what was left of the capsules in your cup."

The closeness of my close call was beginning to sink in. "Did she tell you—"

"That she warned you about getting hurt?" Pierce interrupted again. It was getting to be an annoying habit. "Yes, she told me. Did the coffee taste okay when she gave it to you?"

I looked at him sharply. Connie was a suspect? No, not possible. "It tasted fine," I said truthfully.

"So, who else had a chance to drop something into your cup?"

"Melanie Cole stopped by the office."

"Did she—"

"Not there," I said with a sigh. "She was never alone with the coffee in my office, but she was in the meeting room talking to Will Slater when Connie called me out. But she wouldn't want to hurt me."

Pierce hoisted himself up on the edge of the bed. "Remember that little tidbit you picked up about her growing up in the same town as Hamilton? Well, I did some checking."

"Really?" I was inordinately pleased that he'd taken me seriously and followed up on my clue.

"I had to pull more than a few strings to get some sealed records unsealed." He paused to let the suspense build. It worked.

"And?" I prompted.

"And your hunch was right. Seems young Jake Hamilton had a real wild streak as a boy. When he was a senior in high school, he cornered Melanie under the bleachers at a football game."

"Did he...did he rape her?" I dreaded his answer.

Pierce nodded. "The local judge wrote it off as a boys-will-be-boys thing, because Hamilton testified she was asking for it, then changed her mind too late. She said he'd assaulted other girls, but none of them came forward. Probably too ashamed or didn't want to be the subject of gossip. The judge ordered the records sealed so Hamilton's record would be clean. He had excellent grades, was the track star. And Hamilton's adoptive father was the judge's cousin by marriage."

"I see. So Melanie is emotionally scarred and Hamilton goes on to national glory. Doesn't seem right, does it?"

"No, but you know as well as I do, Robyn, that justice isn't always served. However, it does give Melanie Cole a motive to commit murder. And if she realized later that she'd revealed too much of herself to you, well…" His expression told me he thought I'd brought it on myself.

"She's not the only one who had opportunity." I told Pierce about leaving my coffee unattended and how the room had been rearranged and was dark when I returned five or so minutes later.

Pierce threw up his hands. "Why don't you just tape a bull's-eye to your chest and hand out rifles?"

As I'd told the story, I started to feel incredibly stupid. Pierce's reaction didn't help any. "I didn't think—"

"That's right," he snapped. "You didn't think. Do you know how close you—" Pierce slid off the bed and paced the room as if trying to get his temper under control. "Okay. Who was at the meeting?"

I rattled off a half dozen names before he raised his hand to stop me.

"In other words, half the hospital," he snarled.

That was an exaggeration, but I didn't think this was the time to point that out. "So, Detective," I said as brightly as possible. "Where do we start?"

"We?" He gave me a long, hard look. "You're not going to do anything. It's your unwillingness to leave the investigation alone that put you in this position. Now back off."

Feeling thoroughly chastised and contrite, I nodded.

"Good," Pierce said. "Let me do my job. I'll start by looking for the person with the most to lose if you live."

That seemed as good a place as any.

TWELVE

I WOKE UP GROGGY AND disoriented. Where was I? Then, I remembered. The hospital. I was a patient.

Someone had poisoned me.

After wiggling my toes, I tested my hands and arms, then cautiously rolled my head from side to side. Relieved that everything still worked, I still wasn't ready to try sitting up.

I gradually became aware of the heated discussion going on outside my room.

"I want to take my mother home." Josh's low voice was controlled, but fiercely intense.

"That's not advisable." Larry sounded just as direct, but not unkind. I knew he was shaking his head and wearing his "serious physician" expression.

"Why not? You said she's okay. Her heart rate's stable."

"She is stable, Josh. For now. But if there's a problem, she's better off right here."

"There's something you're overlooking, Doc," said a third voice. So, Pierce was still here.

I breathed a sigh of relief. His presence felt like a safety net. The hospital, on the other hand, was no longer a friendly place.

"Someone poisoned her," he said. "The longer she's here, the greater the chance they'll try again."

I heard only grim silence. Pierce had spoken the inconceivable.

It was one thing to have a stranger murdered in our hospital. In an odd way, we had emotionally detached ourselves from the crime. We'd focused on the murder's effect on the hospital's reputation, and speculated on who did it as if it were a mystery dinner theater.

This afternoon was different, shocking me into reality. One of us had deliberately tried to murder *me*. From Larry's silence, he must have felt the same way. Dismay. Horror. Disbelief. Not *here* at Madrona Bay. Not *our* staff. We knew each other. We laughed and complained together, shared birthday lunches and budget woes. We were all good people, caring and compassionate.

Now we faced the chilling reality that someone we considered a friend and colleague had committed one murder and had attempted a second one.

A wave of nausea swept through me and I swallowed hard. It finally sank in how close I had come to dying. Connie and Detective Pierce had both warned me to mind my own business, to let the police conduct the investigation. But no, I'd thought I knew more and could do better than the professionals.

The three somber-faced men entered my room, three people I knew I could count on. I glanced at Larry, and, for a moment, my confidence wavered. Could I really trust him? Then, I remembered he hadn't been at that meeting. He couldn't have poisoned my coffee. But the momentary doubt brought a sense of loss. I shuddered, knowing I must be on guard with everyone in the hospital until the murderer was identified.

Larry looked at me, and his dark-brown eyes burned with an intensity I'd never seen before. He must have caught that brief questioning in my expression, and no matter how much he might understand, his feelings were hurt.

"Sorry." I reached out.

He took my hand, giving it a reassuring squeeze. "It's okay. I understand."

I shook my head. It was not okay and we both knew it. But there was nothing we could do about it now.

"I'm taking you home," Josh said.

Larry opened his mouth as if to say something, then snapped it shut. Instead, he scribbled away on a clipboard, pulled off a piece of paper, and handed it to Josh. "Here are the discharge instructions."

He turned and pointed his finger at me. "Rob, you are to rest through the weekend. No stopping by your office to pick up work. No calling Connie for messages. Go home and do nothing. It'll take a day or two before the digoxin is completely out of your system."

I rolled my eyes and glanced at Pierce in search of support from him. Instead, he gave me that don't-you-dare look and shook his head.

Resigned to my helpless damsel fate, I asked, "Anything else?"

Larry looked at Josh again. "If she so much as shivers, I want her in here."

"There's a fire station two blocks from us. I'll call them," Josh said. Then he grinned. "Unless Detective Pierce wants to loan me a siren so I can race Mom back here myself."

Pierce clapped Josh on the shoulder. "Call the aid car, son. Don't go playing Richard Petty on my streets."

The relaxed camaraderie between them surprised me. Josh was usually reserved around strangers. But then, I suspected Pierce had a way with distraught family members. I remembered how I'd felt consoled by his solidness after finding Hamilton's body.

While Larry reviewed the discharge instructions with

Josh, Pierce approached my bed. "I'll feel a lot better once we get you out of here," he said quietly.

The anger behind his words caught me off guard. His professional detachment had slipped, and I was comforted that he might have a personal interest in my well-being. I nodded as he returned to listen to Larry and ask a few more questions.

They left so I could dress with the help of a nurse's aide, then returned with Larry pushing a wheelchair.

"Oh, no," I said. "I'm walking out of here."

"Hospital rules," Larry insisted.

"And I'm the one who breaks the rules, remember?" The last thing I wanted was to look like a victim as I left the building. The grapevine would have already reported my collapse, but I couldn't bear the concern or speculation on my colleagues' faces. Besides, if I came across the poisoner, I wanted to look him straight in the eye. Maybe I would recognize his disappointment and identify him from that. Wishful thinking? Probably.

"Get in the wheelchair, Rob," Larry said again.

"We'll take the service elevator," Pierce said. "If there're any reporters hanging around, I don't want them to see us."

I hadn't even thought of that. Dear God, had I made the evening news again? I didn't want to know. "The service elevator would be fine."

We rode down in silence before I realized I couldn't leave yet. "I don't have my purse," I said. "It's in my office."

"I'll get it," Josh said.

"We'll do it later," Pierce countered.

"But I need it now," I insisted.

Pierce scowled at me. "What could possibly be in there that's so important?"

Exasperated, I said, "My keys and wallet."

Pierce laughed shortly. "You can survive without them."

"Then how am I going to drive home?"

The elevator doors opened, but no one moved. Josh and Pierce stared at me as if I had lost my mind.

"You are not driving, Mom."

Josh startled me. He'd used the same no-nonsense tone I used with him when I denied a request and made it clear the discussion was over. When had he assumed the mantle of a responsible adult? He was not my little boy anymore.

We left the building, and Pierce stayed with me on the loading dock while Josh went for his pick-up truck.

"I don't want to be stranded at home," I grumbled.

"You won't be stranded," Pierce said. "You're not supposed to leave the house anyway. We'll get your car and your purse later."

I muttered to myself at being at the mercy of these two concerned tyrants.

Josh pulled up and Pierce helped me into Josh's truck, then added, "Stay home and rest, Robyn. Let me handle this."

I nodded reluctantly.

"Call me if she gives you any trouble, Josh." He slammed the door before I could give him a piece of my mind. In a short time, they had bonded and were now ganging up on me.

We bounced and jostled our way home in silence. My bones felt like they needed a chiropractic adjustment by the time we reached our driveway, and I would've given Josh money to buy new shock absorbers that night. If I'd had my purse.

From the garage, we entered the kitchen and after Taffy greeted us with her boundless enthusiasm, I absorbed the safety of being home. I never comprehended before how helpless patients are in the hospital; strange and stark surroundings, clothes taken away, and dependent on strangers for even the most basic of needs. The bright colors in the kitchen cheered me. The lack of an antiseptic smell was as welcoming as the fragrance of fresh baked bread.

All the stress of the week exploded, draining my remaining energy for anything more strenuous than a hot shower and climbing into bed, too tired even for a comforting cup of tea. In a daze, I kissed Josh on the cheek and said good night. He hugged me then, a bone-crushing hug that told me how scared he really was.

I patted his back. "Worried about your old mom?"

He nodded.

"I'm okay," I said.

He lifted his head and I saw tears welling in his eyes. "Someone almost killed you, Mom."

Despite his grown-up façade, he sounded as vulnerable as a five-year-old. I reached up and smoothed his hair into place.

"But they didn't, did they? I'm all right, Josh."

The phone rang.

"I'll get it." Josh reached across the counter, picked up the phone, and checked the number before answering it. "Hi, Granddad. Yeah, she's here."

I took the offered phone. "Hi, Da."

"Robyn Anne, are you all right?"

"Yes, Da, I'm fine." I wasn't really, but I would not give him something more to worry about.

"Don't lie to me. I called your office this afternoon and talked to that Connie who works for you. Been calling the house for hours. You were poisoned!"

When he said it like that, I winced. "The important thing is, I'm okay now. Really."

"Humph. Do you want me to come?"

"No, Da. I'll be fine, really," I repeated. "Josh is here and the doctor thought I was well enough to come home." I didn't add that a murderer still running loose in the hospital was the best reason for getting me out of there.

After several more reassurances, and promising that Josh and I were coming for Christmas, we hung up.

I looked at Josh. "I wish he hadn't heard."

Josh shrugged. "He was going to find out sometime. Think how mad he'd be if we'd deliberately kept it from him."

"I suppose. Okay, you should probably do what you need to for school tomorrow."

"But Dr. Bridgeway said—"

"Larry is a very conscientious physician. I'll be fine. You don't need to stand watch tonight or tomorrow. If something happens, I'll call you."

"But—"

"No buts. I'm going to the shower."

He nodded, but I felt his troubled gaze follow me from the room.

He had come close to being an orphan today. On a practical level, I'd made all the necessary arrangements years ago: a will, life insurance to pay off the mortgage and provide an income, a trustee to manage things until Josh was twenty-one. He wouldn't be homeless and he'd have funds to finish his education without burdening my father. But, he wouldn't have a mom or dad. Of all the things that had almost happened today, that scared me the most.

I pushed from my mind the somber thoughts of what might have been. Instead, when I reached the bathroom, I debated between a long soaking bath or a quick shower. The shower won only because I didn't think I could stay awake long enough to fill the tub. I shed my clothes and dropped them into the hamper, then stepped under the pounding spray of hot water.

For once, I didn't even consider conserving water. I let it beat on me, warming me to the core. My mind drifted, a meditative trance, until I realized I was falling asleep. I dried off and pulled on my comfort pajamas, white flannel with pink teddy bears, and toddled off to bed. Slipping between Egyptian cotton sheets and fluffing the floral duvet dispelled the remnants of my hospital stay.

If I had expected to fall asleep immediately, however, I was sorely disappointed. I lay on my back, covers up to my chin. I curled into a fetal ball, covers over my ears. I tried the same position, opposite side. A quick glance at the clock told me only thirty minutes had passed.

Sitting up, I flipped on the table lamp and picked up my current book. I usually chose my bedtime reading based on its sleep-inducing potential. This book, an acclaimed literary novel, had been outstanding, putting me to sleep every night for the last two weeks in no more than four pages.

Tonight, it failed. I couldn't focus on the angst-filled characters who continued to do nothing to solve their own problems. Instead, my mind drifted back to the hospital and to a subject guaranteed to ruin a good night's sleep.

Who wanted me dead?

I put the book down, turned off the light, and slid back under the covers to stare at the dark ceiling. Again, I asked myself, who wanted me dead? It only made sense that it was the same person who killed Congressman Hamilton. We didn't have two murderers running loose in the building. And why me? Because I was getting too close to the truth was the obvious reason.

True, I'd been sleuthing, but I'd been subtle, or at least

I had thought so. Was someone tracking my Internet searches? No, that couldn't be it. No one I worked with was that computer literate. And I hadn't talked to anyone about my suspicions except Detective Pierce, and he wasn't about to leak information.

That line of thought wasn't helping, so I switched to who had the opportunity. A mind-numbing list of people had access to Hamilton. The list of possible poisoners was considerably smaller, but more distressing. No wonder Pierce was so annoyed with me. It had been dumb to leave my coffee cup unattended, but who would've thought I'd be in danger among my colleagues? The only drugs we used at meetings were caffeine and sugar.

Larry wanted me to stay home tomorrow and rest through the weekend. Pierce wanted me to leave the case alone. Both reasonable pieces of advice, given the circumstances.

The problem was, despite it all, I wasn't ready to stop. This attempt on my life had happened because I'd come too close to the truth. If that was the case, then the murderer wouldn't believe I'd been scared away. It was awful to accept the idea that a co-worker was the murderer. But, whoever poisoned my coffee had to know I wasn't the kind of person who backed off. As a patient rep, I worked within the system, but was persistent, looking for different ways to reach the best result for everyone involved. Why would the murderer expect me to behave any differently in this case?

I sighed as another thought came to me. Maybe I was wrong to be this way. Maybe what I considered to be the best solution wasn't viewed the same way by others involved. Was I wrong to push so hard for my vision of "justice"? Was I actually as arrogant with my convictions as some of the people who annoyed me with theirs? It troubled me that I might be considered difficult to work with. Probably not difficult enough to motivate murder, but enough that some people chose to avoid me.

Even if this was true, I thought as I fluffed my pillows, now might not be the best time to change. I could already have the clues needed to solve the case and just not know it. Had I been looking at the clues the wrong way, or in the wrong combination or sequence? I needed to find the connection to tie it all together.

Well, I decided, I would play the game. I would lay low for a while, take a break to sort through what I knew, then begin again, more subtly this time. I would figure out who murdered Congressman Hamilton and who tried to murder me. Before they tried again.

THE KNOCKING on my bedroom door finally broke through the layers of unconsciousness, dragging me to awareness. I wasn't happy about it. My alarm clock said seven-thirty. At least an hour before the sun came up. I closed my eyes again.

The door opened with a painful groan. I winced at the noise. I'd been meaning to take some WD-40 to that hinge.

"Mom?" Josh whispered. "Are you awake?"

Taffy brushed past him and landed on top of me.

"I am now." I shoved Taffy to the other side of the bed and propped myself up on my elbow.

Josh stepped into the room, carrying a potted azalea covered with hot-pink blossoms. He set it on the nightstand, then turned to face me.

I fingered the leaves. "That's pretty. Where'd it come from?"

He looked different. I couldn't put my finger on what it was exactly. Tidier, maybe?

"Chuck brought it and wants to say hi," he said.

"Chuck? Your friend from school?"

He nodded. This was very strange, but then, the whole week had been bizarre. I wasn't sure about entertaining a guest while wearing pajamas, but it wasn't as if I was wearing something frilly or see-through. Actually, it was rather sweet of him to want to wish me well, so I decided not to make a big deal about it.

"I'm not exactly dressed to receive company. Give me a minute to freshen up."

Josh nodded again, then disappeared. I made my way to the bathroom and brushed my teeth, washed my face, and ran a quick comb through my hair. I climbed back into bed and propped myself up with pillows.

When Josh returned, he said, "Mom, this is Chuck."

I gawked. This was Chuck?

Petite, blond, and cute as the dickens, the girl standing next to Josh was the furthest thing from a Chuck I could have imagined. She wore the college uniform, faded jeans and a UW Husky sweatshirt. Her skin had the fresh bloom of youth, and, as she approached, I saw that her make-up had been applied with a light touch, accentuating her corn-flower-blue eyes.

"Hi, Miz Kelly. I sure am sorry to hear you're doing poorly."

Her drawl was soft and gentle on the ear. I glanced at Josh and from the heated look in his eyes, it was obvious he was smitten. Was I ready for this?

"Thank you, Chuck. I'm glad to say I'm feeling better than I was yesterday." I wondered just how much Josh had told her.

"Food poisoning's a mighty dangerous thing," Chuck said. I appreciated Josh's spin on my near-death experience. "I remember my granny warning me all the time about not canning properly and not leaving potato salad in the sun. She was always careful about what she served to folks. Do you know what it was that made you sick?"

I wanted to say, Yes, it was *digoxin-laced coffee.* Instead, I shook my head and changed the subject. "So, tell me, how come you're called Chuck?"

She laughed, a twinkle lighting her eyes as she glanced at Josh, and I could see why he was captivated. "Oh, Miz Kelly. I'll bet you thought I was a boy, didn't you?" She turned to Josh. "Shame on you, letting your mama think that."

Josh frowned in puzzlement. "I never said you were a boy."

"But you didn't tell her I was a girl, either." Chuck laughed again and squeezed his hand. I noticed he didn't let go. "My real name is Charlene. Daddy calls me Charlie, and somehow my friends changed it to Chuck."

"I can understand that. My first name is Robyn, but my friends call me Rob."

"I like that." Chuck glanced at her watch. "Oh, wow, look at the time. That bridge traffic is going to be backed up something awful if I don't leave right now."

"I'm staying home today to keep an eye on my mom," Josh said. "Can I borrow your notes this weekend?"

"Why, of course, sugar. I'll call you when I get home." Chuck stood on tiptoes and pecked Josh's cheek before she dashed off.

Josh glanced at me, then mumbled something incoherent as he followed her out.

I smiled broadly. If Chuck was in the engineering program, she was smart, and she had charm and good looks. If she set her sights on Josh, he wouldn't stand a chance. I wasn't ready to turn my baby boy over to another woman, but unless Chuck was hiding some deep, dark secret, Josh could do a lot worse.

"Taffy, old girl, looks like you and I are going to be spending a lot of evenings alone." I patted her on the head and she rolled over so I could rub her tummy.

Before I could turn completely morose, the phone rang. I leaned across Taffy to reach it. "Hello?"

"Robyn? Matt Pierce. Is Josh there?"

"Yes, he's saying good-bye to his girlfriend."

"I thought I'd swing by and pick him up so we can get your car. Can he be ready in fifteen minutes?"

"He's ready now." I hung up the phone and clambered out of bed. From the bedroom door, I hollered, "Josh! Josh!"

Josh sprinted down the hall. "What? Are you okay?" He stopped and held out his arms as if expecting me to collapse.

"I'm fine. Detective Pierce just called. He's picking you up in fifteen minutes to get my car."

"Are you sure you'll be all right by yourself? I mean Dr. Bridgeway said—"

"I'm fine," I repeated. "In fact, after you get my car, go on to school. I'll hang around here with Taffy."

"We'll talk about that later." From his tone, he was not into compromise.

"I'm going to take a shower."

Josh opened his mouth to argue about that too, so I shut my bedroom door on him. I took a hasty shower and was dressed and made up by the time Pierce rang the doorbell.

I started to answer it, but Josh barreled past. I sank onto the couch and waited for the detective to come in.

It's a funny thing about our homes; we get so accustomed to our things that it takes someone new coming into the house for us to see it from a fresh perspective. In his line of work, Pierce had to see all kinds of homes.

What would he see here? Furniture upholstered in

warm earth tones, designed more for durability than for fashion. Hardwood floors with large area rugs. A few knick-knacks scattered on the mantle over the used-brick fireplace, items that showed a touch of whimsy or were family heirlooms. *House Beautiful* it wasn't, but it was comfortable, and it was mine.

I watched Pierce's quick survey of the room, the slight stretch of his neck to confirm the layout of the rest of the house, before his gaze rested on me.

"Do I pass?"

He glanced away as if embarrassed to be caught. "You look a helluva lot better than you did yesterday."

"Thanks. Would you like some coffee?"

"If it's made."

"It'll only take a few minutes."

"That's okay. I'm on duty so I shouldn't stay." He perched on the arm of the sofa.

A wild idea struck me, and for once, I acted on impulse. Pretending to be totally engrossed in a stray thread on a sofa pillow, I said, "Pierce, I was thinking. If you're not working next Thursday, and if you don't have other plans, would you like to join us for Thanksgiving dinner?"

The silence was so loud and lasted so long that I finally looked up. He had the nicest smile on his face. It changed my impression of him again.

"You're inviting me for Thanksgiving?"

I shrugged and gave up on the loose thread. "Josh has invited his girlfriend. I'm a reasonably good cook, and we have all the usual turkey day fare. Plus baked yams with melted marshmallows on top."

"Yams? Really?"

I nodded and he thought for a moment.

"What kind of pie?"

I struggled not to laugh. "I'm not sure yet. Does it make a difference?"

"Not really," he said, looking sheepish. "I'd like to come. Thank you."

"Good. Come around two or whenever the ballgames start." Pleased with how that went, I put the pillow in its place and looked straight at him. "So, have you figured out who tried to kill me?"

"Robyn, it's not even nine o'clock in the morning."

"The detectives on TV would've solved it last night." Despite my teasing, my stomach clenched with fear. "Someone out there wants me dead, and I have to say, Pierce, that's a bit unsettling."

"As long as you stay home and don't let anyone in, you're safe."

"I have to go back to work on Monday. Will it be safe then?" I snapped.

He gave me a hard stare.

"Look Pierce, I have a job to do. I have a son to support. I have one person out on vacation and my assistant is alone in the office. You have to solve this thing, and quickly. I don't have time to wait." *And the longer it takes, the more terrified I am.*

He sighed in exasperation. "Doc Bridgeway said to stay home and do nothing this weekend. Now I'm adding, don't worry about it. I'm doing the best I can. You have to trust me. Now, back off and be a good girl."

Josh returned before I came up with a flippant response. I watched them go, knowing I had behaved peevishly, but I didn't care. I hated the restriction. I loved my house, but I wanted it to be my choice to stay home, not forced imprisonment.

Still fuming, I went to the kitchen, Taffy close on my heels. It took a few minutes, but I finally found the discharge instructions Larry had given Josh. Nothing about limiting what I ate, and I was hungry. I fixed myself a cup of tea, decaf just in case, and made a batch of scones. I tried to convince myself that the routine of mixing and lightly kneading the dough was reassuringly normal, but I wasn't successful. With the scones in the oven, I whipped up an omelette. While it finished cooking, I flipped on the TV and checked all three national affiliates for local news, but found nothing except weather inserts. Wet and drippy. What else was new?

Zipping through the non-English channels, an image flashed by. Stunned, I backed up until I found it again.

Peter? On a French-Canadian cable station? I watched for a few minutes, not understanding a word he said, but recognizing the familiar backdrop of war in a Third World country.

I shook my head. How like him to land on his feet. Within a year, the major stations would forget his breach of journalistic ethics and he'd again be on top.

I was pleased with how I was reacting, the same degree of detachment I'd feel for a movie star. Nothing personal, good or bad. To paraphrase my grandmother, I had mistaken a goat's beard for a fine stallion's tail.

Satisfied that I was truly over Peter, I sat down to eat and watched television until Josh came home.

"Take that coat back out," I said when he came in through the garage. "You're dripping all over the floor."

He seemed distracted and looked surprised at the amount of water on his raincoat. "Sorry." He left to hang it on the clothesline we'd strung up in the garage for just that purpose, and returned with Taffy's foot-wiping towel to sop up the excess water.

"Are you hungry?" I asked, knowing full well what the answer would be.

He perked up. "Sure."

"Breakfast, coming right up!" I cracked three eggs into a non-stick frying pan and felt a twinge. How many more mornings did I have to fix meals for him? I had to pay more attention, treasure the time we still had.

Josh set the table for himself and poured a glass of orange juice. "We got your car okay."

"Thank you." I put three scones on his plate. "What about my purse?"

He didn't look over, but I saw his face and neck turn red.

"Sorry, Mom. We forgot it," he mumbled.

Something about the way he refused to look up led me to think they'd done it on purpose, that if I didn't have my keys and wallet, I really would be confined to home while Josh was at school.

I slid his eggs onto the plate and handed it to him. Leaning against the counter, I watched him wolf down his breakfast, despite years of telling him to eat slower.

After cleaning up the kitchen, I took his dirty dishes and said, "Go to school."

"But—"

"I'm fine." The phrase was becoming my mantra. I placed the dishes into the dishwasher and turned to face him. "Really."

"But Dr. Bridgeway said—"

"Larry said the first twelve hours were the most critical. It's been that long, and nothing's happened. I'm okay."

"What will you do?"

"Josh. Dear." I draped my arm around his shoulder. "I have been known to entertain myself. I don't need you to keep me from getting bored." *Or worrying.*

He looked at me with a suspicious frown. "I don't know."

"Look. I've had a shower, I'm dressed, I fixed my breakfast, I fixed your breakfast. I cleaned up the dirty dishes. And nothing's happened. Go to school." He still didn't look convinced, so I used my last resort. "Won't the other boys work real hard to be sure Chuck doesn't miss you?"

"Oh, Mom, I can't believe you said that," he said with a tinge of disgust. "That's so high school."

There it was again, signs he was growing up. "Sorry. But really, I'm fine. I don't need you to hover over me. Go. Please."

He stood there, my big strapping son, looking torn between duties, between his work and his family, the adult dilemma.

I patted him on the back and said nothing more. In a few minutes, he was out the door.

After making my bed and tidying up, I felt at loose ends. I always brought something home from the office to work on, but obviously not this time. I picked up a book, a hot new bestseller; it didn't hold my attention. The TV was all talk shows and real judges and soap operas and news. Except for the formats, it was hard to tell the difference.

Restless, I stood at the window and watched sheets of rain scrub the street. It took all of five minutes to choose what I wanted to plant in a bare corner of the yard, bulbs that would bloom from early spring through the fall. I thought about taking a nap, but I wasn't the least bit tired, despite tossing and turning all night. I considered cleaning a closet, finally deciding I would save that for a snowstorm.

By noon, Taffy was the only one happy with my restriction, but a person can bond with their dog for only so long. I had no ill effects from yesterday, no symptoms, expected or unexpected. I basically felt fine, no worse than if I had a mild cold. I was well enough to dig out the spare car key and go to work for a couple of hours.

The problem though, the real reason I would follow Larry's directive to stay home, was simple: I was too terrified to go back.

THIRTEEN

THE WEEKEND DRAGGED by in half-hour increments. I called out-of-town friends to catch up, never mentioning "the incident," as Josh and I referred to it. I cleaned out my personal E-mail in-box, a chore I'd been meaning to do for months, but never seemed to get around to.

On Saturday night, Josh stayed home, something he had rarely done since he obtained his driver's license. He went to the video store and rented some of my favorite movies. We watched and ate popcorn, saying little, but clutching the memories of happier times.

During the marathon of Sunday football games, I organized boxes of pictures, labeling them as to who, when, and where. It struck me that this was a task people finally got around to doing when they knew "the end" was near. Whenever my mind drifted to how close I had come to my own end, I pushed the thought aside and refocused on the pictures scattered across the table.

Underlying all the busyness was unspoken fear.

At last—or too soon—Monday morning came. Josh had picked up my purse and keys on Friday on his way home. I waited for him to leave for school, something I rarely did, then found odd chores that needed to be done *now*. Critically important things like changing the sheets and starting a load of laundry. Emptying the dishwasher. Sorting the recycles.

By early afternoon, I admitted I was dragging my feet, that I was too emotionally paralyzed to leave the house.

It bothered me to acknowledge the fear gnawing at me, and I didn't like the dread that held me captive. The longer I waited to return to the hospital, the harder it would be.

Finally, I resisted the temptation to do one more thing, the task that would last long enough to say it was too late to go at all.

I had to return. I needed to go back today, before the events of last week scared me away forever.

IT FELT STRANGE when I pulled into the parking lot and looked at the building where I had worked for the last ten years. After all that had happened the past week, I felt detached from this place. I didn't know it anymore. Maybe I never had.

Grasping for a reason to leave the security of a locked car, I thought about the work waiting for me. I sighed with relief; the State Insurance Commissioner case was sitting on my desk. The response letter was due in Olympia today, and I had yet to draft it, let alone have Dr. Weiser review it. Focusing on work was good. Maybe it would help me to avoid intensive psychotherapy in the future.

Despite my attempt to be logical and rational, my thoughts were still jumbled as I slid from the car and approached the rear entrance. People were coming and going; it was shift change. It all looked so normal.

Not wanting to see anyone yet, I took the service elevator and arrived undetected at my office door, noting how easy it was to move around in broad daylight without being seen.

How easy to find the private minute or two necessary to end a life.

Shaken, I entered my office. "Hi, Connie."

"Rob!" Connie jumped from her chair. "Thank God, you're back. I was so worried, but I didn't want to call, in case you weren't feeling well."

I was not about to tell her the truth, that physically I was doing okay, but emotionally I was a wreck. Instead, I smiled wryly and said, "Staying home isn't near as much fun as we thought."

Connie came from behind her desk. I'm not really old enough to be Connie's mother, but I am her first real boss, and she hugged me with a desperation that reminded me of Josh when he brought me home.

"I'm okay, Connie."

Like Josh, she nodded against my shoulder, and I wasn't surprised to see tears when she pulled away.

"Detective Pierce came by earlier," she said with a sniff and a quick swipe at her eyes. "I haven't heard if he's found anything."

"What's the talk around here?" I asked.

"That's just it. No one's talking." She grimaced as she shook her head. "Everyone's so appalled by what happened to you. I mean, it didn't take five minutes for it to get out that you'd been poisoned. It was okay if you'd fainted, but that…." She shuddered.

"So everyone knows it was deliberate?"

Connie nodded. "Uh-huh. And since it had to be someone at that meeting, everyone's gone totally weird. All of this week's meetings are cancelled. The excuse is that it's a short week and a lot of people have taken off early for the holiday. That doesn't explain why no one wants to take a break together. And at lunch, a few people sit alone in the cafeteria, but mostly, they grab a tray and leave. Everyone's afraid."

Something she said niggled at my brain, but I couldn't put my finger on it. "You can't blame them, though. It's frightening to realize that one of us is a murderer."

"That's just it. No one wants to think about it, so they're avoiding everyone."

It made sense. As I walked to my office, I called over my shoulder to Connie. "How's it been in here?"

"Not too bad," Connie said. "I've referred most of the stuff that's come in. I took some messages for you and Margie, ordered medical records, that sort of thing."

"I better be careful. Pretty soon you'll be running this place so smoothly you won't need me anymore."

"Don't kid yourself, Rob," Connie groused from her desk. "I want nothing to do with those big messy cases you and Margie love."

I plopped into my own chair, closing my eyes for a moment, glad that Connie couldn't see me now. Despite how rested I'd felt when I left home, I was exhausted.

Resisting the urge to put my head down and take a nap, I started looking for the Insurance Commissioner case file, sifting through the bits and pieces of paper and folders on my desk: a hodge-podge of phone messages, hand-written notes, half-completed report forms, letters from patients and medical records. What a mess. I should come in over the long Thanksgiving weekend and clean it up.

The phone rang as I found the file. I picked up the receiver, noting that the call was on my direct line, not a transfer from Connie. "Hi, this is Robyn."

There was a pause, then, "Oh, you finally showed up." So much for Will's sympathetic response to my ordeal. There was another brief pause, before he said, "Come down to my office. Immediately." The phone slammed down.

I stared at the receiver. "Yes, Will. I'm feeling much better, Will. Thank you so much for asking." I dropped the receiver into its cradle. How like him. I'd never seen him show the slightest concern for any of his staff. Whether it was an accident, illness, or a death in the family, it all occurred below his radar and remained unacknowledged.

I sighed heavily. Okay, so Will was upset about something. I really regretted answering that phone. Why did he need to talk with me now? Maybe it was nothing important; maybe he wanted to delegate something so he could be done with it. I could always hope.

I shrugged out of my coat and took a moment to run a comb through my hair and to add some lipstick. If I was going to be seen in the building, I wanted to look good. At least I'd worn my gray suit, which added to a professional demeanor.

During the short elevator ride, my anxiety increased. I tried to figure out if he was upset with me personally, but except for finding Congressman Hamilton's body and being poisoned myself, I couldn't come up with anything. Okay, so maybe that was more than enough to send even the most reasonable of bosses over the edge.

Feeling an affinity with Anne Boleyn on her way to the executioner's ax, I walked into the administrative-office suite.

Arlene, Will's secretary, looked up. "Oh, am I glad you're here."

That caught me by surprise. "You are?"

"He's just been on a tear all afternoon," she whispered. "Of course, he was already upset, what with the murder, and…and then the thing with you. By the way, how are you feeling?"

So, they'd sanitized the poisoning to "the thing with you." "I'm doing okay. Is he upset with me?"

"Oh, it's probably the whole thing," she said with a brush-off wave. "But now a hospital board member's called and the police were here questioning him again."

I saw a glimmer of hope. Maybe I'd been paranoid for no reason. "Why does he want to see me?"

"I don't know for sure, but—"

She stopped as Will flung his door open and stepped out.

"Robyn." He turned and disappeared back into his office.

I looked at Arlene. We both shrugged and rolled our eyes, then I walked around her desk and into Will's office.

"Shut the door." He was already seated. The normally sterile desk was overflowing with papers. His usually perfectly styled hair was a mess, as if he'd repeatedly run his fingers through it. His eyes lacked their typical hardness, and his anxious gaze darted around the room. What surprised me most was that Will called me, of all people, in an apparent moment of panic.

I pretended not to notice the chaos. "What's up?"

He picked up a copy of the Quality Report and tossed it at me. It was a fumble, but I caught it before it hit the ground.

"Is there a problem with my part of the report?" I asked.

"What's there is okay, but the chairwoman of the Quality Committee called. Samantha Duke. She wants more information."

I relaxed. It wasn't an unusual request. "That's fine. What does she want?"

"She wants specifics. Names. Details, like what kind of medical problems these patients had. Plus demographics. Are we discriminating against a particular patient group. That sort of thing."

The request stunned me. "I can put together the demographics, but she can't have names and diagnoses. We never release those. The committee knows that. That's all part of the patient's right to confidentiality. It's—"

Will raised his hand to stop me. "That's the past. This is the new chairwoman and she doesn't care. She's convinced the report is a whitewash."

"A whitewash! Are you kidding? That report gives them everything. Tables of numbers, qualitative summary, corrective actions taken." I ticked off the items with my fingers.

My earlier fear was gone; I was back in the saddle again. The new chairwoman obviously needed an orientation to the federal patient-confidentiality laws as well as the purpose of the report. "Don't worry about it. I'll talk to her."

I wasn't sure what the penalty was for patient reps who were found in contempt of oversight committees, but I had no choice. It went with the badge.

Will leaned back in his chair and said, "Apparently she has some basis for concern."

Warning bells clanged in my brain. "What do you mean?" I asked cautiously.

"It seems her sister-in-law filed a complaint with your department, and the family's consensus is that you covered up a physician's gross negligence with a lot of nice words."

"So based on that she questions the veracity of everything coming out of my office?"

Will nodded. He tented his fingers and looked at me with speculation.

"What was the patient's name?"

"Emma Jamison."

I laughed out loud. "You're kidding? That woman—"

I caught myself before going any farther. I couldn't tell Will anything. He wasn't part of the medical staff review. I couldn't reveal that the woman was certifiable and under a psychiatrist's care, without violating her right to privacy. Her complaint had been groundless. What she claimed could not possibly have happened.

But I was stuck. Just as I wouldn't reveal specifics to

the Quality Committee chair, I couldn't discuss a mental-health case with Will.

"I've been thinking about this situation, Robyn. This and other incidents that have occurred. In fact, I had a call from corporate this morning." He had that this-hurts-me-more-than-it-hurts-you look.

"What do you mean?" I was nervous now. I didn't like the "gotcha" gleam in his eyes. An icy cold wave followed by searing hot dread swept through me. I doubted it had anything to do with the digoxin overdose.

"It happens sometimes. Even to good managers." His tone implied I was not one of those good managers.

"What happens?"

"Oh, they get set in their ways. Resist new approaches." He looked at me with feigned sorrow. "What I'm trying to say, Robyn, is that maybe it's time you found a different position."

If he had made a pass at me, I wouldn't have been more surprised. "You're firing me?"

"No, no, of course not. I'm merely suggesting you look for another job more…more stimulating. Something different. We're part of a large organization. I'm sure you can find something by…let's say by the first of the year?"

I choked. "You're giving me five weeks during the holiday season to find a management position?" The cold-hearted bastard.

"I'm sure you'll do just fine." Will stood and walked to the door. He turned to me with a glazed smile. "I'm glad we could reach an agreement on this."

Shocked, I left Will's office, thankful that Arlene was busy on the phone. I gave a token wave and strode from the Admin suite. Holding myself together, I took the elevator to the third floor, but couldn't bring myself to return to my office. Instead, I went down the hall to a conference room. Not the one where I had been poisoned, but the one next door.

It was empty. Leaving the lights off, I approached the window and stared at the trees swaying in the wind. Rain pounded against the glass, blurring the bleak view that matched my beaten spirit.

Cold seeped through from the outside, chilling me. Or maybe it was the cold inside my heart that made me shiver. So much to deal with. Hamilton's murder. Peter. The poisoning. And now this.

Will's words had left me numb. And hurt. He made it sound as if I deliberately went out of my way to make his job harder by finding the dead congressman and being poisoned myself. How could he continue to have so little comprehension of who I was or what I did?

Then, I started to get angry. He said he received a call from corporate, but he got those calls every day. He didn't say the call had been about me. He'd only inferred it, the slimy bastard. But what if it had been about me? He said we'd reached an agreement. What agreement? What a euphemism! We hadn't reached an agreement. He had issued an ultimatum.

The reality was that Will could simply fire me. The threat hung over every middle manager. We had no union, no mandatory disciplinary process. If an administrator didn't like someone, he could strongly encourage them to pursue their career goals elsewhere, and if they resisted, he made life impossible. It happened all the time.

He was right about one thing: Madrona Bay was part of a much larger organization. But the job options for someone like me were not terrific. I was not a trained and licensed provider, so the clinical jobs were out. There were always openings for billing clerks and claims processors, but management positions that required my skills and experience were rare.

If I wanted to stay with the company, I could either take a disastrous cut in pay or relocate to another state. Neither appealed to me. Besides, applying for management positions took months, much longer than Will's end of the year deadline.

But I didn't want to leave. I loved my job, and I was good at what I did. I liked Madrona Bay and the people I worked with. Except for the one who tried to murder me, of course.

For the sake of argument, for a moment I would assume Will wasn't the murderer. The bottom line was Will didn't like aggravation, and I had been a nuisance since he became administrator five years ago. After last week, he probably viewed me as trouble with a capital "T." Will considered this problem with the new committee chairwoman as the last straw. Somehow, in his mangled little accountant brain, he had rationalized that if I disappeared, so would all his problems with corporate, the press, and who knew who else. Simplistic, yes, but understandable given the week he'd had and the pressure of applying for a federal position and hoping no one at corporate noticed.

I had two choices.

I could give in quietly and slink away, try to find a new job within the company which would not disrupt my entire life and endanger everything I'd worked hard for.

Or, I could fight. I could talk to someone in Human Resources and make a nuisance of myself by insisting on a formal process. Make Will identify in writing what I was doing wrong, and meet with me on a weekly basis to review my progress. Nothing aggressive, just calmly assertive.

There was no guarantee he wouldn't fire me at the end

of the process, but maybe it would buy me some time. He might get that federal job, or transfer to another hospital, or simply get bored and the whole thing would become moot. It was time to advocate for myself the way I championed a patient's cause.

I felt much better. Outside, the wind and rain had abated, leaving small branches and leaves strewn across the parking lot.

As I turned to leave, I had another thought. I could talk to Larry about the Jamison case. She'd been a nightmare patient for everyone involved. Maybe Larry could say something to Will without violating her confidentiality. Will had to believe it wasn't my fault if Larry told him, right? Eternal optimist, that's me.

When I returned to my office, I told Connie that Will's thing had been no big deal. No point in worrying her. In fact, I decided to say nothing to anyone until after I talked to Human Resources. I looked up Sarah's number in the directory and called. The phone rang a few times, then went to voice mail.

"Sarah, this is Robyn Kelly. It's Monday afternoon. I need to talk to you soon. It's important. Thanks."

I hung up and wondered if there was something else I should do. I couldn't think of anything at the moment. My watch said it was almost five o'clock. Where had the time gone?

I called home. "Hi, honey," I said when Josh answered.

"Mom? Where are you?" He sounded so angry, so worried, that I winced.

"I'm at work."

"You should've left a note." Yes, he was definitely overreacting.

"Perhaps, but you knew I was coming in."

"Are you okay? You were supposed to leave right after

me, but I could tell you were here for lunch. That's why I was worried. I thought you got sick or something."

"Of course, I'm okay," I lied. I hesitated. We'd had several long talks over the weekend, and he had surprised me with his perceptions. I'd come away with a new awareness that I really should be treating him as an adult, and be honest about what I was thinking. I took a deep breath and said, "I was afraid."

After a moment's pause, Josh said, "I think I understand. But I wish you'd've told me. I'd have gone in with you."

The sweet sincerity of his offer brought tears to my eyes. "That's very thoughtful, Josh, but I needed to do this alone."

"I guess. Call me when you decide to come home, okay?"

Warmed by his efforts to keep track of me, I said, "I'll do that. See you later."

I smiled as I hung up the phone, but the smile faded quickly as I faced the threatening future.

If someone at the corporate office was asking for my head because of Hamilton and the poisoning, then the surest way to redeem myself was to find the murderer. I went over Connie's earlier comments, but still couldn't grasp what had to be a most important clue.

Hoping it would come to me—and wanting to avoid a complaint from the Insurance Commissioner about my handling of that case—I picked up the Stone file and started the letter. The format was very straightforward, outlining the basics of Mrs. Stone's complaint and then the results of my investigation. As Dr. Weiser had said, the problem had been primarily a matter of what had not been said. The patient had been given the wrong impression, not only that her surgery was covered by the new insurance, but that Dr. Chin had her best interests at heart.

The letter went quickly, and after spell-checking and re-reading it one more time, I gave it to Connie to print and prepare for mailing. Dr. Weiser had to review it first, so I would drop it off at the Medical Staff offices on my way home.

I went back to my office and stared out the window.

What was not said. Giving the wrong impression.

Was that what this was really all about? Since I still couldn't figure it out, I pulled out a pad of paper. If I wrote down everything I knew, maybe the elusive answer would come to me.

The easy part was narrowing the list of suspects. The murderer was at last week's meeting. I hesitated. Did I really want to do this? The answer was a resounding "YES!" By sleuthing on my own, I had helped prove Pham Nguyen's innocence. When I was poisoned, it became deeply personal. I didn't want to live with this fear any longer, and I didn't want my friends to live with it either.

I took a deep breath, then another, and forced myself to think logically. This was just like any of my other investigations. I frowned. Sure it was, only the stakes were much higher.

I quickly jotted down the names of everyone I could remember being in the room when Connie had called me away from the meeting. I tore that page off the pad and started with a fresh page for the first suspect.

It was, of course, Will.

FOURTEEN

WILL'S NAME LEAPED off the page as a suspect. He had both motive and opportunity. Congressman Hamilton had thwarted Will's attempt at a federal job, which gave him plenty of motive. He also had an open calendar at the time of the murder, giving him opportunity. He could easily have slipped the pills into my coffee. I wrote in the margin: *does Will have a Rx for digoxin?* When Will failed to kill me, he'd tried another way to get rid of me.

I stopped writing. If Will wanted to get rid of me, he could have fired me to begin with. Why bother with the poison? *Note to self: to be on the safe side, do not go to any meetings where he will be.* The thought nagged that maybe I was seeking a way to avenge his shabby treatment of me, but I honestly didn't think so because it all fit, it all made sense. Besides, proving Will was the murderer would be karmic justice for his being a jerk.

As satisfying as that would be, Will's whereabouts at the time of the murder had probably been thoroughly dissected by Pierce. I flipped to a fresh page to consider another suspect.

Melanie had a strong motive to kill Hamilton, and she had followed me into the meeting room, ostensibly to arrange an interview with Will for later that day, giving her ample opportunity to drug my coffee. Were the two in cahoots?

I shook my head, doubting this was a conspiracy. Murderers usually worked alone. Besides, the idea that more than one person might be involved was beyond the pale.

Furthermore, everyone knew Melanie was a reporter. She'd stick out like a sore thumb around the patient rooms, and be quickly escorted off the unit.

I flipped to the next empty page and started over.

Cynthia Martin. I knew she'd been on the unit, but she had caused such a ruckus that she was ejected from the area and told not to come back. If she'd tried to sneak into Hamilton's room, Susan and her nurses would have caught her. She'd reacted frantically at the idea of an autopsy, but she was the dramatic type, and she was young and in love.

New page.

Susan had opportunity to kill Hamilton too, but I couldn't think of her motive. We didn't go around killing patients just because they annoyed us. Besides, Susan had been my friend for a long time, and I simply couldn't picture her holding a pillow over a helpless patient's face until he died.

I shivered at the thought. From what I'd learned, Congressman Hamilton had gone out of his way to be obnoxious to anyone who couldn't vote for him. He championed funding cuts for some unlikely groups. If his youthful behavior with Melanie was any indication of his character, he'd probably left a string of unhappy women around the country. It surprised me that he hadn't been nailed with sexual harassment allegations. But then again, Cynthia adored him, and he presumably used that same charismatic charm on all women.

It had taken someone with cold determination to see the job through to the end, someone willing to risk discovery to accomplish the task. Someone desperate enough to kill again when they thought I was too close to identifying them. After scanning the list, I went back and stopped at each name. Who fit those criteria?

I studied the list again, finally stopping at one name, and I knew who the killer was. At least I thought I knew. Karmic justice aside, it had to be Will. His disheveled appearance and erratic behavior were signs of a guilty conscience. But how in the world was I going to prove it? I didn't think Pierce would take my word for it. And no matter how much sense it made, I had no proof.

What I needed was to find a bottle of digoxin capsules in Will's office. Maybe a lab could compare what remained in my coffee with the ones in the bottle to see if they were from the same lot. I didn't know if they could do that, but it sounded good.

Soon, everyone would be gone for the evening and I'd have my chance. Now was the time for patience.

"Here it is." Interrupting my thoughts, Connie came into my office and dropped the printed letter to the Insurance Commissioner on my desk. "I'm leaving now."

I skimmed over the letter and checked to be sure she had attached an extra copy for the Medical Staff files. "Thanks," I called after her. "I'll take it downstairs for Dr. Weiser to sign." Setting the pad upside down on my desk, I picked up the letter and tapped it against my hand.

Pierce had told me to stay out of it, but I had to share what I knew rather than wait for him to discover it on his own. He would be annoyed for a variety of reasons, but it couldn't be helped. I refused to stay on the sidelines when my life was at stake. I knew I was putting myself at risk, but I didn't like the fear that was becoming my constant companion. I'd be careful, I promised myself. I wouldn't take any unnecessary chances.

Picking up the phone, I dialed Pierce's cell phone number. Annoyed when his voicemail answered, I left a detailed message as instructed. Maybe his exasperation with me would be diminished before he called back.

Stiff with tension, I rolled my chair away from the desk and stood up to stretch. It felt so good. In fact, it felt good simply to be alive.

For my own sanity, I needed to resolve this tonight. If I found any evidence, I would leave it where it was and call Pierce again and tell him to bring a search warrant. He'd probably be even more annoyed with me, but I couldn't wait for him to work his methodical way, hampered by rules I didn't have to abide by.

Taking one last deep breath, I glanced at the clock. It was time. I turned off my computer, knowing it was secure with the new password I had chosen. If Peter somehow found his way into my office again, it would take a million years for him to figure it out: Slime. I would change it again, but for now, it was a grim reminder of what people can do to someone they claim to care about.

I slipped on my coat and picked up the letter and my purse. Checking to be sure I hadn't forgotten anything, I flipped light switches off as I made my way from my office to the door. Before stepping into the hall, I glanced around the suite and felt an incredible sadness that everything I had worked for could be ruined by one jerky boss. The sadness was not only for myself, but for all of us. Having a murderer in our midst had changed everything. Would we ever regain that special camaraderie we'd had?

I decided the best approach to the Admin suite was the least trafficked. To avoid evening visitors, I walked the long way towards the clinic, my steps echoing in the empty hallway, and then took the elevator to the first floor. When I stepped off the elevator, the specialists'-clinic doors were closed and their check-in desk area dark.

I passed other departments, also closed and darkened. The front reception desk where Nicole sat during the day was occupied by a security guard I didn't know. From the uniform, he looked like a temp. He didn't bother to glance up from his *Sports Illustrated.*

Across the hall from the Admin suite stood a janitorial cart. The men's room door was propped open. I wondered if Pham had been released and when he would be back, if he wanted to come back here. Trying to prove his innocence was what had involved me in the first place. His arrest in my office seemed years ago, not just a week.

I stepped quietly to the Admin suite door and tested it. The knob turned in my hand. I opened the door and slipped inside, closing the door gently behind me. All the office doors were closed, and no light shone underneath. A quick peek at the usually overflowing recycled-paper bin told me this area had already been cleaned. Good; I shouldn't be interrupted.

I crossed the darkened reception area and moved toward Will's office. When no one answered my knock, I opened the door and slipped into his office. I didn't want to turn on the lights, so I raised the blinds. A nearby parking-lot light illuminated the room.

The top of the desk was still a mess, and I doubted Will would leave evidence there. I started searching his drawers, disappointed, but not surprised, to find them full of folders bulging with paper.

I opened the last drawer on the bottom and saw it. A prescription bottle. But I couldn't read the label without holding it up to the light. Remembering all the detective shows I've seen, I pulled a tissue from my pocket and carefully lifted the bottle from the drawer, holding it by the edges. It felt as if it was almost empty. I turned it toward the light and read the label.

Digoxin. Will took digoxin.

Now I had proof. Now I could call Pierce and give him

the evidence he needed to make an arrest. I bent down to replace the bottle where I'd found it.

Suddenly, the office door opened and the lights came on.

I froze.

"Robyn?" Brenda stood in the doorway, a stunned expression on her face.

"Ah, Brenda. Hello."

"But…but I…Wh—"

I held up the letter and smiled brightly. "I'm dropping this off for Dr. Weiser to sign."

Brenda raised a skeptical eyebrow, then she stared hard. "Robyn, his mailbox is not in Will's office."

That was the downside of working with smart people. It's really tough to put something over on them.

Shaken by what I'd found, evidence that proved beyond a doubt that Will was the murderer, I sighed heavily. "I know. I came looking for this." I held up the bottle of digoxin, making sure I touched only the tissue to keep my fingerprints off.

Her eyes narrowed. "What is it?"

"I…it means that Will is the one who tried to kill me. I think he killed Congressman Hamilton too."

If Brenda had looked stunned when she first entered the office and saw me, now I could have knocked her over with a feather. "Will? You think Will's the murderer?"

I nodded. "He had motive and opportunity to murder Congressman Hamilton and to kill me. And this bottle could prove that he poisoned my coffee last week. I have to call Detective Pierce."

"Yes, I see." Brenda's expression softened. "Come into my office. You can call from there."

I set the bottle back exactly as I'd found it and closed the drawer.

"I'm surprised to see you so soon after what happened last week," Brenda said as she held the door open for me to pass. She turned out the light and started toward her office. "How're you feeling?"

"Better."

"That was a terrible thing," she said, shaking her head. "What a shock for you. You should've taken more time off. Catch your breath. I'll make us some tea, then we'll call the police."

"Sounds good." I appreciated Brenda's mother-hen fussing over me.

I followed her into her office. The overhead lights were off. No wonder I'd thought the Administration suite was vacant when I hadn't seen light from under her door. Only a green-shaded banker's desk lamp illuminated the room. I took the chair between a small round table and the desk while Brenda fussed with a hot pot and tea bags.

The tightness in my shoulders started to ease, tension I hadn't even been aware of. Soon it would all be over. I rubbed my hands over my face.

"Are you okay?" Brenda's voice was filled with concern.

"I'm just tired," I said. "It was hard to come back, and it hasn't exactly been an easy day."

She nodded. "I imagine not." She returned to fixing the tea.

For a moment, I felt safe. Brenda was the protector, the staunch advocate for her nurses' safety and well-being. Now that I was convinced it had been Will who'd poisoned me, I could trust Brenda. Nothing could happen as long as I was with her.

As I began to relax, I absorbed the calmness of the room. I'd always liked Brenda's office. She had decorated it with some small impressionist prints that added pink splashes of color to the walls. A planter filled with peach-pink silk flowers sat on the wide windowsill. A Bible sat next to the ceramic planter. The feminine touches had always seemed at odds with her no-nonsense clothing and hairstyle, revealing a side of her that was otherwise shrouded.

Like my office, the work area was cluttered with the ubiquitous stacks of papers and journals and myriad manuals covering everything from hospital policies to OSHA regulations to clinical nursing topics. Her dark wood desk was immaculate, in sharp contrast to the rest of her workspace.

"Sugar?"

When I shook my head, Brenda brought two cups and set one in front of me before sitting in her chair behind the desk. I picked up the cup and pretended to take a sip. Even though I knew Will was the murderer, several days of suspicion were hard to forget.

"So, let's talk about what's been going on," Brenda said. "Why do you think Will murdered Congressman Hamilton and tried to murder you? A lot of people take digoxin." She leaned back in her executive-style chair, her hands resting gently on leather-covered arms.

I set the tea cup on the table and took a deep breath, then told her everything, a rehearsal for what I'd tell the police—from my search for Will's motive to murder Congressman Hamilton, to checking his calendar for opportunity, and finally, to the attempt on my life. I concluded by saying, "And when that didn't work, he told me to find a new job by New Year's."

Brenda's eyes widened. "You're kidding."

"I wish I was," I said with a heavy sigh. "I never expected that someone I worked for could be a murderer."

"I'm sure you didn't."

"I just hope when this is all over I'll still have my job," I said, noticing a brass picture frame on the corner of the desk. It was a recent photograph of Brenda and Cynthia, both laughing into the camera.

"She's a beautiful girl." I picked it up to take a closer look.

"Thank you," Brenda said with a slight lift of her chin.

"She looks a lot like you, especially around the eyes." I set the frame back on the desk.

Brenda smiled softly with maternal pride. Absently, I glanced at the newspaper lying on top of the paper recycling box next to her desk. *Rep. Hamilton Murdered in Local Hospital,* the headlines screamed. I pointed to it and said, "I can see it now, the next time a patient complains about the care they received, they'll throw in that everybody knows we murder our patients."

A colored picture of Hamilton at a recent rally was splashed across the middle of the page. Hamilton was smiling and waving. Behind him, beaming with happiness, was Cynthia.

I picked up the newspaper and shifted closer to the desk lamp so I could see the picture better. I looked at Hamilton, then at Cynthia, then at Hamilton again. I'd never seen the two of them together before. Then I remembered the video I'd watched repeatedly on Hamilton's website.

And suddenly, I knew. It all fell into place. Darlene had said the meeting I had seen on Brenda's calendar, the reason I never considered her as a suspect, had been canceled.

She was the last person to see Hamilton alive. She had access to my coffee cup. And, besides Pierce, she was the only person who knew I was investigating the murder.

Jake Hamilton had a mannerism of lifting his chin. So did Cynthia. And so did Brenda.

Brenda was related to Jake Hamilton.

I had been so smart, thinking I had figured out who the murderer was, sending Pierce off on a wild-goose chase. But I'd been wrong, terribly, terribly wrong. Will wasn't the murderer after all. And now, I was alone with this woman who had murdered once and had tried a second time.

A cold swirl of dread seeped into my bones. Afraid of what I might see, but unable to stop, I slowly looked up at Brenda. It was the eyes. The eyes, and the lifting of the chin, that innocuous gesture.

I had to get out of there. Could I fool Brenda? Could I leave without her knowing that I knew?

I casually tossed the newspaper back into the recycle box and stood up. "Thanks for the tea, Brenda. It was really nice to have someone to talk to."

Brenda stood up. "Do you have to leave so soon?"

"Josh is waiting for me at home. I called before I left my office and told him I was on my way." If she thought he was expecting me, would she let me go? I forced a smile. "It's interesting to see him worry about me for a change."

I walked from her office, desperately trying to appear casual. I remembered to put Dr. Weiser's letter in his mailbox; surely that had to look unconcerned. I turned to see Brenda had followed me and was standing outside her office. "I'll walk you out."

In my years of dealing with the public, I had faced a lot of moods and attitudes. Frantic, distraught, angry—I had worked through them all. I didn't worry about my safety when a person was ranting and raving because there were techniques for bringing them around. I became uneasy, though, when a person spoke calmly, when they had nothing to lose. I heard that calmness in Brenda's voice. If she knew I'd figured out the truth, then I was in big trouble.

I should have known better than to trust Brenda. It was just common sense: when a murderer was loose—and it was probably someone you knew—you didn't hang out with anyone when no one else was around. I should have thought of that earlier, but I'd been so sure the murderer was Will that I'd never considered Brenda.

Wordlessly, we walked to the elevators. The elevator signs displayed "4," meaning both cars were on the top floor. Fear welled up inside me.

I had to get away from her. I started for the stairwell door and pushed the door open. "Well, good night, Brenda. I'll see you in the morning."

To my dismay, Brenda continued to follow me through the door and down the stairs. Now I was really worried. Did she know? Was she planning to follow me all the way to my car? I forced myself to walk at a normal pace, holding onto the railing. My heart was pounding, and I prayed it was from anxiety, not from the digoxin that might still be in my system.

We reached the landing and I glanced at her as I reached for the exit door. I was going to make it.

She shoved me. I went flying down the stairs, grabbing for the metal railing, but missed. I bounced on the hard concrete steps, banging my head.

Brenda followed me down, kicking and screeching about devil spawn and cursing me for revealing her secret. The stairwell echoed with her voice, the words repeated over and over. None of it made sense as I tried to escape her attack. I twisted away from her kick and landed awkwardly on the next step. Something snapped and white hot agony seared down my leg.

I couldn't stop my descent, couldn't protect my head,

let alone my broken leg. I landed in a heap on the landing, fighting the pain and the blackness that threatened to overwhelm me.

Would she leave me now? If I played dead, would she be like a bear and go away?

I wasn't that lucky. Brenda continued down the stairs toward me. "… cursed from the moment he was born, but I did nothing," she ranted. "Now, we all must pay."

She bent down and rolled me and pushed me toward the next set of stairs. I knew I wouldn't survive another fall. I was on the edge of the landing now. This was it, the end. She put her hands down to push one last time. I reached out and grabbed her collar, pulling her over. She stumbled, then fell headfirst down the stairs.

Silence filled my ears. Had I blacked out? I looked down to the bottom of the stairs. Brenda lay still.

I couldn't worry about her; I had to get myself out of here. It was a holiday week; a lot of people had taken vacation. It was evening; the usual hustle and bustle was over until tomorrow morning. I could lie there for hours before someone came into the stairwell.

Panic bubbled through me. Taking deep breaths, I fought for control. Hysteria wouldn't help; calm assessment would. My head hurt, but my vision was okay. I could breathe through my nose, so it wasn't broken. I ran my tongue around my mouth and all my teeth were in place. That was good.

I wiggled my arms and hands, pleased with the movement. My left leg was okay, but my right leg throbbed. That was a good sign, but with a bone sticking through the skin, I had a compound fracture. It needed treatment soon, before infection set in. I didn't want to think about what could happen then. No need to borrow more trouble than I was already in.

I had to save myself.

Blackness closed in, and I put my head down on the cold concrete. It felt good, so easy to just let go….

No! I struggled to stay conscious. And to not let terror take over. I had to breathe, and think my way out of this.

I grimaced. The same way I had figured out Will was the murderer.

Leave it to the professionals.

Pierce's voice came through loud and clear. I vowed to do that next time. But right now, I had to get out of here.

Where was my cell phone? My purse was six steps up, but it might as well have been ten miles. I wouldn't have a signal anyway.

I had to do something. Even if it meant losing my leg in the end. I shoved that thought away. Escaping was most important. Slipping out of my raincoat, I wrapped it around my leg and tied it together with the belt. At least it would keep all the pieces together, although a splint would have been better.

Lying on my left side, I held the raincoat sleeves to keep my leg stable, and hitched myself toward the stairs. I lifted my rear onto the bottom step, and nearly passed out from the pain. The raincoat didn't support my leg as well as I had hoped.

I had no choice but to continue.

Inching my way up, I reached my purse and pulled out the cell phone. I was right: no signal down here.

A few inchworm steps later, I glanced toward my goal: the door that led to the cafeteria and the parking lot, a heavy metal fire door. Even if I reached it, I might not be able to pull it open. And if I did, there might not be anyone around.

Three steps later, I was ready to lie down and die. Anything to stop the pain.

But, I couldn't stop. Someone had to tell Pierce about Brenda. I wasn't finished raising Josh. I convinced myself that people needed me, that I would be letting them down if I gave up now.

Then I saw the little red box on the wall next to the door. The fire alarm. All I had to do was reach that box and I would be saved.

Five more steps, and I was underneath the little red box. Struggling not to fall again, I held onto the metal railing and drew myself up, stretching until my fingertips curled over the little handle. I pulled it down.

The alarm ricocheted around the concrete stairwell. I sank to the floor and covered my ears. Help had to be on the way.

It seemed like forever, but finally the alarm bell stopped. The fire department had to be in the hospital lobby. Someone would come soon, as soon as they identified which alarm was pulled.

At last, the stairwell door one flight up banged open.

"No smoke here," said a male voice.

"Help me," I called out.

"Hold on, there's someone down there." Several sets of feet hurried down the stairs.

"Robyn?" Pierce's voice. "Are you okay?" The fireman who'd come with him was calling for a paramedic.

"I am now," I said, closing my eyes. My last thought before losing consciousness was of Thanksgiving dinner.

And candied yams.

EPILOGUE

I SANK AGAINST THE cushions, my tummy full of turkey and all the trimmings and just enough wine to feel mellow. My leg ached, so I shifted position and listened to the debate going on around me.

"It goes like this, son," Pierce said with a deadpan expression. "Guests bring a contribution to the meal, and the family cleans up afterwards."

Josh roared with laughter. "You think one can of cranberry sauce and a bottle of wine saves you from dishes?" Josh eyed Pierce with a mischievous grin. "Consider this, Matt. Would you want to eat here again knowing that *I* had washed the dishes? My idea of clean is to let Taffy lick the plates."

From my perch, I groaned silently, but vowed to stay out of this discussion. After all, I still had one leg in a cast. Supervising from a distance was all I was good for.

"I'll help you, sugar," said Chuck.

Josh squeezed her hand. "The point is," he said to her, "Matt's been here so much the last couple of days that I think he's shifted from the honored guest category to the like-family category."

Pierce's face reddened, but he didn't look displeased. "Okay. Chuck, you scrape and stack. Josh, you load the dishwasher. I'll wash the other stuff."

"Deal."

The kids trooped off to the dining room to get started. Pierce stayed behind.

"How did the investigation go?" I asked. This was the first time I'd had both the time and the inclination to hear the rest of the story.

"I managed to talk to Brenda before she died. She wanted to confess her sins and she hoped her family would forgive her. Her husband knew a lot more than she thought he did."

Pierce shook his head. "It was a real mess. She got pregnant in high school, back in the times when that was still a disgrace. To complicate matters, her parents were extremely religious, and they shipped her off to her aunt's place in Montana. The aunt wasn't much better. I guess she harangued her all the time about being a sinner and disgracing herself in God's eyes. It was the aunt who arranged for a local farmer and his wife to adopt the baby."

I remembered something I read while investigating Hamilton on the Internet. "Wasn't Hamilton involved with some bill that caused them to lose their farm?"

"I wouldn't be surprised. He was a real piece of work." Pierce shrugged. "Have to wonder, though, if he wasn't a victim too. After you told me that he and the reporter were from the same town, I had several conversations with the local sheriff back then. He told me the adoptive parents were interested only in cheap labor. They'd adopt a new child every two years as the oldest graduated from high school and left. They gave the kids enough food to stay healthy, and clothes and schooling to keep the authorities from getting suspicious, but Hamilton and the rest worked hard for their keep."

I let his words sink in. How awful for Hamilton. I had grown up on a ranch, and was expected to work hard, but I knew my parents loved me. "Others have it tough and turn out okay."

"But some are born with a mean streak, and he sure

turned out to be one of them. Brenda went to visit him partly because of her administrative position and partly because her daughter worked for him and was obviously falling for him. When she glanced at his chart and saw his date and place of birth, she knew immediately he was her son."

"So she said something about him and Cynthia."

Pierce nodded. "After she realized he was Cynthia's half-brother, she told him who she was. It wasn't a joyous reunion. He told Brenda that seducing Cynthia would be his revenge for being abandoned. Brenda panicked. She left, then doubled back and waited in the stairwell for Officer Tomlin to take a break. That's when she slipped into Hamilton's room and smothered him."

"And she couldn't warn Cynthia to stay away from him because that would mean exposing her mistake," I added. "That poor woman, murdering one child to protect the other."

Dismayed, I shook my head. I could understand why she felt she had to kill Hamilton. He wasn't a nice person. If he'd knowingly planned to seduce his half-sister, then he was more than not nice; he was evil.

It was more difficult to rationalize her two attempts to murder me, so I set that aside. Maybe later I could forgive her in my heart.

"Her poor family," I said, feeling compassion for them that I couldn't feel for Brenda.

"Yeah. Her husband, he's taking this hard. And from what he's said, the daughter's going to need some psychiatric help. She was on the edge anyway, and this pushed her over."

Pierce helped me resettle the pillows supporting my leg, then said, "Explain to me why you thought Will Slater did it."

"He had motive and opportunity. When I first started investi—"

"—snoop—"

"—investigating to clear Pham, I checked all the calendars when I was in Admin. Will's time was the only one that was unaccounted for at the time of the murder. I looked at Brenda's calendar and scratched her as a possible suspect because it showed she had a meeting with Darlene."

Pierce nodded. "We saw that too, but hadn't gotten around to cross-checking it with Darlene."

"Two days later, Darlene said she hadn't had a meeting all week. I didn't put it together and Brenda certainly didn't say anything to correct the misperception that she was someplace else at the time of the murder."

"Next time you think you've figured it out, call me and stay in a locked room alone. Don't go off with someone until the case is really solved."

"Believe me, there's not going to be a next time," I vowed.

"Hey, Matt," Josh called from the kitchen doorway. "You going to help or sit there with Mom all night?"

"I'm coming, I'm coming." Pierce heaved himself off the sofa. "Pushy kid. Just like his mom," he mumbled as he headed toward the kitchen.

Alone, I thought about how much I had to be thankful for. I still woke in the middle of the night in a cold sweat, but I was alive.

I had other things to be thankful for. Sarah, from Human Resources, had called to say my job was secure. Will had been offered the federal job, and he said nothing to her before he left for the holidays. She figured he'd be too busy with other things in the few weeks before he moved to D.C. to fuss with me.

Laughter erupted from the kitchen, reminding me how thankful I was for family and friends who were as honest as anyone could be. Josh and I were talking more openly, less like parent and child. There was no masquerading between Pierce and me. He knew about David. I knew about his wife. He knew about Peter. No secrets that could cause problems later.

Josh slid onto the couch next to me and draped his arm over my shoulders, searching my face for signs that I was tiring. "You okay, Mom?"

"The best I've been all week."

He rolled his eyes. "That's not saying much."

"Guess you're right," I said with a quiet laugh. Then I gave him a hard look. "This was a very different Thanksgiving for us, Josh."

"Yeah, but it felt…right." He thought for a moment before saying more. "I think it's okay to remember Dad without being sad every year."

"I agree," I said over the lump forming in my throat. I patted his hand. "You better get in there and help Pierce."

He left me alone then, alone with my thoughts. He was right. We'd kept Thanksgiving frozen in time in David's memory. I had frozen that part of my life for too many years. I'd refused to let go, and Josh had followed my lead. It was time.

With a sigh, not of sadness, but of acceptance, I removed the claddagh ring from my finger and turned it around, heart turned outward. One chapter of my life had ended, and another was beginning. It didn't mean I was looking, but I had to live all the facets of my life.

A loud crash from the kitchen jolted me upright.

"It's okay," came three voices in unison.